"Is there something troubling you, Cleone?"

Saxon's strong arms encompassed her, snaring her in a mesh of desire. In another minute he would have succeeded in completely distracting her from her purpose.

"You still haven't been entirely frank with your daughter," she plunged on recklessly. "She's always asking me *how* her mother died. It seems to trouble her. She—"

Eyes narrowed, lips tightly drawn, Saxon stared down at her.

"How can I tell the child that I was responsible?"

"For Tessa's death?" Cleone gasped in dismay. "Then you *were* . . . ?"

"And you claimed not to listen to gossip!" Saxon said bitterly. "Yes. So now you know. I *was* responsible for my wife's death— and since I've confirmed your idle speculations, what do you intend to do about it?"

Books by Annabel Murray

HARLEQUIN ROMANCE

These books may be available at your local bookseller.

Don't miss any of our special offers. Write to us at the following address for information on our newest releases.

Harlequin Reader Service
P.O. Box 52040, Phoenix, AZ 85072-2040
Canadian address: P.O. Box 2800, Postal Station A,
5170 Yonge St., Willowdale, Ont. M2N 6J3

The Cotswold Lion

Annabel Murray

Harlequin Books

TORONTO • NEW YORK • LONDON
AMSTERDAM • PARIS • SYDNEY • HAMBURG
STOCKHOLM • ATHENS • TOKYO • MILAN

Original hardcover edition published in 1984
by Mills & Boon Limited

ISBN 0-373-02717-6

Harlequin Romance first edition September 1985

For Muriel,
Nola and Valda

The lion on your old stone gates
Is not more cold to you than I
Tennyson

———————————————————

CHAPTER ONE

'I SHALL conduct this interview alone,' Eric Morton pronounced pompously. 'In fact, if it wasn't that my driving licence is temporarily suspended, you wouldn't even need to be here. I'm your uncle's chief assistant . . . and it's my place to make these negotiations . . . and besides, women are just no good at this sort of thing.'

Cleone Bancroft forced back a sharp rejoinder as she manoeuvred her uncle's heavy old Humber around the narrow Cotswold lanes, an exercise which was a considerable tax on her slight young strength. At twenty-two, she had a slender, boyish figure, which, to the casual observer, made her seem considerably younger than she was.

There was much she could have said, in reply to Eric's chauvinistic speech, but since, if this coming interview proved successful, they would have to work together there was no point in creating a hostile atmosphere.

'In any case,' Eric continued, 'this fellow, Turville, will take some pretty slick handling. Don't forget, I've met him before, took an instant dislike to the fellow too . . . impossibly arrogant type. Just because he owns more than his fair share of land, he thinks he owns the rest of the world too.'

Cleone's heart sank. For all Eric's claims that he was the one to handle the coming interview, it did not seem to her that he was in the right frame of mind to handle someone reputed to be difficult. Apart from his strong, socialistic views, he was not overly blessed with tact.

'Perhaps,' she suggested diffidently, 'we should have waited, until Uncle Amyas was free to interview Mr Turville?'

'Certainly not!' Eric contradicted sharply. Apart from the slur it implied on his capabilities, Cleone had known he would not accept the proffered opinion of a 'mere woman'. 'Amyas is far too soft,' he continued, too conciliatory with these people. He'd only meet with the same boorish reaction as I got last time. Supercilious, high and mighty, bigoted. . . .'

'Perhaps Mr Turville has an excuse for his pride,' she suggested mildly, knowing that Eric was capable of extreme boorishness himself on occasion. 'You did say he was the largest landowner in these parts.'

Eric snorted.

'That's no excuse in *my* eyes, far from it. All men should be born equal, with equal rights, equal possessions.'

Cleone's conviction grew, that, in this instance, Eric, as a negotiator, was going to be, once again, a dismal failure—that the coming consultation was very likely to erupt into an undignified confrontation, very probably culminating into an even more obdurate refusal from Saxon Turville to allow any investigation on land belonging to him.

'If Mr Turville was reluctant to grant permission last time you were here,' she persisted, 'he's hardly likely to have changed his mind, is he? But if Uncle Amyas were to, well, I mean, he might be more courteous to someone like uncle. . . .' Her voice trailed away at Eric's contemptuous snort.

But she felt sure she was right. She could not see any reason so far, why Saxon Turville should have changed his mind, or should do so now, not in response to Eric's methods, which had all the subtlety of a bulldozer. And this second attempt *should* have been left to her uncle; he had wanted to make one more attempt, in person this time; and an appointment had been made, one, which, unfortunately, Amyas had not been able to keep. A respected and well-known archaeologist, much in demand as a consultant, Amyas was completing important investigations in Scotland and he had telephoned, asking Eric and Cleone to postpone their arrangements to accompany him to the Cotswolds and to contact Saxon Turville to settle on a new date.

Eric, however, had argued with Amyas's decision and had finally persuaded the older man that he should be allowed another attempt at negotiation.

'I can very well deal with this. I've got Turville's measure now,' he had asseverated.

Cleone's spirits fell still further as she stole a glance at Eric's pugnacious profile. If only Amyas were here.

Cleone had worked for the last four years with and for her uncle Amyas, her mother's brother; had lived in his home, in fact, ever since she had left boarding school. Her father was in the diplomatic service and thus her parents were scarcely ever in England. With no desire to travel around Europe in their train, Cleone, who shared her uncle's passion for things ancient, was quite happy to keep house for him, assist with his paperwork and accompany him on his 'digs'. She was not actually qualified in archaeology herself, as Eric Morton was, but after all these years and with her uncle's guidance, she had considerable knowledge of his subject and had acquired expertise in the skills required.

Her passion for archaeology, nurtured by living and working in her uncle's company, was nearly as great as Amyas's own; and even before that, her imagination had been fired, at a very early age, by stories of Heinrich Schliemann's search for the remains of Troy, the discoveries of Sir Arthur Evans at the Minoan palace of Knossos, of Howard Carter and the tomb of Tutankhamun. She was as eager as her uncle and Eric could be, to be involved in a major discovery—was as enthusiastic as Amyas about his current pet project, his theory that there were still important discoveries to be made in the Cotswolds, an area to which the Romans had been particularly partial, looking upon it as a sort of holiday playground. His chosen area was that around the village towards which she and Eric were now bound.

Amyas had so fired with his own fervour, his team of half-a-dozen young assistants, culled from among his students, that all had willingly volunteered to spend the whole of the Long Vacation working on their leader's envisaged project, if—and this was the stumbling block—*if* he could obtain prior permission for his investigations from the landowner, whose jurisdiction encompassed the village, its immediate environs and, far beyond, many acres of Cotswold downland. The landowner in question was one Saxon Turville, a man notorious for being something of a local lion, both socially and by temperament.

It was for this reason that, a few months previously, Amyas being engaged with lectures, Eric, as her uncle's chief assistant, had been sent to Salpeth, his mandate to open negotiations with the great man.

'This Turville lives in a great, ostentatious place.' Eric was continuing his indictment of the landowner. 'Tudor, of course, built on land, no doubt, that used to belong to the common folk. I wonder how many honest Yeomen were beggared, so that some arrogant "gentleman" could have his country seat? I hate those great, showy places. He's an arrant snob too . . . had the utter gall to call me a scruffy student . . . *me*!'

Cleone made no comment, but she wasn't surprised at the landowner's mistaken reaction. Eric never made any secret of his socialistic beliefs, beliefs with which Cleone could not agree; and part of his flouting of convention, despite his twenty-five years, took the form of wearing deliberately faded jeans, topped by a duffel coat of doubtful age and origin, purchased from an Oxfam shop. She supposed he was good looking, in an unconventional kind of way, but it was a way that had never appealed to Cleone, used to the society of an older man and his friends, with their more restrained tastes in clothing and hairdressing. Sometimes Eric made it obvious that he would be prepared to be more than just friendly with his chief's niece, but Cleone had always politely but firmly repressed his attempts.

'He told me he didn't want to see Salpeth overrun by a "bunch of tatty, long-haired weirdos".'

Cleone could just imagine the landowner's view of Eric's flowing black locks, which were all part of the image he cultivated and though his hair was perfectly clean and well cut, its possession would not have improved his standing in the eyes of the man Saxon Turville sounded to be. His wealth and position would indicate a man of about her uncle's age, she had decided, but of a crustier, less approachable disposition.

'I told him I wasn't a student, that I happened to have

a BA in archaeology, moreover that Amyas placed every confidence in me. D'you know what he said?' Eric did not wait for Cleone's reply, but went on: 'Said his tenants also had every confidence in *him* ... that he'd be doing less than his duty by them, if he allowed their peaceful lives to be disrupted by the presence of people like me. Toffee-nosed, that's what *he* is, and I told him so. I told him that was the trouble with monied people. They think they have the right to stand in the way of progress.'

Cleone flinched, as she imagined Saxon Turville's reaction to Eric's heated retort. However could Eric imagine that this interview would proceed any differently? He had already been judged and condemned—and Amyas's project with him.

'Fellow sneered at me, then, asked me if I called digging up the past, progress.'

Cleone was not left long in doubt as to Eric's reply to *that* remark.

'I said, since his own views were so obviously outdated, that I would have expected the idea of ancient remains to suit *him* down to the ground. I told him what I thought of his insulting remarks too. So then, he had the effrontery to say he didn't find courtesy very useful in dealing with "persons of my type" ... that a blunt refusal worked better.'

So that explained the outcome of Eric's 'diplomatic' mission to Salpeth, Cleone brooded. Eric's reaction to all that Saxon Turville represented had not helped, of course. But it did sound as if the landowner had his faults too ... had been particularly obstructive ... even provocative.

'What's he like ... to look at, I mean?' she added hastily.

Eric shrugged.

'Big, powerful chap, typical of your upper classes, all millionaire tan and tweeds. The *sans culottes* of the French Revolution would have known what to do with his sort,' he concluded savagely.

Cleone was almost positive now that the breakdown in negotiations had been Eric's fault, for he had an undoubted knack of antagonising people, particularly

those whom he considered belonged, most unfairly in his
view, to a privileged race. Eric was not poor, he
commanded quite a good salary, and he was certainly not
uneducated, but he directed the energies of his agile
brain, his knowledge of history and social mores, to the
provocation and condemnation of what he labelled the
'have-it-alls'.

She sighed. She hoped there was going to be no
unpleasantness. It was far too nice a day, the
surroundings too glorious, to be spoilt by conflict.
Maintaining a thoughtful silence, in the hope that Eric
would do likewise, she drove on.

A great deal of their route had lain along the ancient
Fosse Way, the Roman road which ran the full length of
the Cotswolds, carving a line across England and taking a
direct route across the successive waves of the wolds; not a
road originally, but a frontier that marked the Roman
subjugation of south-east England. Like many Roman
roads, it was well suited to traffic and that day it had
been heavy with cars and lorries, so that Cleone, at the
wheel of her uncle's heavy car and having finally left the
main road, was uncertain which she found more tiring,
driving in busy conditions, with the concentration
entailed, or negotiating her way along the narrow lanes
that ran among the pale stone villages.

Professor Amyas Pringle could well have afforded a
more modern, less cumbersome vehicle, but with absent-
minded complacence he never noticed the inconvenience
it caused his niece, who acted as combined assistant,
housekeeper, secretary and chauffeuse for her eminent
relative. Amyas never drove himself, not because of any
incapability or because of advanced years, Amyas was
only fifty-two, but because, with his propensity for falling
into reverie, it would have been far too dangerous an
undertaking ... for himself, his passengers and for other
road users.

Like the streams and rivers of the Cotswolds, they were
penetrating deeper now into the high wolds and it was
here, up these valleys, that there had once existed a land
of villa estates and Romano-British hamlets. The lanes
linking the villages seemed to grow even more narrow

and winding, curving unhurriedly over the flanks of the hills, contouring along the valleys. These lanes and the ever-present brooks crossed and re-crossed. The rural highways harmonised with their landscape setting, sweeping up the bed of the valley in gentle curves and gradients, gaining height slowly but steadily, until, nearing Salpeth, the deep lanes plummeted down again, down through a wooded hollow to the village, a venerable hamlet, secretive and peaceful with cottages and a little pub, the honey-coloured buildings set in random, leisurely fashion about a large green.

Salpeth was an isolated hamlet, set among the sheep-spangled slopes, near the upper reaches of the River Coln; and, another reason for Amyas's pet theory, not too many miles distant from Chedworth, where the most completely exposed villa in the West of England was sited. It was Amyas's dream to discover, not just another Chedworth, but an even finer example of Roman domestic architecture.

The village was beautifully cared for, Cleone noted, verges and central green neatly trimmed. The Cotswold stone of the cottages was enlivened by many-hued, climbing roses; front paths were edged with a wealth of dark, Hidcote-blue lavender.

They could see the wide sweep of a church roof now, the stone tiles as closely interlocked as the feathers of a bird's wing and beyond was the spread of a manor complex—stone buildings of gleaming silvery grey against the dark wooded heights beyond.

Then, behind the leafless branches of tall, guardian lime trees, Cleone could identify the high, Elizabethan chimneys of the manor. As in many Cotswold villages, the great house and church stood almost side by side, forming a group set apart behind a farm at the end of a short by-lane.

'Slow down! Stop!'

Surprised, Clone obeyed Eric's command, as he craned his neck for a better view.

'I want you to take a look at that church . . . traces of Anglo-Saxon, with Norman additions . . . but predominantly Perpendicular. It's not as large as some of its kind

... but unless I'm very much mistaken ... and I bet I'm not ... it's a "wool" church.'

'*Wool* church?' Cleone queried.

'Yes. You've noticed all the sheep on the wolds, of course? But there used to be a lot more, once they were *the* most important animals in these parts. These showy churches were built by the successful sheepmasters and wool merchants of the Middle Ages; and a lot of these unnecessary great manor houses were built with fortunes made in the cloth trade. Probably that's where this blighter Turville's money came from.'

'I know your views about privilege, Eric,' Cleone said hesitantly, feeling that she must make some attempt to secure the success of this visit, 'and you're entitled to them. But please, don't get on your hobby horse with Mr Turville, don't antagonise him, for the sake of uncle's project, Eric, *please*.'

'I know what I'm doing,' he replied loftily.

The manor house was a traditional, Cotswold, Elizabethan house of steeply pitched roofs, pointed gables and mullioned windows. The drive approaching the house was flanked by grass, a smooth, green, velvet carpet. To reach the house, they had to pass through the farmyard, where excited, barking sheepdogs accompanied their progress and where hens foraged among rusting, outdated implements. Then they were driving between massive gateposts, topped by great stone lions rampant, which seemed to look down upon the newcomers with haughty hostility.

Cleone braked cautiously on the gravelled area before the front door, switched off the ignition and turned to Eric, a rueful expression on her pointed little face, her tawny-gold eyes slightly apprehensive as she studied his set face. It was the first time she had ever experienced this niggling sense of doubt as to the success of such an interview. Perhaps it was because, besides Eric's unfavourable description of Saxon Turville, the rumour had reached them, even in Oxford, of the man's unapproachable nature. People had hinted at a mystery, said to have soured his disposition.

'Well, here we are, fingers crossed,' she quipped, in an

attempt to hide her unease, her doubts of Eric's capability.

He made no reply to her words of encouragement; he was staring up with distaste at the house they were about to enter.

'See what I mean?' he snorted. 'Ostentation.'

Personally, Cleone thought the grey stone house with its five gables and air of quiet, compelling dignity, was a charming building, with little of ostentation in its architecture and she felt oddly drawn to it; but her main concern was not with the manor, but with the man who owned it—his reaction to Eric's renewed endeavours.

A grim-faced housekeeper answered the bell's summons and seemed dourly unimpressed by Cleone's politely expressed claim that they had an appointment with the master of the house.

'Wait here!' she dictated sourly, leaving them to cool their heels in the large, square entrance hall.

'I hope Saxon Turville's more forthcoming than his staff,' Cleone commented, when they were alone.

'It's probably *his* fault the woman's the way she is. Being in a menial position *does* things to people.'

Trust Eric to find a subject for his anti-establishment theories, Cleone thought with a touch of irritation, as she took the opportunity to look around her. The floorboards on which they stood were polished to the colour and lustre of old tortoiseshell; and equally lovingly cared for was the large, oak table, holding an enormous copper jug, filled with an arrangement of dried grasses and ferns. The ceiling was rich with plasterwork and the mullioned windows with armorial glass, while panelled walls held hunting trophies and sporting prints—mainly featuring red-coated huntsmen in full cry.

Eric's eyes had perceived these too and he moved to inspect them more closely. The curl of his lip spoke volumes and Cleone could read his thoughts. Hunting was an upper class pursuit and therefore, in his eyes, a decadent one.

The housekeeper returned at a leisurely pace, to inform them, in grudging accents, that 'Mr Turville would see them now.'

'Not you, Cleone,' Eric reminded. 'You keep out of this.' He turned to the sour-visaged housekeeper. 'Is there somewhere Miss Bancroft can wait?'

'Hallo . . . are you with that man?'

'Mmmm?' Abstractedly, Cleone raised her tawny-gold eyes from the old map spread out on the library table and which she had been studying, during her enforced wait for Eric. She regarded the child, perhaps about ten years old, who stood on the far side of the table. Her gaze was absent at first, past centuries still drifting before her eyes, then held growing interest.

There was diffidence here . . . a sense that the child was poised for flight, should Cleone prove unsympathetic to approach. The body was that of an elf, slight and fragile as a woodland flower, the square little face soft, wistful, mouth gently drooping, grey eyes full of curiosity.

Cleone's wide, generous mouth curved into a friendly smile. She felt that the waif-like child before her needed reassurance.

'Yes, I'm with Mr Morton. My name's Cleone Bancroft . . . and you are . . .?'

'I am Ianthe Turville . . . Saxon Turville's daughter.' Her manner of speech was oddly adult.

Cleone held out her hand.

'How do you do?' she said gravely. 'My friends usually call me Cleo.'

Her hand was taken tentatively by one so small, so delicate that the bones felt like those of a bird, their touch so brief, so light as to seem almost a figment of the imagination.

'And you're an archaeologist too?' the child enquired.

'Not exactly. An archaeologist's assistant would be nearer to the truth.'

'My father doesn't like archaeologists,' the child stated flatly; the grey eyes were wary, assessing Cleone's reaction to her words.

'So I believe,' Cleone replied, amused by this frankness. 'But we're rather hoping that he'll change his mind. Do you know *why* he doesn't like them?'

Ianthe shrugged, a curiously unchildlike gesture.

'Not really. I just know he doesn't. I don't think my father likes anybody very much.'

'Except you, of course,' Cleone suggested.

For a moment, the child's eyes were bleak.

'He t ... tolerates me,' she stumbled over the word. 'That doesn't mean he likes me.'

'Parents *love* their children,' Cleone said.

'Do they?' Ianthe sounded unconvinced. 'I think my father puts up with me ... because he has to ... because I live here. I wouldn't be at all surprised if he sent me to boarding school, when I'm eleven.'

Cleone looked at her sharply. Was this child dramatising herself, as young children often did, or did she seriously believe what she said? Either way, Cleone felt it would be tactful to change the subject and she cast around for a happier topic.

'Are *you* interested in archaeology?'

Apparently this was not such a good idea either, for Ianthe's face puckered painfully.

'I'm not allowed to be. I once found some books in the loft, about ancient Egypt and the pyramids, about an archaeologist who discovered Tutankhamun's tomb. My father saw me reading them and and took them away.' Ianthe looked troubled, puzzled. 'I think he burnt them.'

Cleone's small, shapely breasts lifted on an indignant breath. What a brute Saxon Turville must be, to deny his daughter this interest. That was the trouble with elderly, intolerant parents. She was tempted to tell Ianthe of the vast number of books she had brought in her luggage, for Eric had insisted on coming prepared to stay in the area, having no doubt about the success of their mission. She almost told the child she might borrow any book she chose, but the thought of Saxon Turville's wrath, if he found her suborning his daughter, made her reject the idea, for the moment at least.

'That man came here once before, didn't he?' Ianthe said. 'He has long, black hair. I saw him from my bedroom window.'

'Yes.' Cleone wondered if the child knew the details of that first visit.

'Do you understand old maps?' Ianthe had rounded the table to stand at Cleone's side. Obviously, she had decided the older girl was harmless.

'I know how to read a map, yes,' Cleone told her. 'Perhaps you'd like me to explain it to you?'

Ianthe nodded, but she was not looking at the map. Instead, her grave eyes were on Cleone's face.

'My father refused to let that man work in Salpeth, didn't he? that first time he came. When my father is rude and unkind to people, they don't usually come again. Why did he come back? Why are you here?'

'We came on behalf of my uncle ... because archaeology is my uncle's profession ... and we both help him.'

'And do you have to go wherever your uncle says? After all, you are grown up.'

'No, I'm not forced to go anywhere, but I like working with my uncle. He's a very nice man ... *you'll* like him when you meet him.' If you meet him, she amended silently, wishing she could be as certain as Eric that they would be working here.

'Oh, I doubt it.' The voice was cynically weary for a child of such tender years. 'I don't think I like men very much at all.' She considered for a moment, then added: 'Perhaps if I had an uncle I should like him ... but I don't think I like fathers. I think they're rather frightening people.'

Throughout her conversation with Ianthe—the child had left the library door ajar—Cleone had been conscious of the hum of voices from another room, near at hand; and it had soon become apparent that this was not the buzz of harmonious conversation. Voices were being raised, acrimoniously on Eric's part, in condemnation on the part of Saxon Turville, whose tones came to her as only a deep rumble, several keys lower than that of the young archaeologist.

'I don't think my father is going to change his mind,' Ianthe observed, her head slightly on one side.

'You could be right,' Cleone agreed despondently.

But Ianthe was no longer paying attention; a sound from outside having drawn her to the window.

'A taxi,' she commented now, 'with an old man in it. I wonder who he is? I've never seen him before.'

Cleone, joining her at the window, was able to enlighten her and as she did so, felt a burden lift from her shoulders. Perhaps, after all, it was not too late to save the project; Amyas had arrived, unexpectedly, but most fortuitously and now his slim, distinguished figure was mounting the front steps. Followed curiously by Ianthe, she hastened out into the hall just in time to see him admitted by the dour housekeeper.

'Oh, uncle! Thank goodness you're here,' she exclaimed, at precisely the same moment in which a roar of wrath came from the adjoining room.

'Typical upper class bigotry,' she heard Eric pronounce shrilly. 'Trying to keep culture away from the masses.'

'Don't try to give me any of your socialist claptrap, young man. I am not impressed by such posturings.'

'No, your sort never is impressed by reasoned, modern thinking. Conservative in outlook, and in politics too, I bet.' Eric was shouting now.

'My beliefs are none of your business. This interview is at an end. I suggest you return to Oxford and spend your long weeks of idleness in annoying someone else.'

'For the last time, I am *not* a student. I am a professional . . . I work extremely hard. . . .'

'I am not interested in how you spend your time.' By the sound of things, Saxon Turville was moving towards the door, his tone impatient. 'Now, if you will kindly leave . . . mine is a working farm and. . . .'

'*You! Work!*' Eric exclaimed disbelievingly. 'Surely you mean you ride around your estate, overseeing the serfs?'

'Get out, Mr Morton!' Saxon Turville said with weary dignity, 'before I throw you out.'

And with these words, Eric appeared in the hall, with such celerity that it almost seemed he had been propelled by an unseen hand; and strode through the front door, barely acknowledging Amyas's presence.

Amyas had been swift to assess the situation, even before Eric's rapid exit. He fingered his pepper-and-salt beard, which he had worn for as long as Cleone could remember.

'Not going too well, eh? I had my doubts, that's why I decided to cut short the Edinburgh business and get down here. Eric's all very well in the field, but ...' He shrugged expressively. 'But why aren't you in there? You've got more diplomacy in your little finger than ...'

'Eric wouldn't let me,' she explained. 'He said ...'

'Yes, well ... never mind that. Let's see if we can save the day.'

Taking a firm hold of Cleone's arm and before she could protest or draw back, Amyas entered the room from which Eric had issued.

The room in which Cleone found herself was, like the hall, delightfully panelled and which, despite the summer's day, was warmed by the blaze from a fireplace of monumental proportions, above which was carved some heraldic device ... Saxon Turville's coat of arms perhaps? Cleone thought afterwards, for he had the air of a man of long and ancient lineage.

A modern carpet, in a soft, sage green covered the floor and the furniture, though not modern, was certainly not antique, chosen obviously for comfort rather than for show. Nor, apparently, was Saxon Turville a particularly fussy man where his furnishings were concerned, for two King Charles spaniels sprawled across a settee, drawn up at an angle to the fire, their fine, liquid eyes regarding the newcomers with indolent intelligence.

From the window a man turned to accord them a haughtily surprised, chilly greeting; a man, thought a stunned Cleone, of whom the word handsome could not possibly do justice to his looks. *This* was no crusty, elderly person.

He was tall—six foot two or three, Cleone guessed—with a superb physique, his shoulders broad and powerful, his carriage erect, arrogant. But it was his face that held her startled gaze: rugged planes weathered to an almost summerlike tan, below thick, fair hair the colour of sunbleached wheat; broad, slightly crooked nose; chin belligerent, protruding. It was the kind of face which should have held instant appeal to a woman; all the necessary well-shaped component parts were there; but it was a face which, after her heart's first startled beat of instinctive attraction, struck a chill into Cleone's innermost being. For it seemed a soulless, empty shell, its expression cold and unfriendly, the mouth set into stern lines; haughty grey eyes humourlessly observant had Cleone under cool surveillance.

On seeing him, her tawny-gold eyes had widened and even under that chill gaze, she was aware of a wish that she had arrayed her coltish, boy's body in something a little smarter, a little more feminine than the tightly hugging pants and sweater, clothes which she had chosen with more reference to driving an old car with persistent draughts and a faulty heating system, than to impressing the man they had come to visit. Despite her knowledge, gained from Eric of course, that he was cold, hostile and implacable, Cleone felt her nerves tauten, quiver with an electrifying sensation of some curious, magnetic impulse. It must be her imagination, she told herself, this sense of danger, of tense undercurrents in the atmosphere. But instinctively, her hand went up to check the single, heavy braid, in which she always secured the waves of her gold-tinged, auburn hair.

'Turville?' Amyas Pringle enquired. 'Forgive this intrusion ... but you were, originally, expecting me. My name's Pringle. I wrote to you about the possibility of conducting a preliminary survey in this area. I see my assistant has forestalled me, not too tactfully, I apologise. But I only discovered at the last moment that I could, after all, manage to keep my appointment.'

The cool, hard planes of Saxon Turville's face had not relaxed one iota; indeed it seemed that his square jaw was set more firmly and the grey eyes did not even turn towards Amyas, but remained fastened upon Cleone, taking in, she felt sure, her unsophisticated appearance, her young leggy grace, with what was almost certainly a sneer quivering the corner of his shapely mouth. His voice, with its cold tones, in which sounded the ring of steel, matched the overall glacier-like quality of his appearance and manner.

'I regret even agreeing to see him. It's quite out of the question, quite impossible. I can't allow it. Schoolgirls and students. . . .' He gave a dismissive wave of a large

hand as if expecting them to depart forthwith. His
accents were icy, though cultured, his remark about
schoolgirls obviously aimed at Cleone.

Though she had a passionate, fiery temperament to
match her flame-like hair, Cleone was determined not to
allow this proud, aloof man to anger her, even though his
reference to her as a schoolgirl had flicked her on the raw,
sensitive as she was about the slender, apparent
immaturity of her body.

'Actually, you're wrong,' she informed him. 'Mr
Morton isn't a student, nor am I a child and we've both
had considerable experience in investigating archaeological sites, making preliminary surveys, and negotiating with site owners—like yourself.'

Except. she added internally, that no site owner had
ever been quite like Saxon Turville, either for looks or
unapproachability.

Her cool, reasonable manner seemed to effect no
change in his expression though he continued to watch
her steadily.

'Miss . . . Miss . . .?' Thick, crooked eyebrows arched in
enquiry.

'Bancroft,' she said shortly.

'Miss Bancroft. I don't know where you've suddenly
appeared from, but your intervention is totally useless.
I've given up quite sufficient of my time to that . . . that
young man . . . on two occasions now, and I . . .' As he
spoke, his eyes had at last, to Cleone's relief, turned
towards Amyas and now they widened slightly. 'Good
Lord,' he exclaimed, taking a swift step forward, his
manner totally unlike its former, unbending hostility.
'Surely it's The Badger? What are *you* doing here? You
don't mean to tell me that you're . . .?'

The nickname 'Badger', Cleone knew, was widely
applied to Amyas, behind his back of course, by his
students, on account of the uneven colour of his beard,
which had gone grey at an early age. But she had never
expected to hear the informal mode of address on the lips
of this man.

After a few moments of blank amazement, recognition
had begun to dawn in Amyas's eyes.

'Is it? ... it is ... isn't it? The "Terror of the Tigers"? Never knew your real name.' He turned to his niece, enthusiasm, generally reserved for ancient artefacts, enlivening his studious features. 'The best forward St Teresa's Tigers ever put in the field.'

'*You?* played rugby? For St Teresa's?' Cleone could not help the note of incredulity. She couldn't imagine this arrogant man indulging in the sometimes undignified antics of the rugby field.

'Long before *your* time, I should imagine,' Saxon drawled, mockingly, his sweeping glance once more taking in her fresh, youthful appearance, and Cleone bristled.

It was perfectly true that when he had been performing the feats over which Amyas now enthused, she had been in her second year at infant school. But that didn't mean he had to treat her as a schoolgirl now. But she bit back the indignant retort. Miraculously, the two men had found a common meeting ground, which augured better for the success of their visit and Cleone had no wish to undermine their unexpected rapport. Besides, why should she worry what Saxon Turville thought of her? As he himself had pointed out, there was a great difference in their ages. He was quite old.

That she should think with pleasurable vindictiveness of Saxon as being old, yet not accord the same epithet to the much more senior Amyas, did not occur to her as being at all strange.

'Of course Turville was never one of my students,' Amyas explained to Cleone, as, uninvited, he sank into the embrace of a shabby chair, which, like the settee, showed evidence of doggy predeliction for its comfort. 'History was your penchant, wasn't it ... history and literature?' he enquired. 'Though I seem to remember my department did have some attraction for you.' Amyas's brown eyes twinkled, as he turned to his niece. 'Pretty little student I had at that time. Half the young men in Oxford must have been wild for her ... quite a Helen of Troy, what? But I seem to remember you topped her popularity poll, eh, Turville?'

Saxon Turville had become much more relaxed at this

encounter with her uncle than Cleone would have believed possible, but now his striking face had set once more into inflexible planes.

'You could say that, I suppose.' He sounded . . . angry? But with whom?

'Whatever became of her, I wonder . . . promising lass.' Amyas seemed to have forgotten the purpose of their visit, Cleone thought and with his recognition of Saxon had fallen into a state of pleasurable reminiscence. 'Teresa was her name, if I remember rightly?'

'Tessa, actually.' The words came out, coldly clipped. 'And I married her.'

'Well now!' Amyas sounded fatuously gratified, Cleone considered, with a spurt of unexpected . . . could it be . . . irritation? It was an unpleasant sensation, whatever it was. Why should her uncle find it such a source of satisfaction, that some poor girl had had the bad taste, or the misfortune to fall for Saxon Turville—for Eric had been right about one thing . . . the landowner's arrogant manner. But, she reflected, it shouldn't have been a shock to find that Saxon Turville was married, after all there *was* Ianthe. What had become of the child? she wondered. She had disappeared as unobtrusively as she had appeared.

Amyas was still enthusing about Tessa.

'I shall look forward to renewing our acquaintance.'

'I'm afraid that won't be possible,' Saxon said abruptly, then: 'Now, about your visit . . .?' He seemed almost anxious to change the subject, Cleone thought. Perhaps he was a possessive husband, resenting any other man's interest in his wife.

Recalled from one of his frequent lapses of attention to the task in hand, unless it were of an archaeological nature, when his mind did not often waver, Amyas shot his niece a guilty look.

'Ah . . . yes. Well, m'dear fellow. Eric Morton came down to see you before . . . about March, wasn't it, Cleo? . . . about this pet project of mine.'

Once more, as her uncle addressed her, Saxon looked directly at Cleone, thoughtfully, his intent gaze making her colour up. But, as though unimpressed by what he saw, he shrugged and returned his attention to Amyas.

'So *you're* the professor who wants to come and disrupt our peaceful way of life?'

There was no reason why she should make any favourable impression on him, Cleone thought with some bitterness. No one had ever referred to her as 'a pretty little thing' . . . not even as 'striking'. She had heard her face described by a friend, more frank than tactful, as 'pleasantly ordinary', by yet another as a 'nice little face'; but never had anyone compared her to the beautiful women of history. If Helen of Troy had possessed Cleone's features, she told herself wryly, those thousand ships would have been sunk, rather than launched. She was totally unaware that she had her own particular claim to beauty, not that of classical good looks, but in her vivacious yet candid expression, the lovely, wicked twinkle that frequently lit her golden eyes.

Nevertheless, she felt impelled, for some reason, to ensure that Saxon Turville did not go on ignoring her.

'Are you really refusing us permission to assess the possibilities of this area? Is that your final, considered word?' She felt her uncle looking at her in some surprise, since she did not usually usurp his prerogative.

'My words are always considered.' There was remote assurance in the cold voice.

Yes, I bet they are, Cleone thought with sudden savagery. She was willing to bet too that Saxon Turville had never done an impulsive thing, spoken an impulsive word in his life—a robot had more warmth and spontaneity. But they couldn't give up, not yet. This was too important.

Cleone too could be haughty, when she chose and when annoyed was rarely at a loss for words to express her annoyance. In the past she had dealt with many awkward people, on behalf of her vague, preoccupied uncle and she would have felt perfectly well qualified to deal with this one, if it were not for the disconcerting effect he seemed to have upon her. Even so, she persisted, albeit rather tremulously.

'You do realise,' she asked, 'that you could be hindering very important work, perhaps preventing a major discovery?'

'Oh, I doubt that. Archaeologists have propounded totally unfounded theories before this.'

'But suppose,' Cleone said, in a last desperate appeal, 'suppose my uncle is right? Suppose there are artefacts and buildings of importance, somewhere on your land?'

His eyes narrowed.

'You're Badger's niece?'

She nodded ... and then he shrugged broad, muscular shoulders.

'If there are artefacts as you call them, if they've been lying there undiscovered for many hundreds of years ... does it really matter if they remain so? Especially if the alternative is to have my property overrun by long-haired "reds".'

'Eric isn't a Communist, actually,' she said, trying to sound reasonable. 'He just believes in fair shares for all ... and the abolition of privilege.'

'A conviction which you obviously share?' Saxon commented.

Cleone bit her full lower lip and forced a shrug. Let him think that if he liked. She dared not let herself be drawn into an argument with this man. For some unaccountable reason, he made her see a red far more vivid than that of the creed he attributed to Eric. She felt that it would give her great satisfaction to see this man's haughty pride lowered to the dust. But since that was not possible and because, to indulge her feelings would be to damage her uncle's cause, she would keep quiet, even if she burst a blood vessel in the effort; and fortunately, Amyas now chose to intervene.

'Turville, I came here in the hope of persuading you to change your mind ... about letting us examine the area for traces of Roman occupation.'

'Why should I?' Saxon asked, 'change my mind, I mean ... unless you're basing your hope on the fact of our previous acquaintance?'

'Nonsense, my dear fellow!' Amyas flushed, the nearest Cleone had ever seen her even-tempered uncle to annoyance. 'I came here with that purpose in mind, before I had the slightest suspicion that we'd met before.'

'But you must admit the fact has since given you hope?'

Saxon's voice was drily sardonic and Cleone could willingly have slapped the rugged, unsmiling face.

Amyas shrugged.

'All right ... all right ... I have to admit it. I wouldn't be human if the thought hadn't crossed my mind ... that in the circumstances you might relent. But I should never have mentioned the fact, if you hadn't.'

'Hmmm.' Saxon eyed first Cleone, then Amyas. 'And if I did withdraw my veto, just what would that involve me—and Salpeth—in?'

'Not a great deal, initially,' Amyas replied, his voice becoming more intense, eager, as it always did when he was launched upon his favourite topic. 'You must know enough of archaeological principles to be aware that the true scientist does not launch himself into the landscape at random? Nor does he move in with bulldozers. It's a slow process. As a first step, I should want to acquaint myself with the geology and topography of the area, consult maps, make soil tests. Maps often give place names which reveal, or at least hint at, the existence of ancient sites. I assume you will have certain maps and deeds to your property?'

Saxon inclined his blond head. He had all the mannerisms of royalty, Cleone thought crossly, without their graciousness.

'Then, as a preliminary, I would ask that you allow my assistants access to these. For my own part, I should like to walk the terrain, get the feel of the place.'

'Some of the maps and deeds you refer to are extremely ancient and therefore fragile, irreplaceable too,' Saxon informed him. 'I could not agree to their being removed from the premises. They would have to be consulted here, in my library.'

'Naturally,' Amyas agreed. 'That would be quite acceptable.'

Saxon turned his attention to Cleone's face yet again, his eyes analytical—just what was he looking for? This continual assessment was becoming embarrassing. It was as though he sought to see beneath her outer appearance. She became aware that she was sitting tensely on the edge

of her seat. Suddenly the whole atmosphere had changed.
Tentatively, negotiations had begun, but Saxon Turville
had not given a definite affirmative. Would he do so? and
under what conditions? She had a feeling that Saxon was
a man who would always make conditions.

CHAPTER TWO

As Cleone had guessed he would, Saxon imposed
conditions, before he would lift his ban on their proposed
activities.

'You spoke of assistants?' he said.

Amyas nodded.

'Yes, my niece and Eric Morton.'

Saxon issued his ultimatum with such uncompromising
finality that Cleone could only feel relief that Eric was
not there to hear it.

'I will not have that young man in my home. His beliefs
are an offence to every tradition which I uphold. I will not
have him contaminating my household, examining my
possessions, denying my right to their ownership.'

'My niece then . . .' Amyas began and Cleone held her
breath, hoping that the veto applied to her too. She
disliked intensely the idea of working under this man's
roof, under his cold, grey, disapproving eyes, whose gaze
played havoc with her usually steady nerves.

'Your niece isn't tarred with the same brush?'

Good, he *was* looking for a reason to reject her too.

'No!' Amyas said positively. 'I can't allow you to think
that. Both Cleone and I have a great respect for Eric as a
colleague. Where his work is concerned, he really is a first
class chap. But we do *not* share his political beliefs. We
have as much veneration for the old order of things as
you yourself, perhaps more, since our researches take us
deeper into the past.'

Saxon turned that direct, piercing gaze on Cleone.

'Is that so? Do you associate yourself with your uncle's
remarks?'

Cleone met his eyes steadily enough, though she felt her cheeks flush a little under the penetration of those steely grey orbs; a combination of indignation and embarrassment, she told herself. It was humiliating to have to placate this man. Though her uncle had spoken only the simple truth, some perverse instinct made her feel she would like to defy Saxon, to tell him that she too found his position, his wealth, his local autocracy as distasteful as did Eric. She longed to cry revolution, not because she held reactionary convictions, but merely, deliberately to disassociate herself from anything that Saxon Turville held sacred. But commonsense prevailed. She had to support Amyas, could not, in any case, tell a direct lie. So she lifted her pointed chin, determined to outface his critical gaze, to ignore the disproportionate unease it caused her.

'What my uncle says is quite correct.'

'And is she capable of carrying out this documentary research unaided; does she realise the importance of care, where old papers are concerned?'

The question was levelled at Amyas this time; and Cleone quivered with the desire to make the heated assertion that of course she was perfectly capable, as she was also capable of speaking for herself. But she managed to curb her tongue.

'Naturally, my dear fellow,' Amyas replied, 'or I should not suggest that she handle such valuable items. But if you would prefer your wife as an expert herself, to oversee Cleo . . .?'

'No!' The interjection rang out forcefully. 'If you are prepared to guarantee Miss Bancroft's suitability for the task, then I am satisfied. When do you wish to begin?'

Amyas spread his hands.

'Any time. We are all of us free agents for many weeks now. But as far as I am concerned, the sooner the better. Shall we say . . . tomorrow? I confess I am eager to begin.'

Saxon signified his assent by a brief nod of his handsome head.

'How many will there be in your party?'

Amyas reflected.

'Let me see ... there's myself, of course, Cleo here,
Eric, and six of my students. I'll telephone them tonight
... tell them to get down here ... and my fiancée, Miss
Kennedy, may join us later.

Nerys Kennedy! Cleone had forgotten Nerys moment-
arily, but now her brow furrowed. Why, after a bachelor
existence of fifty years plus, Amyas had suddenly
succumbed to the lure of matrimony, his friends and his
niece could not imagine. His affianced, a lecturer in
English literature, was some twenty years younger and
Cleone could not like her.

It wasn't jealousy, she had often assured herself, the fact
that Nerys must, some day, supplant her as her uncle's
general factotum. No, it was more that she doubted Nerys's
ability to make Amyas happy. It would take a very special
kind of woman to cope with his impractical lifestyle, his fits
of abstraction. His wife would have to resign herself to the
fact that she must always take second place to his
archaeology. Cleone couldn't see Nerys in a subordinate
role. Then, too, the older woman had a sardonic quality
which Cleone mistrusted; she always had the feeling that,
subtly, Nerys was deriding her, but very carefully, so that it
was apparent to no one else. Not that Amyas would notice.
He would be completely oblivious even if they fought tooth
and claw under his very nose.

Cleone had been hoping for these next few weeks
totally divorced from the irritant of Nerys's presence, for
the other woman had never made any secret of the fact
that she found it faintly ridiculous that adult people
should enjoy wallowing in muddy trenches, retrieving the
commonplace minutiae of former civilisations. Amyas
had smilingly admitted that it was not a dignified pastime
and had never seemed perturbed by his fiancée's
determination not to become involved. But for some
reason, to Amyas's quiet delight and to his niece's horror,
Nerys had announced her intention of joining them at
Salpeth, if and when they were safely established.

'Nine ... possibly ten. ...' Saxon sounded thoughtful.
'The local inn can cope with six, seven at a pinch, if two
of them don't mind sharing. You and your niece had
better stay here.'

'Oh, my dear fellow,' Amyas protested, 'we wouldn't dream of. . . .'

'But I insist.'

Cleone, who had recoiled inwardly at the idea of actually living in at the manor house, in such close proximity to Saxon Turville, thought she could guess at the motive behind his invitation. It was no proffering of the olive branch, nor the courtesy of *noblesse oblige*. Quite simply, he wanted to keep his cold, beady eye on the archaeologists, to be able to keep a tight control over any proceedings which might affect his property or his tenantry.

'You could accept Mr Turville's invitation, uncle,' she said hastily. 'I can put up at the inn. I could easily share with one of the girls. Nerys could stay here with you then.'

So anxious was she not to sleep under Saxon's roof, that she was even willing to throw Nerys and Amyas even closer together, whereas, up till now, she had hoped that her uncle's infatuation for the lecturer in English literature would evaporate before he irrevocably committed himself.

But Saxon immediatey dispelled her hopes of avoiding his hospitality.

'There are several bedrooms which can be made available at very short notice,' he stated. 'When Miss Kennedy arrives, it will be a simple matter to accommodate her also.'

'While the *hoi polloi* lodge at the inn!' Thinking of Eric's segregation, Cleone could not have prevented the sarcastic remark to save her life. Though she was well aware that Eric would have refused point blank to stay at the manor, she felt that he had been somewhat harshly discriminated against.

Her unwanted host's eyebrows rose sharply.

'You would scarcely expect me to house your entire workforce? and may I remind you that only seconds ago, *you* were proposing to form one of the so-called *hoi polloi* yourself, a prospect which apparently *you* did not find damaging to your *amour propre*, so why should they object?'

It was annoying to find herself, uncharacteristically, at a loss for an answer, but so it proved, and Cleone was glad to note that her uncle was making a move to depart.

'I must find my assistant . . . calm him down . . . and put him in the picture. Then I'll see what arrangements we can make at the inn. No, no . . .' to Cleone, 'no need for you to move, Cleo. You've had a long drive today. You stay here and get better acquainted with our host. Bring him up to date with news of Oxford. Perhaps you could tell him a little more about the work we propose to do, what we hope to find?'

And before the horrified Cleone could protest, or think of an adequate excuse for accompanying him, he was gone.

With Amyas's departure, an awkward, beating silence fell and though Cleone, her nerves knotted tightly, sought desperately for something to say, her mind seemed to have gone completely blank. She couldn't remember anyone else ever having this tongue-tieing effect upon her before. It must be her dislike for Saxon Turville, she told herself, making her so unusually nervous. She disliked him, yet in some way she could not define, he disturbed her, threw her into a ferment of uncertainty. In self-disgust, she reflected that her behaviour must be increasing his belief in her youthful gaucheness, but it would be even worse if she were panicked into speaking just for the sake of it and as a result uttered something totally insane and meaningless.

Hoping, by nonchalant movement, to conceal what amounted almost to unreasoning terror in this man's presence, she stood up and approached the dogs, which still lay, apparently relaxed, but in reality alert to every sound and movement in the room. Warily, they eyed her approach, but Cleone was accustomed to dogs and did not rush them. She allowed them to nose at her hand, before attempting to caress their silky heads.

'Gwynne and Castlemaine!' Saxon's voice broke in upon her absorption with the dogs and she looked at him with a puzzled frown. 'The bitches,' he explained. 'They're King Charles spaniels, so I named them after Charles the Second's mistresses. There was a man who had the right idea. He took his pleasure in various places, not confining himself to the whims of one woman.'

'Oh!' Ridiculous to blush at his statement about the dogs. Cleone felt naïve and childish. Was he trying to embarrass her? or had it been his stilted way of making conversation? As for the remark about Charles the Second's mistresses, she could only deplore his sentiments, which revealed all too clearly the kind of man he must be. She ventured a surreptitious glance at him and surprised him in a very comprehensive assessment of her appearance. Her throat seemed to close up. Goodness, this was awful. In a moment, she would be shifting from foot to foot and fiddling with her clothing like a self-conscious infant. She took a deep breath, forcing sound to pass the incomprehensible blockage inhibiting speech.

'I ... I suppose I couldn't see my room ... the room I'm to use, I mean,' she amended hastily, in case that sounded presumptuous.

Perhaps it was cowardly, but she felt that, once upstairs, she could find an excuse to linger there alone, until she heard Amyas return, thus avoiding this uncomfortable *tête-à-tête*, for which, she was sure, Saxon could have no more inclination than herself.

She expected that it would be the housekeeper's task, or that of the so far invisible Tessa, his wife, to escort her upstairs. But not so ... and then she remembered him telling Amyas that it would not be possible for him to renew his acquaintance with his former student. But why?

Saxon summoned no one; instead he moved towards the door, indicating that she should precede him. Her ploy to avoid his company had failed and she scolded herself for being so easily disturbed. Why should she permit this man to upset her normal self-assurance?

A deep-treaded, creaking staircase made a gradual ascent to the first floor and Cleone had time to admire the rich patina of lovingly cared for wood. Upstairs the old house seemed to be on a multitude of different levels, with steps up and down, unexpected recesses and windows, all of which had been given a character of their own, by a carefully chosen ornament or floral arrangement. It seemed the dour housekeeper took a pride in her work.

After what seemed like miles of corridors, her host stopped and threw open the door into a small but charmingly appointed bedroom. It was necessary to descend two steps to enter the room, which was carpeted in a rich red, which contrasted strongly with white walls and black beams. The curtains were of a deep pink and a multi-coloured patchwork covered the small, modern bed.

Saxon opened the small latticed window, then stood aside, so that Cleone could admire the view. It was breathtaking. Her room was at the back of the house, looking upwards towards mile upon mile of woodland and above the swaying tops of the trees, could be seen the rolling downs, their softly rounded slopes rising steeply from the valley floor, and dotted here and there, minute in the distance, yet startlingly white against the deep green of the grass of summer, were placidly grazing sheep. It was an idyllically peaceful, typically English scene and Cleone felt strangely soothed by it.

'And does the accommodation meet with your approval? Do you think it will come up to the standard of the Inn?'

She looked up sharply at the ironic note in Saxon's voice. Did he really expect her to be dissatisfied, or rude enough to express that dissatisfaction?

'I think it's charming,' she said quietly, 'thank you.' Then, because the question had been exercising her mind for some time and it seemed natural that the thought should formulate itself into words, she asked: 'Tell me something, Mr Turville ... why did you change your mind?'

His reply was unexpected.

'In answer to that, let me ask you something. What is it about archaeology that appeals to you?'

On familiar, safe territory, Cleone was able to answer unhesitatingly.

'It's the utter fascination of formulating a theory, examining it, trying to prove it right. Then, there's the excitement, the satisfaction of discovering ... not something unexpected exactly ... more "suspected" ...

yet nonetheless wonderful for all that.' She looked at him enquiringly. 'Does that answer your question?'

He returned her gaze gravely, assessing, though she did not know it, the almost childlike candour, the clear innocence of the golden eyes. Somehow, Cleone did not believe those beautifully chiselled lips of his were capable of smiling; but there was an odd expression in his eyes . . . almost . . . almost triumphant? But what had he to gloat over?

'Very adequately! It also answers your own!'

Once again, Cleone sat in the library, poring over an old map, only now there were dozens of them, some rather dusty, she thought, with a rueful regard for the dress she wore.

She was wearing a petrol-blue, summer dress today, which conferred a more flattering outline to her slender body. But, of course, it was worn solely for comfort . . . her own pleasure . . . not in any way to amend Saxon Turville's view of her. To convince herself of this, she had left her red-gold hair in its normal single braid. Unbound, her glorious hair was long enough to sit upon. But she had allowed herself a modicum of make-up, just enough to emphasise her most attractive features, the tawny eyes, which shone like gold when she was happy and dulled to moody brown in moments of distress, and her mouth, discreetly reddened, drawing attention to its full, passionate, though unawakened curves.

'My father let you stay here.' Once again, Ianthe had attached herself to the newcomer and it seemed that when Ianthe pursued a topic of conversation, she did so with single-minded determination. 'But he didn't let the man with the long, black hair stay. He has to stay at the Inn, with the rest of the working party.'

The child seemed very well informed, considering she claimed to find her father alarming and unapproachable.

'How did you know that? Did your father tell you?'

Ianthe gave a world-weary little smile, which Cleone found exceedingly pathetic in one so young.

'Of course not. I talk to servants . . . listen to their

gossip. My father wouldn't approve, of course; but who else is there to talk to? He invited you to stay here,' Ianthe now persisted. 'I wonder why? He doesn't like girls either you know. Why do you suppose my father hates everybody, Cleo?'

Cleo stared at her helplessly. The child was incredibly like her father, the face as square as his, bore the same golden tan, was capped by the same sunstreaked hair. The eyes regarding Cleone were the same shade of grey, but where the father's face was granite-like in its implacability, the child's was wistful; the mouth, that in the father was arrogant and tight-lipped was gently drooping in the daughter and the grey eyes were not bleak and humourless, but full of anxious enquiry.

All Cleone's inclinations were to assure the child that she must be mistaken. Despite Saxon Turville's un-approachability, she could not believe that somewhere beneath that icy surface there was not an inner, warmer core. He was so good-looking, she thought wistfully. The most attractive man she had ever encountered. But suppose Ianthe was right, and the child must know her own father better than she, Cleone, ever could. What a dreadful atmosphere for a ten-year old to live in. How could Ianthe ever be expected to form satisfactory relationships in her life, with only her father's misogynistic example to go by? Yes, Cleone sighed, undoubtedly Saxon's daughter knew him too well to be reassured by anything a stranger might say.

'You don't think perhaps my father likes you?' Ianthe said, 'that perhaps he changed his mind, about letting the archaeologists come, because of you?'

What an idea!

'Most certainly not!' Here Cleone could make a positive assertion. 'He doesn't like me, any more than I like him,' she added, in case the child might be under that illusion and perhaps jealous on her mother's behalf. 'I don't know why he decided to let us come, but he did, quite suddenly, except that he refused to allow Eric to work on these documents.' She indicated the maps before her.

There was a few minutes silence as Cleone pursued her

studies, but somewhere at the back of her mind a question still lurked, preventing her from giving the maps her full concentration. With a sigh, she abandoned the attempt for the moment and, tentatively, set about satisfying her curiosity.

'I've met you, and I've met your father,' she said to Ianthe, 'but I haven't seen your mother. Is she away at present?'

'I don't have a mother,' Ianthe stated flatly.

'But. . . .'

'At least, I'm not sure if I have,' the child qualified slowly. 'When I try to ask my father about her, he gets very angry. *I* think she's dead . . . and sometimes, I think my father killed her.' She stared defiantly at Cleone, as if daring her to contradict—or perhaps hoping that she would?

Cleone was appalled and if this had been another type of child, she might have suspected malice, but there seemed to be no vindictiveness in Ianthe's voice, no intention to mislead. Instead, there was a kind of sorrowing fear, as if she wept for what she suspected and feared what it pained her to believe.

'Oh, Ianthe! That can't be true! What on earth gave you an idea like that?'

'Something I overheard the housekeeper telling the gardener. I told you,' she said with self-deprecation, 'that I listen to servants' gossip. It's the only way to find things out in this house.'

Cleone did not, she told herself, believe Ianthe's outrageous claim, but the fact that Tessa was no longer in residence at the manor did explain why there had been no hostess available to show Cleone to her room; and remembering who had shown her the way upstairs, she found herself dwelling upon Saxon's parting shot, and puzzling over it. What theory did he hold? she wondered again. What did he hope to prove or discover—and what had it to do with the presence of the archaeologists in Salpeth? Altogether, she thought, there was a great deal here that she did not understand, least of all his surprising *volte-face*. She had certainly not expected to be here now, to have been granted access to the documents spread out before her—and what about Saxon's dislike for members of her uncle's profession? his daughter's more than normal awe of a stern parent; the unexplained absence of his wife. She followed this last train of thought through.

'When did you last see your mother?'

'I've never seen her,' was the surprising reply. 'I don't remember her at all. I don't even know what she looked like . . . there are no photos of her anywhere.'

Cleone did a rapid calculation. Ianthe was ten years old. Most children could recall incidents from about their fourth or fifth year, some even earlier. Which meant that Tessa Turville had not been around for some five or six years, perhaps longer. Surely, if she had disappeared under mysterious circumstances, someone would have been interested enough to notice her absence, comment on it? . . . even take action if foul play had been suspected. But now she was allowing Ianthe's fanciful words to colour her thinking. That could be dangerous.

'Shall I explain this map to you now?' she suggested, in an effort to divert her own vivid imagination from the path it was taking. 'If you're going to be an archaeologist some day, you'll need to . . .'

'My daughter is not going to be an archaeologist.' The cold pronouncement made them both start nervously. For a large man, Saxon Turville had the uncanny knack of moving silently. 'Ianthe!' he continued, his tone rough, condemnatory, 'what are you doing in here? you are keeping Miss Bancroft from her work. You were told . . .'

'I don't mind . . . honestly,' Cleone interrupted, smitten by the look of dismay on Ianthe's face, her immediate, nervous retreat. 'I'm quite . . .'

'For the duration of your study, the library is off limits to my daughter.' He had taken absolutely no notice of Cleone's attempts to smooth over his rebuke to the child. He moved towards the door, holding it suggestively wide, indicating by his attitude that he expected Ianthe to leave. She did so and he closed the door firmly behind the small figure.

'Let us get one thing quite clear, Miss Bancroft. I do not wish my daughter's head to be filled with ridiculous notions. I. . . .'

'And just what is ridiculous about wanting to be an archaeologist:' Cleone asked, her voice deceptively mild, whereas, in reality, she was inwardly seething, not just at the implied denigration of the profession, but also at Saxon's callous treatment of his daughter.

'It's not something with which I wish my daughter to be associated.'

He was a snob. That was his trouble. Cleone's golden eyes darkened to moody brown as she glared up at him.

'You make it sound like an occupation pursued by people of inferior birth,' she told him. 'Many eminent men, and women, have been archaeologists. I thought Mrs Turville herself studied the subject. What could be more natural than for her daughter to . . .?'

'We will leave Mrs Turville's idiosyncrasies out of this, if you please. I do not wish Ianthe to be involved with this matter *in any way*. She understands this and . . .'

'No! I don't think Ianthe does understand,' Cleone contradicted, without stopping to consider her own temerity. 'She may understand that you have forbidden her to take any interest in the subject, but she doesn't understand why and neither do I. . . .'

'It is not necessary for you to understand my . . .'

'That child is utterly bewildered,' Cleone swept on, ignoring his words, 'both by you and your attitude towards the whole thing—and by the way you treat her.'

Goliath could not have been more thunderstruck by David's defiance than this large man was by Cleone's audacity in defying him in his own home.

'Miss Bancroft, may I remind you that you are a guest in my house—a guest moreover, who is here on sufferance. The rules I make for the members of my household do not concern you. Kindly confine yourself to your task. The sooner this whole insufferable business is concluded the better. I do not wish to hear my daughter discussing archaeology with you again, nor, should there be any excavations—and I sincerely hope there will not be—do I want her on the site. I hope I make myself quite clear?'

Transparently so, Cleone thought, as he marched out of the library, with so much celerity that she suspected he feared that he might not have the last word in the discussion. These last few moments had been full of revelation. Saxon's antipathy towards archaeologists and archaeology in general was because he had not liked the fact that his wife followed that profession. But why had he objected to this fact ... why on earth had he married her? One thing was very evident; he did not intend that Ianthe should pursue her hereditary interest.

It was some while before Cleone could concentrate fully on the task before her. She had no liking for Saxon Turville of course, despite the undeniable magnetism of his good looks. But she could not help reflecting on the tragedy of it—that such a man should be so embittered, had become an emotional cripple. One would expect him to have everything going for him. He had a beautiful home, set amidst acres of good farmland, a decidedly appealing small daughter. By all accounts he was popular locally, with a loyal tenantry; and last, but by no means least, he had his magnificent appearance. If only his manner and character had the same charisma as his face and physique, he would be an exceedingly disturbing man ... to an impressionable woman that was. Hastily, Cleone added the rider to her thought. She thanked her stars that she was not impressionable, otherwise, before she knew where she was, she might find herself actually feeling sorry for Saxon. But his words had given her considerable food for thought and in her mind's eye, she could still see the forlorn little figure of his daughter, whom she most certainly did pity.

There was no way, Cleone told herself fiercely, that she would refuse to answer little Ianthe's questions; nor would she drive her away, that was, if the child had the hardihood to defy her father's edicts.

But, in spite of these turbulent thoughts, the lure of the past drew her back under its spell at last and for a while she was able to forget her unsympathetic host and his apparently unfeeling behaviour towards his daughter.

The older maps interested Cleone most, for, over the centuries, names had become distorted or modernised, while certain features had been omitted, probably because later cartographers had attributed them to legend rather than to fact.

The best method of working, she had discovered from past experience, was to draw up her own master map, filling in the relevant information from the assorted documents. It was rare for settlement patterns not to have rhyme and reason and she hoped that in this way such a pattern would emerge, pinpointing the most likely site for Amyas's investigations.

The village itself, she noted on her sketch, had once been spelt 'Salpaeth', its present name obviously a corruption, which might be worth researching later on. Basically, its layout seemed to have remained much the same for several centuries: buildings encircling a green, a church, not in its present form of course, and latterly, since the fifteenth century, the manor house and farm.

Once the Cotswolds had probably all consisted of entirely deciduous forest, with beech the dominant tree, and from documentary evidence, Cleone could see that the beechwoods flanking the manor grounds had originally been more extensive than those shown on the up-to-date Ordnance survey. But even so, there were still considerable stretches of woodland; and one of them in particular interested Cleone, a huge area lying between the house and the wold, divided by a minor tributary of the Coln. On an eighteenth-century map it was described as 'Barrow Wood' while another showed it as 'Priory Wood' with a field closely abutting upon it as 'Abbotsfield'.

It would seem, Cleone reflected, that there had been a religious settlement here if nothing else. But as she had hoped, her research was to take her even further back, via a piece of parchment so frail that someone had had the good sense to frame it under glass. It was undated, but, subject to Amyas's expert opinion, Cleone judged it to be a seventeenth-century copy of an older map, how much older, she wished she knew. Represented on the parchment was yet another version of Salpeth, but the woodland was still identifiable—not as 'Priory Wood' this time but as 'Diana's Grove'.

Was it just wishful thinking on her part? Was she making facts fit theory? or had this stretch of woodland once been named for the Roman's virgin huntress and patroness of chastity? Increasing the radius of her scrutiny, a magnifying glass was necessary for the faded ink and crabbed writing, she found that 'Abbotsfield' had once been the 'Grove of Libertina'. Cleone drew in an excited breath. Libertina—the Roman goddess of burials! This was further support of her theory. Had later generations followed Roman tradition? for new settlements were often built on top of earlier occupation sites. The Priory—if Priory there had been—and this was something which could be confirmed quite easily, might well have stood upon the former site of a temple to Diana; and it was quite within the realms of possibility that 'Abbotsfield' or 'The Abbot's Field' as it appeared on some documents, had been the monks' burial ground, their Christian bones mingling with pagan, in ground once sacred to Libertina.

Cleone was tempted to rush out at once in search of her uncle, but Amyas could be anywhere, covering the area with his long, eager strides, his soil-testing equipment in his haversack, his shrewd eyes seeking out landscape formations. Finding an archaeological site could be difficult. Not every ancient settlement left identifiable surface features, even to the keenest gaze. Her present study would be of inestimable help, so she must complete her work here, even though her eyes felt strained and gritty, her head clouded from poring over the ancient documents.

Her perseverance was rewarded. In the area she now thought of, though she knew one should always prove one's assumptions first, as Diana's Grove, she found two small references, very close together and so faded as to be almost invisible, to 'Minerva' and 'Fortuna'. Impossible to guess what these represented, but it was enough, this juxtaposition of several Roman names, Cleone felt, to make an investigation of the beechwood worthwhile.

As always with a new project, she was itching to begin. But over the years, she had learnt to temper enthusiasm with patience. To the general public, archaeology was, as it had been to her in childhood, synonymous with the excavation of treasure-filled tombs, the discovery of lost cities and civilisations, the glittering promise of gold throwing the archaeologists' true aims out of perspective.

But Cleone knew, from her uncle's careful instruction, that pots, temples and tombs were not the main objective. She could not deny the thrill she still felt at the thought of such things, but her uncle, she knew, was concerned, not with their intrinsic value, but in their systematic study as a means of reconstructing the past, in interpreting the context in which they had once existed. One made haste slowly.

Amyas was insistent, with every new batch of students, that they should see themselves, and be seen by others, not as plunderers, but as seekers after knowledge of the past.

'Man needs a tangible past on which to base his future and archaeology is the key to it,' was one of his favourite maxims.

Emerging from the library as dazed by this release from close confinement as a mole that unwarily surfaces in sunlight, she found, as she had suspected, that Amyas was nowhere to be found. Bursting to share her discoveries with someone, she thought of Eric. It was possible of course that he had accompanied her uncle, but somehow she doubted it. More often than not, Amyas preferred to be alone on his tours of reconnaissance, likening himself to an old bloodhound, who worked best when alone on the scent. There was almost something of clairvoyance in the way he projected himself into the past he sought, often intuitively interpreting the smallest clue, so that quite often he happened upon sites in a manner which could only be described as serendipity.

In any case, it was lunchtime, a fact that had escaped her in the pursuit of information; but now she was forcibly reminded of it by gnawing pangs that could no longer be ignored. If Eric was not to be found in the Inn, she was not perturbed at the thought of eating there alone.

Saxon's housekeeper, so he had informed Amyas, did not cook at midday; breakfast and an evening meal would be available for his house guests, but at other times they would be expected to forage for themselves. This would not trouble Amyas, who had been known to miss three consecutive meals when in hot pursuit of some archaeological quest, but Cleone did not share that particular form of his dedication and since she did not normally eat breakfast, food was now a dire necessity.

As she had been instructed, she locked the library door, returned the key to its hook in a cupboard near the housekeeper's room, then set off for the village.

Despite her ravenous appetite, she moved slowly, looking about her appreciatively. On the previous occasions she had passed through the main street, she had been driving and too full of apprehension to admire her surroundings. Now, she had time to notice that, without exception, the houses were all pretty, gabled, with distinctively steep, stone roofs, gently angled corners, proper Cotswold chimneys, windows with stone mullions and delicate drip moulds, stone tiles in deep shades of varying colours.

In the centre of the large green, a wooden seat, built around three large oaks, was made for chatterers, while on the opposite side from the Inn, a brook made a little ford, and at the other stood an old-fashioned village pump, topped by a lamp, presumably once intended for those drawing water after dark; and though no longer in use to supply the village, water could still be obtained, gushing into a large, semi-circular stone trough, edged with water-loving plants.

The village was quiet, but not lifeless; a tractor rumbled by, two men road-trained a lively, quivering, bay mare and in one of the neat gardens a cheerful-faced cottager polished her windows. She turned at the sound of Cleone's footsteps and waved a greeting. As Cleone nodded and smiled in return, she noted the carved inscription above the doorway, indicating that this little building had once been a school.

The Inn, The Golden Fleece, though small, was a handsome building, half-timbered, with small bay windows at the front and an octagonal, projecting stairway and gallery at the back. A sign over the door proclaimed that the hostelry still brewed its own beer. But the interior scarcely matched its exterior attractions, being plain and functional. No ornamentation, such as Cleone had seen in other country pubs, adorned the low, twisted, black beams and the furnishings consisted of simple oak settles and tables, standing upon an uncompromisingly bare floor of white stone flags. The fireplace had a mantel with niches for mugs; and on the walls flanking it were photographs of various village celebrations and of the local hunt. In the public bar a darts match was in progress and outside could be heard the unmistakable noises of a skittle alley.

Eric was not among those present, but as Cleone had more or less expected this, she ordered a ploughman's lunch and a half pint of shandy and retreated to a comparatively quiet corner by a window.

Although she received one or two curious glances from the regulars, Cleone was not troubled or self-conscious about her solitary state. She ate her lunch with relish and allowed herself to speculate upon the potential of the morning's discoveries.

Her reverie was interrupted, as the darts game ended and the little group of players broke up, some to return to their work, some moving towards the bar, to order fresh drinks.

It was not until he paused by her table that Cleone realised Saxon Turville had formed one of their number. She wondered that she had not noticed him immediately; he was not a man one overlooked, but then his height was not so distinctive among these large, brawny country-men, his estate workers, she guessed, most of whom could match him for size if not for those startlingly good looks. He had a plate in one hand and a pint mug in the other.

'Mind if I join you?' It seemed to be a rhetorical question, for he did not await her reply before sliding on to the oak settle, uncomfortably close to her on its short, smooth length, his muscular thigh brushing hers and surreptitiously she edged further into her corner.

While she found Saxon's personality distinctly abrasive, there was no doubt about his physical attractions and their strange effect upon her, and she preferred not to be reminded of them by any accidental contact. How tiresomely perverse of her body to be stirred by the proximity of a man whose manner both puzzled and angered her, but even worse, a married man, even if his wife was not at present in evidence.

His approach to her was a totally unexpected turn of

events. Whereas Cleone could well visualise the 'lord of
the manor' fraternising with his tenants, she had not
expected him to condescend to her, one of the despised
race of archaeologists. Disconcerted, she murmured a
belated disclaimer, annoyed to find herself blushing over
the doubtful honour he accorded her.

'Do you always lunch here?' she asked, feeling that
something was expected of her in the way of conversation.

'Most days . . . except Friday . . . market day . . . when
I eat in Cirencester.'

So he wouldn't be around tomorrow—good!

'Where does Ianthe eat then?' All very well for his
housekeeper to expect a grown man to forage for himself,
but what about the child?

He shrugged.

'Here and there, at friends' houses mainly.'

'Not a very satisfactory arrangement surely, for a child
her age?' Cleone could not forebear to remark.

Well-defined eyebrows, darker than the thick, sun-
bleached hair, shot up in haughty interrogation.

'Children are hardy creatures, Miss Bancroft. I can
assure you, Ianthe does not starve.'

No, Cleone thought mutinously, not for lack of
nourishment perhaps. But she was missing, starved for
other things. She thought back to her own childhood,
before she had been sent to boarding school; the heart-
warming comfort of coming home to the welcoming
atmosphere of a house redolent with the good smell of
cooked food, the family conversation over lunch, the
ironing out of any little, childish problems, that might
have arisen during the morning session at school; and
this, for Ianthe, was not term time, but the long summer
holiday. How did Ianthe occupy herself all day, every
day, with no mother around and, presumably, no one else
to care how she spent her time?

'What does Ianthe do, to amuse herself, during the
holidays?' she asked.

Again, that infuriating, supercilious quirk of brows.

'You seem inordinately interested in my daughter.'

Not because she was his, if that was what he was trying
to imply.

'She's a nice child,' Cleone said aloud, defensively. She wanted to make it quite clear that she was concerned about Ianthe for the child's sake. He needn't think her interest had anything to do with him, that she was using Ianthe to further herself in his eyes. Firmly, she told herself that she couldn't care less what Mr High-and-Mighty Turville thought of her.

'Don't get any ideas about taking her under your wing, Miss Bancroft. You know my views about her associating with your party.'

'Anyone would think we were lepers,' she said indignantly. Then she asked outright the question which exercised her mind. 'Just what have you got against archaeologists, Mr Turville?'

He gave her a long, steady look from eyes totally devoid of warmth or expression—unless it were hostility.

'Very well! Since you ask. I deplore the expenditure of time and money on the resurrection of past civilisations. Our concern should be with today, on improving the conditions of the people living around us, not rhapsodising on those of former times.'

It was the longest speech he had yet made to her and Cleone was surprised by the intensity, the obvious sincerity with which he expressed his views.

'I agree with you, about caring for the living,' she said slowly. Wasn't that why she deplored his casual attitude towards his daughter? 'But surely we can learn from the past; you studied history yourself at university?' Her tawny eyes met his with genuine puzzlement.

'Only,' he said drily, 'because, academically, history and English were my best subjects and my father insisted that I follow the family tradition in going up to Oxford. I would far sooner have gone to Agricultural College.'

'Still . . . if you hadn't gone to Oxford, you wouldn't have met your wife, you wouldn't have had Ianthe or . . .!' She faltered into silence as his lips tightened.

'Not exactly an argument in its favour,' he commented.

Cleone was appalled at his seemingly callous dismissal of his daughter's existence.

'You're very lucky to have such a lovely little girl,' she said with heat, 'some people . . .'

'Oh, Ianthe's well enough,' he interrupted her impatiently. 'It was the doubtful blessing of marriage to which I referred.'

Remembering Ianthe's words about her mother, the child's declared ignorance concerning Tessa's whereabouts, Cleone burned to know the truth; but there was no way this man was going to open up to her about his wife, and that was the operative word—'wife'. It wouldn't do to become too interested in his affairs. Hastily, she finished her meal.

'I must get back to my work,' she excused herself.

He rose, his tall, well-built frame seeming larger still in the close confines of the small bar.

'I'll walk back to the Manor with you.' It was not a request to be allowed to bear her company any more than when he had joined her at her table, and Cleone could see no way of avoiding the situation without actually being rude.

They passed through the bar to the accompaniment of cheerful nods and farewells. Saxon Turville seemed popular enough with those present. Did he not show his dourer side to the villagers, or was their behaviour the outward sign of obsequiousness from tenants to landlords?

'How have your researches progressed?' he asked, as they walked across the green, Cleone setting a brisk pace, the sooner to rid herself of his uncomfortable presence.

From her uncle Cleone had learnt to be cautious about propounding theories, particularly to layfolk who knew nothing of the processes involved in identifying and proving a site. She was not ready yet to share her theory about 'Diana's Grove'—at least not with Saxon Turville, who continually denigrated the profession of archaeologist. But she could not quite disguise the triumphant ring of enthusiasm in her voice.

'Quite well, actually. I've noted down some details of sites, which I think are worth investigating.'

'I see!'

It was difficult to tell if his noncommital tone expressed displeasure, but Cleone guessed he had been hoping that her work would prove profitless, so that he would quickly be rid of a disruptive presence in his domain.

She decided that, for the remainder of their walk, it might be politic to change the subject and she made some admiring comments upon the character of the village and its architecture.

'I'd love to buy a little place like that and have it as a weekend cottage,' she enthused, as she stopped to study one particularly pleasing prospect; a gloriously lopsided cottage, its roofing arranged so that the small slates at the top graduated to larger ones at the eaves, a pattern best suited to the heavy material and steep pitch of the roof and having the same orderly beauty as a fish's scales. The path to the front door was edged with honesty, phlox and marigolds, flowers and foliage making endless permutations of light and shade, of colour and contrast.

But if she thought to please Saxon by her admiration of his village, she was mistaken. Disconcertingly he snorted.

'That's one thing you wouldn't be able to do, you or anyone else, not in Salpeth.'

'Oh? Why's that?'

'Because,' he said grimly, 'we've taken steps to prevent that sort of thing. I've seen too many villages, where derelict cottages have been snapped up by the "cocktail and Jaguar" types, altered out of all recognition with white plastic shutters and garden gnomes.' He shuddered. 'Not only do they ruin the whole character of the place, they raise property prices way beyond the reach of the local population, whose right it is to live here. All these dwellings used to belong to the Turville estates, until my grandfather was forced to sell them off. Then, several years ago, we formed a Trust, under my chairmanship, to buy up the cottages, as they came up for sale. We own nearly all of them now and we maintain them in keeping with their character and rent them at a figure the villagers and the estate workes can afford. It ensures that Salpeth is kept for the local people.'

'How very feudal,' Cleone said scornfully. 'I would have thought the place would benefit from an injection of new blood, and money.'

'The rural Cotswolds are feudal, always have been, we're proud of it. We don't encourage outsiders at Salpeth,' he said flatly, 'particularly those with wagging, malicious tongues.'

That was interesting. To whom was he referring? to someone who had maligned him? and did he mean that the villagers as a whole did not welcome outsiders . . . or that Saxon Turville did not?

Strange that a man who had been up at Oxford, known a different kind of community life, should be so insular in outlook. Had he always been so, or had some experience embittered him, made him shut out the world? From where had his wife originated? Cleone felt that it could not have been from Salpeth, so was she one of the outsiders to whom he referred? Was this creed of his totally rooted in the foundations of an unhappy marriage? or could it be that this closed little community had something to hide from the outside world? Vague thoughts of latter day smuggling or other illicit activities flashed through her mind.

Annoyed by her continuing obsession with Saxon's affairs, she tossed back her head with its long braid of auburn hair in an irritated attempt to clear her brain of these unsettling imaginings; but one lingered. She could not entirely banish the effect of Ianthe's words . . . 'I think he may have killed her'. Was it Saxon Turville alone who feared outside intrusion?

But that was nonsense, she tried to reassure herself. If that were so, he would hardly have rescinded his refusal to allow the archaeologists on his land; and, on the subject of archaeology, she thought, she must not allow herself to be diverted from her work. Her brain should be occupied with the interpretation of the clues she had discovered, not in idle speculation upon Saxon's motives, his private life, which, once again she must remind herself, was no concern of hers.

Cleone had hoped that when they reached the farmyard her companion would leave her to continue on alone. Surely his claim that his was a working farm implied that he himself took an active part in that work? He must have more important things to do than to accompany her?

But he seemed intent on seeing her to the library door and Cleone hoped that he wasn't going to ask her to detail her discoveries for him.

If that had been his intention, it was driven from his mind by other considerations.

'I thought you were told to lock the library door in your absence?'

'But I did . . . I. . . .' Her voice trailed away as she saw the key in the lock. Could she have forgotten? No! She distinctly remembered putting the key back on its hook. 'I did lock the door,' she repeated firmly. 'Someone has unlocked it again. Perhaps one of your staff? to do some cleaning?'

But he was not listening. With a swift movement, he threw open the library door and behind him Cleone gazed in appalled silence. The documents were scattered and one or two lay on the floor. Who had been in here and done this? Was somebody trying to get her into trouble?

'Pick them up!'

She turned to look up at Saxon Turville, about to ask him who the hell he thought he was talking to, but something in the cold, concentrated fury of his expression stopped her. Outwardly meek, but inwardly seething, she did as he bade her, acutely aware, as she did so, of him standing over her. Not until every document was once more spread on the table did he turn away.

'Kindly complete your work at the earliest possible moment. I should like to return my papers to a place of safety . . . since it seems you are not a fit and proper person to have access to them . . . that you are totally irresponsible . . . like all females. I have no patience with irresponsible behaviour.'

It was fortunate, Cleone thought, that he had made his exit on those words, because otherwise she might not have been able to repress the angry retort that sprang to her lips. As it was, she worked with furious haste to complete the details of her map. Saxon could not be more eager than she for his papers to be safely stowed away, but it was a pity the incident had occurred; it only increased his antagonism towards the archaeological party. That it had injured her in his eyes was not, she convinced herself, an important consideration.

More and more she wondered at his complete *volte-face*

in his sudden decision to give his permission for their investigations, for it was certainly not attributable to good nature on his part, or due to any belief in their aims; and a cold finger of fear feathered her spine, as she came to the conclusion that he had some ulterior motive.

CHAPTER THREE

AT last, with a sigh of relief, Cleone rolled up her completed sketch map and left the Turville papers neatly stacked on the library table.

'This time,' she said aloud, with grim humour, 'I'll lock the door and put the wretched key straight into "his lordship's own hand".'

'Oh . . . *please!*'

The voice startled her, emanating as it seemed to from thin air. Then one of the heavy brown velvet curtains at the window swayed slightly and Ianthe emerged hesitantly from its folds.

'Please don't lock me in.'

'Ianthe! What on earth? Oh heavens . . . it was *you* . . . wasn't it?' Cleone gestured towards the map-laden table.

Ianthe lowered her eyes and her fragile fingers pleated the skirt of her skimpy cotton dress. Had anyone noticed, Cleone wondered, that the child was growing out of her clothes? Ianthe spoke in a breathless voice that held a hint of tears.

'Please don't be angry, Cleo. I didn't mean to get you into trouble, but I did so want to look at the maps. I've never seen them before. I . . . I know it was wrong of me, but I borrowed the key. I meant to have it back in Mrs Griggs' cupboard before you . . . and then I heard you coming . . . and I heard my father's voice too. I was scared. I knew he'd be cross. Then the papers slid off the table and there wasn't time to pick them up before I hid and . . .' She ventured to look up at Cleone, but her lip trembled ominously. 'I suppose I'd better tell my father it was me.'

'No!' Cleone spoke impulsively. She longed to put her arms about Ianthe and hug her, only she wasn't sure how the child would react to such a familiar gesture from a stranger. But she was not going to submit her to what would obviously be an ordeal; the little girl seeemed really terrified of Saxon. What *was* the matter with the man? didn't he know how to treat a child? 'It's all over,' she told Ianthe, 'we'll forget all about it. I'm just glad it was an accident. I thought someone had done it on purpose, to cause trouble.'

'But my father did blame you. Aren't you ... aren't you afraid of him?'

'No ... of course not.' Cleone thought she had made quite a creditable attempt at making her tone convincing, considering her words were not entirely true. But her fear was not that of being in the wrong, of incurring Saxon Turville's wrath; hers was a strange, inexplicable fear, that seemed not to have rhyme or reason. 'He doesn't scare me a bit.'

Ianthe gave a soft, but audible sigh of relief.

'Thank you, Cleo! I don't care what my father says. I think you're very nice.'

That hurt a little, though why it should, she couldn't imagine. What had Saxon Turville been saying about her to his daughter? Cleone brooded. Whatever prejudices he had himself it was unfair to attempt to warp the mind of a child. She longed to ask what he had said, but just because he was unfair didn't give her the right to discuss him behind his back, to encourage Ianthe to criticise her father.

'Will you teach me about archaeology, Cleo?' Ianthe had come closer, now that she knew the older girl was not angry about her accident with the maps.

Cleone hesitated. She hated to refuse a child ... and yet. . . .

'Have you forgotten? Your father has forbidden it,' she reminded her gently.

Ianthe's square little chin came up, in unconscious imitation of her father at his most pugnacious.

'He can't stop me asking you questions and you wouldn't be mean enough not to speak to me ... to answer me . . . I know you wouldn't.'

Cleone smiled wryly. For her age, the child was a shrewd judge of character.

They left the library, Cleone locking up and testing the security of the lock by a heavy push against its solid panels.

'I'm going to give the key to your father now. Better make yourself scarce,' she suggested, 'or he might suspect something.'

In spite of her principles, she was still abetting Ianthe in deceiving her father, she thought, her pleasant little face puckered into a troubled frown, as she made her way to the farm office. But her sense of indignation strove against the promptings of her conscience. Saxon Turville didn't deserve anyone's loyalty, and couldn't command hers anyway. If the child was guilty of deceit it was his own fault, no one else's. Ianthe's fear of him, his impatient tolerance of her existence, were driving a wedge between father and daughter more surely than any outside influence could.

Full of the resentment induced by these reflections, Cleone marched into Saxon's office and unceremoniously threw the key down on his desk.

'The job's finished and the library's locked. You can put your precious papers away just as soon as you like.'

He looked at her, his handsome features cold; it was only convention, she felt sure, which brought him to his feet in her presence.

'You seem to forget you have been accorded a privilege, in being allowed access to them.'

'Yes . . . and I still don't know the real reason for your kind condescension,' she retorted. She sketched him a mocking curtsey, 'but thank you, sir . . . deeply honoured, sir . . . three bags full, sir!'

He was round the desk before she had regained her balance, his large hands taking her forearms in a vicious grip, yanking her forward, so that she had to tilt her chin to meet his eyes. Only inches from him, she could sense the rigidity in his muscular frame, almost as if he found her proximity distasteful. But of course . . . he would . . . he was a woman-hater.

'Irresponsible . . . impertinent . . . ungrateful . . . all typically female traits.'

'You forgot to add "and lacking in deference towards your lordship",' she interrupted with spirit, despite the fact that he was hurting her, that she was disconcerted by this unlooked for proximity.

For a moment, she could almost have sworn that his face twisted in reluctant amusement, but the fleeting expression was gone too soon for certainty and she decided it had been a rictus of annoyance.

'I ought to . . .' he muttered. He did not finish his sentence, but she had the feeling that if he had completed his threat, it would have included a mention of chastisement; and the thought gave her a little frisson of the fear she had denied she felt for this large, dominant man.

What had he been like, before life had soured him? she wondered. Had those handsome features ever been alight with real laughter? Surely he must have been different once, for Tessa, Ianthe's mother, to have fallen in love with him? She tried to imagine those cold, grey eyes warmed by passion, the stern features relaxed, the beautifully moulded lips smiling. Unconsciously she sighed at her failure. Impossible! She just could not see him as anything but haughty and arrogant. Then she became aware that he was still holding her arms, that for several seconds she had been staring up enquiringly into his face. She flushed. Whatever would he think? What was he thinking? those eyes suddenly intent, searching.

'Kindly let me go,' she demanded; and when, to her surprise, he complied, she turned on her heel, secretly shocked at her own reactions to his touch, forcing herself to move with slow dignity, instead of running in the sudden unreasonable panic she felt. Why on earth should she even bother to try and picture him as ever having been any different? What did it matter?

There was no sign of Amyas at dinner that evening and Cleone felt acutely uncomfortable, seated at Saxon's table. For a horrible moment, just before she had entered the dining room, she wondered if perhaps he dressed for dinner and whether her attractive but simple cream dress would be totally unsuitable. So it was an enormous relief, to find him still in the same slacks and jacket he had worn all day; though she noticed he had changed his shirt and

donned a tie, that his blond hair was still darkened by
water from the shower he had taken.

She was relieved, too, to find that Ianthe was to join
them at table. Not that the child's presence did much to
lighten the atmosphere, for her awe of her father kept her
almost silent and she replied only stiltedly to Cleone's
attempts at conversation. Poor, repressed little mite,
Cleone thought. If ever a child needed feminine company
it was this one; and at that moment, Cleone decided,
unethical or not, she was going to make the most of any
opportunity that came her way to make Ianthe's days
fuller and more enjoyable, even to the point of defying
Saxon's edict about discussing archaeological topics.

Frustrated in her intention of retailing the day's
discoveries to Amyas, Cleone decided she would wait no
longer to see her map translated into reality. She wanted
to see 'Diana's Grove', to feel its atmosphere for herself.

Just occasionally, she had found that, to a certain
extent, she shared Amyas's knack for sensing the sites of
the past. Perhaps this would be one of those occasions, she
thought excitedly. Perhaps, alone in the wood, with no
other human distractions, she would be able to relate to
her surroundings, would *know* that here was a place to be
investigated. Her uncle, she guessed, would not return
until he had exorcised whatever preoccupation rode him.

Glad that Saxon showed no inclination to linger after
the meal, she made an excuse to father and daughter,
then slipped unobtrusively from the house, not wanting to
be questioned by either about her destination. Ianthe
might beg to accompany her and while she had resolved,
in general, not to discourage the child, for this first visit to
the beechwood, she had to be alone.

A long, light summer evening lay before her, in which
to make a thorough exploration. Avoiding the wide open
spaces of green lawns, Cleone sped through the protective
cover of a yew walk, its trees clipped into fantastic shapes,
then skirted a large paddock, where horses grazed, until
she reached the edge of the gleaming beechwood, whose
copper giants suddenly blocked half the sky from view.

Then, she was in among the grey, smooth trunks, a
feeling of freedom assailing her, away from the constraint

she felt in Saxon's presence. She seemed to walk for miles, in which densely packed trees flocked with raucous pheasants alternated with mossy clearings, until she began to wonder, a trifle uncomfortably, if she could be going in circles.

But she was not seriously worried; she had plenty of time before darkness would envelope the countryside. A sloping bank in one of the clearings tempted her and she sat down, looking around her, watching with lazy fascination the ephemeral evening dance of gauzy, transparent, woodland insects.

Her urgency for exploration ceded itself to a kind of lethargic indolence which made her content to dream of discoveries instead of pushing on to make them. How marvellous it would be if she could be instrumental in making a major find; *that* would show Saxon Turville that she was a useful member of the archaeological team. It seemed important somehow, that he should recognise her worth, be duly impressed by her skill.

A faint, distant rustling, somewhere behind her, made her start and she had the sensation that unseen eyes watched her, but when she looked round there was nothing to be seen and she relaxed once more; a large bird perhaps, or a rabbit, or even a small deer?

Her thoughts returned to their former preoccupation. Away from the manor house, no longer restrained by Saxon's presence, she felt better able to view him dispassionately. OK. So he was not disposed to be friendly and she could not like his casual treatment of his daughter, but for some reason best known to himself, he had allowed Amyas and his team their visit to Salpeth; so, instead of rising to his abrasive manner, she must attempt to be, not conciliatory exactly, that sort of servility was alien to her independent spirit, but to restrain her normally impulsive nature, keep a curb on her ready tongue. It would be awful if her hot temper were to jeopardise her uncle's projected survey here. However strongly she felt about the way in which he was repressing Ianthe's interest in archaeology, she, Cleone, must not be seen to champion the child's cause openly.

But she had not come to these woods in order to brood

about the Turville's problems; she stood up and moved on, hurrying her pace a little now; and at length she came to a large, damp, wooded hollow, where fungus sprouted from mossy tree roots. There, hidden among its dark cloak of trees, was a building; and if she had any doubt that this was what she sought, the architectural style of the structure reassured her. It was what remained of a medieval chapel, almost certainly part of the priory that once had stood in 'Priory Woods' or 'Diana's Grove' as she preferred to think of it.

Years of neglect had gnawed deeply into the crumbling grey stones. It was just a pile of masonry now that confronted her, robbed of life, of vitality, by encroaching trees and other plant life and Cleone fancied that the ruin had an air of mystery, broodingly silent, unhappily so, an atmosphere not altogether conjured up by her vivid imagination. There was, as she had half expected, the sense of an area sacred to a god, but which god? She shivered. Anchorites, monks, nuns—an overrated section of the spectral life, but she really did feel that something of the sort lingered here. Certainly she had the sense of a life alien to hers; presences waiting for her to go and leave them to their centuries old solitude.

But Cleone was no coward. She was not to be frightened away by spirits, real or imagined. She moved closer, till she stood beneath the outer wall of the edifice and as she did so, her nostrils caught the distasteful, damp smell of dry rot in ancient timbers. Several pigeons fluttered out of the window-like tracery, their deep-throated calls startling her. But she took a deep, calming breath and stepped forward.

Inside, the remaining stonework formed a shell as hollow as an unfleshed skull; elder shrubs grew up through broken flagstones. One window only retained its glass, rheumy with film, like an aged eye. Pigeon droppings fouled the floor and fern-edged, lichen-carpeted steps led down to what must once have been a crypt.

She ought not to linger much longer; already the shadows cast by trees and ruin were lengthening and the warmth was going out of the air; but she simply must venture down a few of those steps, to see what lay below. She dared not go right underground of course, without a torch. In any case, the way might be blocked by fallen masonry.

There was enough daylight filtering down the steps to enable her to creep just below floor level, but it was not a pleasant experience. An evil, musty smell emanated from the crypt and despite her normal common sense, she could not help thinking of mouldering bones. But something pungent, underlying this other odour, did remind her of earlier experiences and she turned back, but not swiftly enough to avoid the cloud of small bats which rose into the space around her.

At that moment, Cleone would have preferred to encounter a ghost. Despite Amyas and Eric's continual assurances that bats did not deliberately fly into hair, she had an illogical certainty that they did just that. But even so, just the close passage of their small bodies, past her head, was enough to send her into panic-stricken flight.

Erupting from the underground area, she startled someone else—someone who had no business to be there. 'Ianthe!' But it was not Cleone's voice that thundered the child's name. It was a deep, masculine voice, ferocious sounding in its outraged anger. 'Come out of there! and you too, Miss Bancroft ... *at once!*' It was Saxon, his two spaniels in attendance.

Cleone was only too ready to oblige, but in her anxiety to quit the ruined building, she was less careful than she had been on entering and stumbling over loose stones, she fell heavily, feeling an excruciating pain through her thigh as she did so, as sharp projections ripped her skirt and lacerated the soft flesh beneath.

It was Ianthe who stretched out to help her and Cleone rose awkwardly putting her hand to her thigh. She could not stifle the dismayed gasp as her hand came away wet with blood. Looking down and seeing the rapidly spreading stain, she felt sick and swayed slightly, her head swimming as it always did at the sight of blood.

'Cleo!' Ianthe's voice was shrilly anxious. 'You've hurt yourself.'

'What is it?' Saxon snapped. 'What have you done?' It was not the harsh tone of annoyance now, but the edgy anger of concern.

'Nothing ... nothing at all,' she whispered, as he loomed over her.

Every time he was near her, he seemed larger than on the last occasion. She tried to conceal the evidence of her injury from him, but to no avail. She might have known nothing would escape his sharp eyes.

Two strong hands gripped her shoulders and forced her down upon a tree stump. Then, before she could antici-pate his next move, he was down on one knee, lifting her skirt above thigh level to inspect the damage. Startled, she tried to remove his questing hands, but he brushed her efforts aside and surveyed the gash in her creamy skin with clinical appraisal. Of course, Cleone thought, it would mean nothing to him that it was a woman's leg he held; it might have been that of one of the animals on his farm. But the warmth of his hand was doing unthinkable things to her nerves, already quivering with shock.

'That looks nasty.'

'It ... it's all right. I'll be OK. Just leave me alone,' she snapped, angry ... with herself? ... with him?

But his hand still rested just above her exposed knee and to her utter horror she was finding it not an unpleasant sensation. His flesh was warm and dry and the contact was sending little tingling feelings through her. How could she experience sensations like that, when she didn't like him; and it was quite certain that he did not intend that she should derive pleasure from his touch.

'Leave me alone,' she repeated.

'Don't be stupid. That's a bad wound. It needs attention.' He whipped out a large, immaculately clean handkerchief and proceeded to bind it tightly over the gash.

Cleone closed her eyes, not because he was hurting her, but because she was becoming even more acutely embarrassed by his nearness, his blond head only inches from her face. She could smell the warmth, the masculinity of him and his hands were brushing her flesh as he worked; it seemed such an intimate service he was performing for her.

But it did not seem as though he was affected by any sensual considerations.

'Perhaps this will teach you not to go blundering

around ruined buildings in the half light,' he observed, 'and with a child too. One of you could have been seriously injured. Do you realise this stone is crumbling badly? Suppose a portion of it had come down on the pair of you?'

Her nerves badly exacerbated by fatigue, by the fright she had received, the necessity of allowing this hateful but disturbing man to touch her, Cleone snapped back.

'That's your fault, isn't it? If your property is in such a dangerous condition, surely it's your responsibility to do something about it?'

'Yes,' he agreed. 'It *is* my property and it's on private land. Nobody has any right to be here without my permission. If you'd told me where you were going, I would have warned you that . . .'

'You gave your permission for on-site surveys,' she began to argue.

'To Badger Pringle, yes. But I understood that you undertook the clerical side of things.'

'Certainly not! I suppose you think that's all women are fit for. For your information, my uncle trusts me with any task connected with his work.'

Saxon shrugged.

'Well, that's his look out, if he allows you to go blundering about in this fashion. But the area is off limits to my daughter and you had no right to bring her here, after I had given strict instructions. . . .'

'Daddy!' Ianthe said, her small face white with desperation and Cleone admired her courage, for it was evident that it cost her an effort to speak up. 'Daddy, Cleone didn't bring me here. I saw her go out and I . . . I followed her. I wanted to see what archaeologists do and . . .'

'Well now you know! They do damn fool things like this.' He indicated Cleone's leg and she realised, with a rush of blood to her cheeks, that her skirt was still pushed back.

Hastily, angrily, she wrenched it down and stood up. She took a few steps away from Saxon, each one of which caused an agonising pain in her damaged thigh.

'It's a long way back to the house, Miss Bancroft,' he said sardonically.

'I know.' She forced the words to issue airily, even though her teeth were clenched against pain that threatened to overwhelm her, making her feel nauseous and giddy.

'You'll never make it,' he continued, with what sounded to her like callous indifference.

'I *will* . . . it if kills me,' she muttered and essayed a few more yards.

An impatient exclamation and sudden movement startled her. Without asking her wishes in the matter, he had lifted her in strong muscular arms and without apparent effort was carrying her out of the hollow, Ianthe trailing somewhat disconsolately in his wake.

'It's a good thing for you that I chose to exercise the bitches in this part of the wood,' he commented.

But she was not interested in his reasons for being there, or what he thought was good for her.

'Put me down!' Though she knew her protest was ridiculous, knew that she needed his help, she did not want to accept it—did not want to be held like this, so close against his broad chest that she could feel the rhythmic thud of his heart, could feel the warmth of him, experiencing sensations that it was not right or proper for her to know.

'Untouchable little thing, aren't you?'

Cleone seethed. She might be small compared to his gigantic build, but she was not accustomed to being treated as though she were helpless, and as for 'untouchable', why should she submit to being man-handled by him?

He caught the ferocious glare and a grunt of amusement escaped him.

'What a face! Anyone would think I had assailed your virtue.'

What he was assailing, though he couldn't know it, was her peace of mind, her unawakened senses which he had no right to stir.

'You wouldn't get the chance . . . or know how,' she muttered under her breath. It was defiance, and it was self-reassurance.

Steely grey eyes locked on to her flushed, mutinous face.

'What did you say?'

'Nothing!'

She stared back at him defiantly; but it was a mistake, for the grey eyes were knowing, derisive. He had heard precisely what she said; and he probably thought she was being deliberately provocative; as if she would want to provoke him into action of any kind. She shuddered.

'Don't worry!' Misunderstanding her reaction, his voice was curt. 'You won't have to endure my touch much longer.'

She was dumped with scant ceremony on the settee, from which the two crestfallen spaniels were temporarily banned.

'Ianthe!' Saxon said, in a tone that brooked no argument, 'Bed!'

And of course, Ianthe, who wouldn't have dreamt of arguing with her autocratic father anyway, went meekly.

'Now we'll do something about that injury.'

Oh no ... Cleone felt herself quiver anew. She didn't have to endure that again. It would be bad enough if she liked the man, but she didn't she told herself ... and to have a man she was sure she disliked so intensely making himself free of her upper leg, touching her, albeit impersonally, where no other man had ever laid hand ... why couldn't he have let Ianthe stay a little longer?

'I can see to it myself ... really ... when I get to my room.' She made as if to rise, but one large hand forced her down again.

'That wound needs cleaning and dressing properly. Situated where it is you can't possibly do an efficient job on it.'

Cleone knew she couldn't move fast enough on the bruised limb to evade him and in any case he was quite capable of following her up to her room and insisting on treating her gashed thigh there. So perhaps it would be wiser to submit meekly here and now. But she felt far from meek, as she subsided with an irritated intake of breath.

His large hands were surprisingly gentle and sensitive,

as they cleaned and probed for dirt and again Cleone had that faint, pleasurable sensation, as his warm flesh brushed against hers. It was all imagination of course—any hands that relieved her discomfort would have had the same effect; a doctor, a nurse. It couldn't possibly mean anything that it was Saxon's hands that made it necessary to conceal a sensuous shudder.

'I can apply a temporary dressing, but I think you should see a doctor tomorrow. Had a tetanus jab lately?'

Cleone nodded. It was a precaution that Amyas insisted all his assistants take. He believed that it was possible, during disinterment, for long-dormant bacteria, when exposed to light and air, to become active once more.

Antiseptic applied and a large dressing taped to her thigh, Saxon rose from his kneeling position by the settee.

'A hot, sweet drink, in case of shock, and then bed,' he ordered brusquely, as if she were the same age as Ianthe, she thought crossly; but he made the drink himself and later, causing Cleone further bewildering unrest, he carried her up the stairs and along the maze of corridors to her room.

'Can you manage now?' he asked abruptly, as he set her down outside her door and Cleone drew an inaudible breath of relief. She hadn't really believed he intended to actually deposit her upon her bed, but. . . . For the last half hour, he had been almost human, she thought. Perhaps he wasn't so bad after all—just reserved?

'Oh . . . yes . . . of course. Th . . . thank you.' With the shyness she still felt, she looked up at him from under the thick lashes fringing golden eyes, unconsciously treating him to one of her friendly, ingenuous smiles, a smile which dug a single dimple deep into her cheek, a smile which she normally reserved for people she liked.

'Goodnight,' he said abruptly, with a sudden retreat into his usual frozen rigidity.

He was almost at a turn in the corridor, when she remembered.

'Mr Turville!'

He was back at her side in a few, swift strides, grey eyes alert.

'Something wrong?'

'No . . . I just wondered . . . is my uncle back?'

He shook his head.

'No. But he did warn me that he kept irregular hours. Not worried about Badger, are you?'

'N . . . no. No. He does go missing for hours, when he's absorbed in a project.'

What *was* worrying her was that she was alone in this house with Saxon, alone that was apart from the child. None of the staff slept in, but just why that should worry her, she couldn't really fathom.

She was a little uncomfortable too, about facing him next morning. Contrary to her normal custom, she went into breakfast. This morning a meal was a necessity, she felt, since she was planning another foray into Diana's Grove, alone if need be, but, if her uncle had returned, she hoped to be able to demonstrate her find. The priory, of course, was not Roman, but Cleone was certain, though certainty was based on intuition alone, that the site had once been occupied by an earlier building, a temple to a Roman deity.

Her thigh was one large bruise now, stiff and painful, but exercise would be the best possible cure, she assured herself.

To her relief, she did not have to breakfast *à deux* with Saxon. As well as Ianthe, there was Amyas, a little pale and fine drawn, as if a day of fasting had told upon him, but otherwise looking exceedingly cheerful. Cleone began to talk animatedly of her find, but after a while she realised that her uncle was only listening with impatient politeness; obviously the previous day had not been unproductive for him either.

'Yes . . . yes . . .' he said, when Cleone came to a rather lame halt, with the suggestion that she would like to investigate the priory ruins, 'another day perhaps? I have a feeling that I've discovered something far more important . . . maybe just what we're looking for. We'll take a walk out there this morning . . . Eric . . . you . . . myself. The students are arriving this afternoon, so tomorrow we can open up a preliminary trench, I . . .'

'Your niece is in no condition to go traipsing about the

countryside,' Saxon interrupted Amyas in full flight. 'Her immediate priority, whether she realises it or not, is to see a doctor.'

Cleone glared at him furiously, about to protest, but Amyas was immediately concerned. He might live for ninety-nine percent of his time in AD120 or thereabouts, but he took his responsibilities where his niece was concerned very seriously indeed.

'She has a nasty injury to her thigh,' Saxon stated in response to Amyas's enquiry. 'It may need stitching and certainly should have a professional opinion. My treatment was only of an interim nature.'

Cleone flushed with remembered embarrassment, as she saw her uncle's eyes full of amused speculation. He knew how she detested Saxon Turville and she could see he found it highly diverting to imagine her reactions to receiving first aid from her *bête noire*.

'So I intend to take her to my own doctor. . . .'

'No!' Cleone said forcibly, then moderated her tone, realising that she sounded most ungracious, that Ianthe was looking at her in astonishment. 'It's really not necessary. I can quite easily drive myself to the nearest hospital, go to outpatients. There's no need for you to trouble.'

'No trouble,' Saxon said smoothly. 'It happens to be market day in Cirencester. I have to go in anyway and you would find driving that heavy car exceedingly uncomfortable. I imagine that thigh is a mass of bruises this morning?'

No point in denying it. She had the dreadful feeling he might insist on visual verification if she did; and besides Amyas was nodding agreement. But a trip to Cirencester in Saxon's company? What on earth would they talk about on the way? Every subject that interested her was controversial where he was concerned. Of course she could keep silent all the way, but when she was silent in his presence, disturbing thoughts visited her.

'Daddy!' It was Ianthe who solved Cleone's dilemma, her request hesitant. 'Could . . . could I go to Cirencester too? With Cleo? I . . . I wouldn't be any bother. . . .'

Heaven bless the child. It shouldn't be necessary for

her to say such a thing. What possible trouble could she be? Cleone fumed. Didn't the man realise his good fortune? Some children of ten were absolutely impossible.

'I'd be very glad of Ianthe's company.' She hastened to support the child's petition.

Cleone thought Saxon looked at her oddly. Perhaps he was wondering why he was not sufficient. She hoped he had no inkling as to why she preferred not to be alone with him. He gave his permission however and Ianthe, more animated in her father's presence than Cleone had ever seen her, sped off at once to fetch her pocket money.

It was a change to be driven instead of being the driver. Comfortably ensconced in the front passenger seat of Saxon's grey Mercedes, with Ianthe leaning companionably over her shoulder from the rear, Cleone had an opportunity to see the countryside through which they passed; a countryside rich with market gardens, whose boundary signs carried the appetising slogans; 'honey and apples'; 'brown eggs'; it was a land of steep beech woods, short turfed downs, miles of unbuilt distances, of Norman churches and stone-walled fields, cornfields like sunlit sand dunes, daubed with the red of a thousand poppies.

Their route took them via inconveniently narrow twists through cottages and barns and several times they were held up by slow-moving, shaggy loads, filling the width of the road.

But Saxon showed no impatience, as they awaited their opportunity to overtake. He was a countryman, of course, used to this kind of hazard; and he was a good driver, alert, but relaxed too. Cleone had driven with men who were tense at the wheel, heedless of the rights of other road users, intolerant of their vagaries. But Saxon was none of these things; she felt perfectly confident in his ability to handle any motoring situation that might arise, without losing his cool self-control. But then, that was the man himself—cold, restrained—she felt he would be so under any circumstances. Any?

She glanced at him surreptitiously. Was he capable of passion? and she was not thinking of temper now, but of a

different emotion. She supposed there must be a fire
somewhere that had begot Ianthe; or had the child's
birth been a clinical attempt at securing an heir? If so, it
had been a failure. Would he have preferred a son? a lot
of wealthy men did. Was that the reason for his almost
indifferent attitude towards his young daughter?

Goodness, she apostrophised herself, how she did dwell
upon this man's character and his problems, when they
were no earthly concern of hers. She must remember, firstly
that she didn't like him and secondly that even had she
liked him, he was married. For she didn't really believe in
Ianthe's theory; it was too far fetched . . . or was it? After
all she knew very little about him, his potential for
violence.

Not only did Saxon take her to his own doctor's
surgery, he insisted on waiting to introduce her, before
going about his own business.

'It really isn't necesssary,' she protested. 'You've gone
to quite enough trouble already.

'I told you . . . no trouble. Besides, I feel it is only my
duty to see that you receive proper treatment. As you
yourself pointed out, I could be held responsible, since
the injury occurred while you were on my property. I've
no wish to be sued for damages . . .'

'As if I would!' Cleone exclaimed indignantly. 'Do you
really believe I'd do a thing like that? when it was
through my own carelessness.'

'One never knows when a woman will stab one in the
back,' he observed, but there was no trace of humour in
the comment; he meant it!

Cleone was tempted to tell him that he must have been
mixing with the wrong kind of women, but since that
could imply a reflection on his wife, she held her tongue,
contenting herself with a withering look, which was
supposed to leave him in no doubt as to her opinion of his
remark.

The necessary introduction made, Saxon left Cleone,
with Ianthe in attendance, to the doctor's ministrations.
He was reassuring. Stitches would not be necessary and
having ascertained the fact that she was immunised
against tetanus, he applied a fresh dressing.

'You'll progress through all the colours of the rainbow,' he told her, 'but there's no real harm done.'

Emerging from the surgery, Cleone asked Ianthe how she would like to spend the time until their appointed rendezvous with Saxon. As the child had insisted on bringing her pocket money, Cleone was quite prepared for a protracted shopping session, while Ianthe deliberated over the layout of her cash; but to her surprise, the child had a very acceptable alternative to offer, one that accorded very well with Cleone's own inclinations.

'Please . . . could we go to the museum? I went once with the school, but they never give you enough time to look at things. You have to keep up with your group and the others in my group were bored, so. . . .' She shrugged expressively.

At Cleone's agreement, given with only the slightest pang of conscience that she was abetting Saxon's daughter in flouting his wishes, Ianthe led the way to the Corinium Museum, stocked with the debris of everyday Roman life: the bones of the animals they ate; fragments of pottery; bone tools and pins; stone figures of their household gods.

Cleone allowed the child to linger at will over sculptured stones, mosaic pavements, more personal articles such as glass phials for medicines and cosmetics, tiny bronze birds and animals. There were tools too and cooking utensils; and all gave a fascinatingly intimate glimpse of Roman daily life.

The layout of the museum was such that only the imagination of the viewer was necessary to bring to life the Cirencester of Roman times, with its temples, baths and public buildings, handsome homes belonging to the wealthier citizens, all enclosed within its ramparts and guarded by four main gates.

Various tableaux included a representation of a family talking in their home, a man working on a fragment from a mosaic decoration and a shepherd's cote. But of greatest interest to Cleone was the model of a villa, possessing two courts surrounded by buildings, the main residence being arranged around an inner court with colonnades on three sides. The villa contained a large hall and from the hall, passages covered with mosaics led to rooms on either side.

'This,' Cleone told Ianthe, 'is what my uncle and I would love to find, a whole villa that nobody else has discovered.'

Ianthe was awed.

'And do you think there might be a villa like that, on our land?'

'Well, it wouldn't look like this model of course, only the foundations would be left, but yes, we do hope to find something similar ... but it is only a hope as yet.'

'Well, I hope so too. Then my father would have to take notice. But would lots of people come to look at it? I don't think he'd like that, you know.'

This was a consideration. Saxon's almost fanatical desire to keep Salpeth exclusive would not be helped by a major discovery on his land.

Ianthe's pocket money was invested in post cards and other souvenirs of their visit and when they finally emerged from artificial into daylight, the child sighed blissfully.

'I did enjoy that, Cleo. I love museums.'

Cleone nodded.

'So did I, when I was your age, I still do. My parents often used to take me. . . .' She stopped, feeling she had been tactless and certainly Ianthe's sigh now held a different emotion to that betokened by the first.

'I wish my father was interested. All he thinks about are his old sheep.'

'We ... ell ...' Cleone said, trying to be fair, 'as a farmer, I suppose. . . .'

'Oh, I know ... and I wouldn't mind that ... but these aren't just ordinary sheep. He says they're special. Sometimes I think he prefers them to people.'

Cleone would have questioned Ianthe further about her father's pet flock, but by now their wanderings had brought them to the market place and the child, all cares apparently forgotten, plunged in among the varied stalls, with as much enthusiasm as she had shown at the museum. There were the usual home-made cakes, jams and pickles, vegetable and plant stalls, side by side with bargains from Midland factories. Fish stalls offered Wye or Severn salmon, Coln trout, wood pigeons and eggs. Fruit from local farms made a colourful display and there was an aroma of many kinds of fresh bread and lardy cakes from village bakers.

It had been arranged that they should meet Saxon for lunch and Cleone was glad he had not chosen an hotel. He had settled for a public house, situated in a side street, an establishment which provided bar snacks and where children were permitted. After the substantial breakfast she had eaten, she could not have faced a formal meal.

Having related the doctor's remarks about her injury, Cleone found herself at a loss for words, tense again in Saxon's presence; but Ianthe, excited perhaps by a more stimulating morning than usual, was surprisingly vocal, commenting on the people who thronged the bar.

'Oh, look, Cleo! That man looks just like one of the gargoyles we saw in the museum. He ... Oh!' She stopped, a hand clapped over her mouth, the grey eyes so like her father's darting to his face for signs of comprehension and disapproval, which were not slow to appear.

He did not break into the condemnatory speech Cleone had expected, perhaps because they were in a public place, perhaps because of the child's presence; but the glint in his eyes as he looked at Cleone left her in no doubt as to where blame had been apportioned and she knew an angry scene had only been postponed, which would be all the more nervewracking, by virtue of the delay.

'Since you're both so keen on "sightseeing", he remarked with heavy irony, 'perhaps you would care to spend the afternoon in viewing some of the other interesting places in Cirencester? It does have an existence apart from its connections with the Second Legion.'

So he wasn't altogether ignorant of local Roman history, despite his professed distaste for archaeology.

Cleone had recognised the sarcasm, but Ianthe took her father's challenge at face value.

'Oh yes please, Daddy!' Her square face, a reproduction in miniature of his own, glowed with enthusiasm.

How very rarely he must offer his daughter a treat, Cleone thought and now that he had, it was not out of any promptings of good nature, but merely induced by spite—aimed at their visitor.

'How about you, Miss Bancroft?' His rugged features showed his acknowledgment of the fact that she recognised his suggestion for what it was; and there was almost, but not quite, a gleam of humour. What a difference it would make to his face if, just for once, he would smile.

One thing Cleone did know. He would be an impossible man to defeat in a battle of wits, but that didn't mean she would not try.

'I'm quite willing to look around,' she said coolly. 'Unlike you, I do find it possible to appreciate other people's interests and their right to indulge them.'

'Really?' he drawled, 'One imagined that nothing after the fourth century would have any value in your eyes.'

'But then it's a mistake to let imagination have full rein,' she retorted sweetly. 'One should restrict oneself to the scientifically proved facts, before making a judgment of things . . . or people.'

'And yet I think . . .' he said softly, moving nearer, the words for her ears alone, 'you have already made up your mind about me, knowing nothing of "the facts".'

Cleone stiffened, at his words, at his proximity.

'I know that you're one of the most abominably arrogant men I've ever met,' she hissed, also with Ianthe's young ears in mind. 'That you're misogynistic, feudal and insular! and totally prejudiced against women.'

'But then you don't know why,' was the insistent rejoinder 'and that is one of the essential facts, so perhaps you should reserve judgment until you do know?'

'I'm not in the least interested in your traumatic experiences, Mr Turville. If you've been injured by some woman, or women, I imagine the fault was not one-sided.'

'Imagine? you imagine? But you have just condemned the overuse of imagination, Miss Bancroft.'

Damn him! He had brought the argument full circle. She'd known he would be a tricky customer; and how did he manage to sound so sardonically, triumphantly amused, without a trace of the humour appearing in his set, rugged features? The man had a basilisk-like stare, enough to turn even the most red-blooded of women to stone.

'Could we stop wasting time and get on with the "guided tour"?' she enquired with icy politeness.

'The time hasn't been wasted,' he assured her, 'just occupied . . . until we are ready to make our way to our first objective.'

Oh, he was insufferable. He had an answer for everything. Cleone decided to ignore him. She refused to bandy words with him any further.

Once back in the heart of the town, Cleone's gaze turned upwards to the spire of the church of St John the Baptist, as impressive in appearance as a cathedral with its splendid Perpendicular tower.

'It's the largest and finest church in the Cotswolds,' Saxon commented. 'Want to go inside?'

She nodded, keeping to her resolve only to speak when strictly necessary and preceded him through the three-storeyed porch and down worn, stone steps into the high, spacious nave, where immensely tall, slim-shafted pillars carried the roof to a breathtaking window of delicate, medieval glass.

'You will have realised that this is one of the "wool" churches? The Trinity Chapel was built partly for the Weavers Company. If you examine this brass here, you'll see it depicts an old man with a pair of shears above his head and a dog at his feet.'

After a comprehensive tour of the church, with Saxon surprisingly knowledgeable and ready apparently to inform, they emerged once more into the market place, where he paused briefly to detail its history.

'A market is recorded here as early as the twelfth century and it was always a centre for the wool trade. It still is a convenient meeting place for the farmers of the south-east Cotswolds. There's a big sheep fair in

September, two medieval hiring fairs in October and a Christmas sheep and cattle fair.'

He took Cleone's elbow in one large, hard hand, to guide her through the jostling crowd, Ianthe skipping at their heels. His was a totally impersonal touch, she knew, but as always at any contact with him, she felt oddly disconcerted and self-conscious, yet very aware and she was not sure whether it was relief or some other emotion she felt, when, pausing before a sombre-faced building, he released her once more.

'This is the Weavers Hall, founded in the fifteenth century for poor weavers and dedicated to St Thomas of Canterbury.' He indicated a small, worn, carved figure, set above the door and the building's only ornament. 'That, presumably, represents St Thomas.'

They moved on and this time Cleone was careful to maintain her distance, keeping Ianthe between them, as Saxon pointed out the tall old mansions, formerly the houses of prosperous wool-staplers, and the smaller, gabled houses of their workers.

'A lot of the architecture is eighteenth and early nineteenth century ... that was the period when wool-staplers and clothiers used their wealth to build themselves town mansions. Their predecessors preferred to use their surplus to rebuild churches, ensuring their "mansions in heaven". The church at Salpeth was rebuilt by my ancestors. You must take a look round, if you can ever spare the time from your absorption with things Roman.'

He was sneering at her again and Cleone was moved to retort.

'You accuse me of being obsessed with Roman remains, yet you seem to have your own obsessions, wool and sheep.'

'Surely, to be accurate, you should put the sheep first?'

Good Lord. He actually did have a sense of humour, albeit rather rusty-sounding and that had almost been a smile. For heavens sake, don't let him suddenly thaw, she begged inwardly. She knew how to deal with a reserved, hostile Saxon—any transformation might be too disconcerting, though in what way she was not quite certain, still totally puzzled, unable to rationalise her reactions to him.

Throughout their conversation, Ianthe's eyes had gone from one to the other, like those of a spectators at a tennis match, a little frown of perplexity creasing her smooth forehead. Now, as Saxon paused to speak to an acquaintance, she looked up at Cleone, her expression wondering.

'I've never heard him talk to any lady for as long as that . . . or tease her. Perhaps he likes you better than any of the others? I do hope so.'

Cleone returned the child's candid gaze doubtfully. She wasn't sure that she wanted Saxon Turville to regard her in any other light than he had at first acquaintance. True, she burned to have him acknowledge her competence as an archaeologist, to prove to him that the science did have its uses, its place in life . . . and to have him admit that there was no earthly reason why his daughter should not show an interest in the subject. But it didn't matter to her whether he regarded her highly as a person—or did it? It shouldn't of course, but despite the indignation he was capable of rousing in her and the manner in which he spoke, she discovered that she had actually enjoyed their verbal duel, even though she had not emerged the victor.

Reflections of this nature were swiftly dispelled, as Saxon rejoined them and suggested that it was time to make their way back to the car and thence to Salpeth.

So absorbing had the interlude been, such a mixture of pleasure and enigma, that Cleone had almost forgotten the retribution that lay in wait for her on their return to the manor; but she was inescapably reminded of the fact, as Saxon braked outside the front door to allow his passengers to alight.

'My office . . . in ten minutes, Miss Bancroft!'

CHAPTER FOUR

SHE watched him drive around the side of the house to garage the Mercedes and her spirits plummeted. What an anticlimax to what had, strangely enough, turned out to be a very enjoyable day. But, almost immediately, she braced herself. She was no coward and nor was she a schoolgirl about to be carpeted by the Headmaster. So what if Saxon Turville was about to lecture her? He couldn't eat her, or inflict corporal punishment, she assured herself; nor would any unpleasantness on his part affect her permanently. In about six weeks time, she would be back in Oxford; their paths need never cross again. Though oddly that thought was not as satisfying as it ought to have been.

She would go to his office, because not to do so would make the incident seem too important; would make it appear as if she accepted that a rebuke was in order, and that, consequently, she feared to face him. But ten minutes! No. She would go in her own good time!

She showered away the stickiness and dust of Market Day and discarded the dress she had been wearing for snug fitting jeans and T-shirt—her 'digging' outfit. Then she brushed and rebraided her heavy auburn hair. There was no way, she vowed, that Saxon was going to keep her away from her uncle's discoveries any longer. She had submitted to visiting a doctor and there were no complications. Walking up to the site should prove no more arduous for her bruised thigh than had wandering around Cirencester all day.

Thus, it was nearly three-quarters of an hour later when she strolled into the farm office, trying to appear utterly nonchalant, as though her heart was not struggling to leap up into her throat in the most disconcerting way. She was not afraid of Saxon Turville, she kept repeating to herself . . . yet if not, why this flutter of apprehension?

Having steeled herself for an uncomfortable confrontation, it was decidedly anticlimatic to be greeted mildly, as though he had not even noticed that the time lapse was greater than he had ordained. He was looking through some papers on his desk and scarcely bothered to lift his blond head.

'Sit down! I'll be through with these shortly.'

Cleone sat and for the first few minutes was content just to look curiously about her. She had been in Saxon's office once before, but not long enough to study his daily surroundings. It was a typical farm office, but, and this was not really surprising, knowing the character of the man, meticulously neat and ordered, the furniture utilitarian and designed for maximum efficiency, not comfort.

Even the walls bore only that which related to his work: a farming calendar and photographs of sheep. Cleone wished she could rise and inspect the photos more closely. Were these the 'special' sheep of which Ianthe had spoken? If she had been alone in the room, she would have satisfied her curiosity, but she was not going to give him the satisfaction of showing an interest. He was about to castigate her for trying to share her hobby with Ianthe, so she would exhibit complete indifference to his.

She withdrew her gaze from the photographs and found herself studying Saxon instead, the handsome, but somehow frightening countenance, the powerful structure of cheek and jaw, the well-shaped but stern mouth. This contemplation made her strangely restless and she wished he would get on with whatever he intended to say.

A glance at her watch told her she had been here ten minutes already. She waited. Fifteen, twenty, Cleone was becoming distinctly annoyed. Twenty-five, thirty. She shifted in her chair and cleared her throat.

Saxon glanced up.

'Yes, it is irritating to be kept waiting, isn't it, Miss Bancroft?'

'You're doing it deliberately!' she accused. Too late she saw the trap.

'As you deliberately kept me waiting.'

She couldn't deny it.

'I didn't see why I should jump to your orders,' she muttered, 'especially as you've only got me in here so that you can be unpleasant.'

'Unpleasant?' He said the word as if he did not even comprehend its meaning.

'About Ianthe ... about me taking her round the museum,' she said impatiently.

'So you admit I had cause to be annoyed!'

'No ... no ... I don't.' Cleone abandoned all caution. She might as well tell him exactly what she thought. 'I can't see any good reason why you should deny Ianthe something which ought to be part of her education ... her heritage.'

'Ianthe's heritage,' he interrupted smoothly, 'is this farm. Her ancestors have worked these lands since the time of Domesday and probably before. I wish her to take an interest in her paternal heritage. I have no desire for her to follow in her mother's footsteps.'

Just what had Tessa Turville done to make her husband so bitter against her?

'But you're condemning the child to living a half-life. She has her mother's genes as well as yours ...'

'Yes. I fear that is so ... which is why I am anxious that she should not come to the same end.'

End? Cleone paled. Did that mean Ianthe was right in her assumption that her mother was dead? and what about the child's other assumption? the manner of Tessa's demise? Oh surely not! Saxon was almost inhuman, but Cleone could not really see him as murderer.

'This conversation is a pointless waste of time,' she told him. She rose. 'We shall never agree in a million years.'

'Heaven forfend that our association should last so long,' he said sarcastically. 'Wait! I haven't finished!' He had risen too, not out of courtesy this time, but to prevent her departure.

'Well, I have. I want to go up to the site and find my uncle and Eric. They ...'

'You haven't time before dinner,' he pointed out. 'Besides, you'll never find it alone. You need a guide. Those woods are more extensive than you might think. You could actually get lost. But, as I said, I haven't finished with you yet.'

This time he did not rely on words, or the interposition of his body between her and the door. He actually grasped her wrists. Cleone did not like the sensation of being held by him ... she didn't like it at all. It was not distaste; he was not physically repellent ... quite the opposite in fact. But she didn't like the knowledge that this man's touch could actually stir her, even though she felt sure that she disliked him. Added to that, no one had ever used physical strength before, to restrain her.

'There's no need for this ... this brutality,' she exclaimed, as she struggled to free herself. 'Let go of me and I'll listen ... but I will not be bullied ... kept here forcibly.'

'I don't think I've ever met a woman quite so frigid and untouchable as you,' he said thoughtfully and Cleone seethed.

Why should he assume that that was the reason for her fighting him?

'You mean that women are normally bowled over by that ice-cold reserve of yours?' she enquired, making her tone heavily incredulous, ironic.

His eyes narrowed and his whole frame seemed to tense.

'Are you being provocative by any chance? challenging me? Because, if so. . . .'

Provocation was the last thing she intended.

'I'm waiting,' she said hurriedly, 'to hear what else you have to say and I'd be glad if you would make it as brief as possible.'

He relaxed, but his eyes were still watchful.

'Very well,' he said curtly. 'I was about to suggest a compromise. It's obvious that the apparent "glamour" of your presence here has had its effect upon my daughter, inasmuch as she has twice defied me. But ...' he paused and Cleone wondered nervously what he was about to demand, 'but if I relax my rules, I must ask you not to glamourise your profession still further, to encourage any ideas that she may have about becoming an archaeologist herself. Children are very impressionable, but if you handle the subject sensibly, it will be forgotten two or three weeks after your departure.'

She stared at him in silence. She didn't think he realised that, for a ten-year old, Ianthe was unusually mature; and she reflected that, at Ianthe's age, she had wanted to be an archaeologist and the ambition had persisted. But perhaps, in view of his concession, it would not be wise to mention that. But surely, his suggestion of tact came a little late. It has been his opposition that had fanned the flames of Ianthe's enthusiasm.

'Well?' he demanded impatiently. 'Do you agree to talk to the child sensibly; not to turn her head?'

'I think,' Cleone said slowly, 'that Ianthe's rebellion is against your personal aversion. If you could bring yourself to take an interest in the site, she wouldn't feel so bound to flout you.'

It was not a stupid suggestion, but she knew it was foolish of her to make it, because he would take no notice of her opinion; and in any case, the last thing she wanted was Saxon Turville on site whilst she was working. You needed a steady hand when disinterring and handling broken shards of pottery and similar finds; and he made her unaccountably nervous. But she made the suggestion for Ianthe's sake. The child desperately needed a common meeting ground with her father and Cleone felt strongly that it was up to him to make the effort, rather than the reverse. She met his eyes, trying to gauge his reaction, but he made no comment; instead, with an inconsequentiality untypical of the man, he remarked:

'Why do you scrape your hair back into that ridiculous schoolgirl's pigtail? It makes you look about fifteen. With it loose, I imagine you could be reasonably attractive.'

It was the first really personal remark he had made to her, and as such she felt it was totally uncalled for. Reasonably attractive indeed! Cleone knew that, unlike his wife, no one had ever compared her to Helen of Troy and she was under no illusions anyway about her own pleasantly ordinary appearance. But it was not up to him to comment on it. She sighed inwardly, but then, neither should she feel so aggrieved by the lukewarm compliment.

'I wear it this way because it's convenient,' she said icily, 'especially on a dig.'

'It must be very long?'

His remark was prompted by curiosity rather than as a criticism, but Cleone chose to resent it.

'I happen to like having long hair.'

And she was proud of her silky, auburn mane, which, when unbound, was fully long enough for her to sit upon. Once, seeing her with it unbraided, Eric had told her she could enter a fancy dress competition—'or undress' he had joked—as Lady Godiva. But she preferred the more romantic description applied by one of her uncle's friends, who had likened her to a pre-Raphaelite painting.

'May I go now?' she demanded.

He nodded absently, apparently regretting the interest he had shown in her for his eyes were once more on his paperwork and Cleone left swiftly, before he could change his mind. Despite her relief at his decision about Ianthe, she felt a little deflated. She had come there in a spirit of defiance, prepared to do battle, but conflict had not ensued, at least, not the kind of conflict she had envisaged. It had been of a more subtle kind, leaving her baffled and bewildered, by her own inconsistencies.

She had half an hour to spare before dinner. But, as Saxon had pointed out it was not long enough in which to go up to the site; but it was long enough to feel restless and dissatisfied, though she could not pinpoint the cause of her unusual unrest. Drifting disconsolately into the house, she encountered Ianthe and the child's face lit up with flattering pleasure at the sight of her.

'Oh, there you are Cleo. I'm sorry I let you in for that.' She lowered her voice sympathetically. 'Did he give you a bad time?'

'Your father? No ... no ... actually he's given permission for me to take you on the dig.'

'Goodness!' Ianthe's eyes were grey saucers of wonder. 'How did you manage that? I was right, wasn't I? He must like you?' Fortunately for Cleone's composure, the child did not wait for an answer, but slipped a hand into hers. 'When can I see the site?'

'I don't know. I don't even know if there is a site yet. My uncle planned to begin investigations this afternoon.

Perhaps we could go up for an hour after dinner, if there's something to see.'

'Super!' Ianthe enthused. 'And when we come back, I'll show you my secret—if you like?'

Cleone was intrigued, as indeed she was meant to be. 'Secret! What secret?'

Ianthe laughed, a pure, silvery sound of excitement, which Cleone had never heard before.

'Ah . . . if I told you it wouldn't be a secret. But I'll give you a clue . . . I found it in the attic.'

Another book on archaeology, Cleone thought indulgently. She only hoped the child had the good sense not to let her father find out, though unaccountably he did seem to be mellowing. . . .

Amyas was at dinner, though Cleone doubted if he noticed what he ate, the food disappearing into his mouth in the brief interval between sentences.

'We're on to something—something big, if the feelings in my bones are right; and they generally are, aren't they, Cleo?' He grinned at his niece. 'I got the students up there this afternoon, didn't even give 'em a chance to unpack! We marked off a small, likely area and began scraping away the top layer. It's early days yet—early days, but just take a look at this. It's only a fragment, but it's identifiable.' He delved into the capacious and now baggy pocket of his old tweed jacket and handed a carefully wrapped object to Cleone.

Her fingers trembling with anticipation, she unwrapped it and immediately recognised the glossy red colour, which she had seen many times before—in museums and on other digs.

'Samian pottery,' she breathed, then, in explanation to Ianthe. 'This kind of pottery was made in Gaul and the Romans imported it to Britain. It's made of an earth which only comes from Samos, a Greek island off the coast of Turkey, in the Eastern Aegean.'

She held out the red-burnished fragment for the child's inspection, then politely passed it to Saxon. He accorded it only the briefest scrutiny, then looked at Amyas.

'So! You have your find! You'll be staying on then?'

His tone was carefully expressionless, so that it was

impossible to tell whether he were pleased or displeased.
But Cleone thought she knew the answer to that. Saxon
had been hoping there would be no discoveries, so that he
could be rid of their disruptive influence on his village
and on his daughter.

'Yes ... we'll be staying on ... with your permission,
of course. In fact,' Amyas said, 'I was hoping you'd come
up this evening and take a look at the site ... give us
formal permission to open up?'

'Oh yes please, Daddy! *Please* let's go and have a look.'
Ianthe's clasped hands and pleading eyes would surely
have moved a monster, Cleone thought, and she was
beginning to realise that Saxon wasn't quite that.

It was a sizeable expedition that set out after dinner,
led by a voluble, swiftly striding Amyas; only Saxon with
his long legs and splendid physical condition was able to
keep pace with the enthusiastic professor. Eric and
Cleone together with Ianthe were in close pursuit, as
were the six students, anxious to a man, and woman, to
hear the landowner's verdict on their chosen site.

Amyas's find, Cleone had learnt over dinner, was in
the same area of the beechwood as the old priory, thus
vindicating her theory that Diana's Grove had Roman
associations; but her uncle had found a different route,
easier of access for vehicles, which would be necessary, if
they were to transport equipment to the area.

'In actual fact,' Amyas told her, 'it's literally a stone's
throw from your ruined priory, as you would have
discovered, if you'd walked just a few yards further on,
just beyond the next belt of trees. I came back that way
and took a brief look.'

'And?' Cleone was keen to see Amyas's site, but she felt
a proprietory interest in her own discovery.

'You could be right,' he told her, 'but I doubt if we'll
have time to investigate your theory this trip. Another
time perhaps,' he added vaguely.

Another time! Cleone felt that she would be very
surprised indeed, if Saxon gave permission for a second
invasion of his territory.

Just beyond the Golden Fleece Inn, a steep, tree-
shadowed lane climbed up to a ridge. It was a genuine

Cotswold 'white-way', whose character had never been hidden beneath tarmac or granite chippings, but was composed only of crushed Cotswold stone of a soft, tawny colour. Scabious, knapweed and vetch grew under dry stone walls that separated the lane from adjacent fields, dusty gold with their crop of corn. The track skirted the upper edge of Diana's Grove, then, narrowing, fell to a damp, coppiced bottom, before climbing yet again until they reached a large clearing, much larger than that in which the priory stood. But a few more steps and a swift glance through the trees assured Cleone that her uncle had spoken the truth, when he mentioned the priory's immediate proximity.

'With a tractor and trailer, it would be possible to get equipment up here,' Amyas pointed out. 'We'll need tents and possibly a small wooden hut where we can list and store any artefacts we find.'

Saxon made no comment and Cleone wondered if he would give his consent. She felt Ianthe's hand creep into hers and knew that the child shared her uncertainty.

The preliminary trench had been opened up on the sheltered and well-drained hillside, certainly a typical site for a Roman villa of the kind they sought. The soil here would have been fertile and there would have been plenty of timber to hand.

'I'm certain we're on to something,' Amyas persisted. 'Eric and I did extensive soil tests today and the findings of pottery shards, though not conclusive proof, are indicative of some kind of occupation. I'd very much like your permission to extend trenching, to establish conclusively if there is a site and to determine its extent and nature.'

'Doesn't trenching have its drawbacks?' Saxon asked.

'Yes, if it's the sole method of excavation—a great deal of information can be lost. Obviously I shall undertake a more complete examination as well.'

'You intend to use open area excavation too?'

He certainly knew the terminology, Cleone thought, learnt, presumably from his wife?

'Yes.' Amyas nodded. 'To show each phase of the site in one operation, we examine, record and then remove each successive layer. Once I have your permission to go ahead, I intend that my working party should mark out a grid of pegs, spaced at regular intervals, to make it easier to record each find.'

Amyas prowled back and forth, darting questioning glances at Saxon, as he did so, as though he too were unsure of the landowner's reaction.

At last, Saxon sighed heavily, as if accepting a burden it was impossible to avoid bearing, his eyes reflectively on Cleone's anxious face.

'Very well. Since the area is well screened by trees, I suppose any unsightliness will not affect the village. But I must make one condition.'

They all watched him expectantly.

'I want no publicity while the work is going on. Nothing is to be released to the news media until work is complete. I do not want hordes of sensation seekers beating a track through my woods, upsetting the even tenor of the villagers' lives. Should there prove to be an important site here, we shall have to consider some permanent form of access, but until then, complete secrecy. Agreed?'

The only voice raised in protest, as Cleone had known it would be, was Eric's. But a word from Amyas quelled his pugnacious assertion that the British public had a right to know things that concerned their heritage; but not before Saxon had bestowed a look of distaste, which left Eric simmering.

'Feudal! Absolutely feudal!' He muttered to Cleone, as they retraced their steps. 'A petty dictator. I'm surprised Amyas puts up with his autocratic ways.'

For once, however, Cleone was inclined to agree with Saxon. She liked to be able to concentrate on her work and hated people clumping about the site asking silly questions; and since Ianthe was present, she felt that Eric should not criticise Saxon in front of the child. On the other hand, she did not want to fall out with Eric. She attempted placation and sweet reason.

'Look at it this way, Eric, if we were to let the press get wind of what we hope to find here and then nothing came of it, we'd look pretty silly. At least this way, it may save us from embarrassment.'

It was dusk now and the village only gabled silhouettes against the sky; but the air was still warm, even sultry and Cleone knew a sudden restless desire to go on walking, not with Eric, yet not alone, but in some congenial company, though whose she was not sure. All she did know was that it was the kind of evening when she was aware of a nameless longing, for what she could not say, but at times like this, it seemed to her that some dimension was missing from her life.

Saxon came up with them shortly afterwards, slowing his pace to match Ianthe's and thus Cleone's. His presence was enough to detach Eric from her side and with a truculent expression on his face the younger man fell back to join Amyas, whose stride was less urgent now that his objective, Saxon's sanction of further work, had been achieved.

'I suppose you're as anxious as Badger to begin excavating?' Saxon enquired.

'Oh yes!' In the failing light, her eyes still gleamed golden, a sudden spurt of excitement lifting her spirits. It was the thought of beginning work of course. 'A new site is always exciting. There's no telling what you might find.'

'So you're unlikely to have any more time for sightseeing?'

Was he just making conversation? or was there some point behind his remark?

'We ... ell ...' Cleone said slowly, 'my uncle does insist that we each have a full day off site once a week ... and I would like to visit Chedworth. I ...'

'I meant something else besides Roman remains,' he said irritably. 'Good lord, girl, what a one-track mind you have. Don't you think it would be a pity, if you didn't see something of the countryside while you're here? At your age, you should be broadening your outlook. Do you never feel the urge for other interests, apart from digging up the past?'

Strange that he should touch upon the very subject that had filled her thoughts a few moments ago—the wish that there were more to her life; and yet, Cleone realised, until she had come to Salpeth, she had been utterly content. At what moment had she conceived these restless urges and why? She looked at Saxon thoughtfully, his profile just a dark shape against the sky, as though this contemplation could provide her with an answer.

'What do your friends think?' he continued, 'of your single-minded devotion? Don't they object? Is there no young man back in Oxford right now, bitterly resentful, because you're spending the Long Vac on a dig?'

Cleone shook her head, the heavy braid of her hair swinging against his arm as she did so.

'No ... that's no problem. All my closest friends are here with me.'

'Including the long-haired Eric?' he asked, his tone sardonic.

'Of course,' she said serenely. 'Apart from my uncle, Eric is my very best friend.' And it was true. While not wanting any romantic entanglements, she did enjoy the young man's friendship—when he was not riding his socialistic hobby horse.

'A strange choice surely.' The expression of distaste was there again.

'I don't see why,' she objected. 'We have a great deal in common.'

'I see,' he said curtly and to her disappointment, he made no further conversation.

Eric and the student party dropped away from them as they reached the Inn once more and Cleone wished that she too were staying there, instead of at the manor. They would all assemble now in the bar and there would be good conversation and much laughter until closing time. She would have been tempted to join them, except that Ianthe reminded her of 'the secret'.

'I must show you before I go to bed.'

Knowing that her uncle would expect her to be up and on site early next morning, Cleone agreed that the secret must be revealed that night.

Up the wide, main staircase, along the many levels of the corridors, until they reached the attic stairs, gained by a doorway whose existence one would never have suspected, unless one knew it was there. For a house of such vast size, the roof space seemed to Cleone to be unnaturally cramped, until Ianthe explained that this was only a small, almost forgotten area, which she had discovered by chance one wet day the previous week.

'I didn't have time to look at everything then,' she explained. 'It's absolutely cram-full. But I went up there again this afternoon, while you were in Daddy's office and I found something very special. I'm going to have it in my room.'

With her torch, Ianthe picked out the furthest corner of the room.

'There! There it is!'

As the torchlight lit up the object of the child's interest, Cleone gasped aloud. For a moment, she had believed that she looked at a living woman. Then, she realised it was a full-size painting that she confronted—the portrait of an elf-like woman, piquant of face, merry of eye, a cloud of long, black hair falling about her like a sable cloak that only served to emphasise her near-nakedness, the swirling draperies only covering her with minimal decency. The portrait was simply inscribed 'Tessa' and the signature was that of an artist well known in Court circles.

'Isn't she lovely?' Ianthe said. 'Can you guess who it is?'

'Your mother.' It could be no one else, though there was not the faintest trace of Tessa's features or colouring in the child beside her. Only her tiny, fragile stature proclaimed Ianthe as Tessa's daughter.

'Will you help me carry her down to my bedroom?' Ianthe asked.

'Oh ... but. ...' Cleone demurred. There must be some reason why the painting had been immured in the dark anonymity of the attic. 'Perhaps you'd better ask permission first.'

'I have,' Ianthe assured her. 'I told Daddy there was something in the loft that I wanted for my very own, and he said I could have anything I liked, as long as I didn't expect him to waste his time sorting through old rubbish.'

Cleone was still doubtful. She was in something of a dilemma. She did not want to offend the child by seeming to doubt her word and if she insisted that they seek

Saxon's permission—and it was already given, he would probably be extremely irritated by the unnecessary repetition. On the other hand, if he had forgotten that this particular item was in the loft, then Ianthe only had permission by implication.

'Come on, Cleo!' Ianthe was looking at her impatiently, almost jumping up and down in her anxiety to have her treasure safely bestowed. 'I can't possibly carry it by myself. Here . . . you take one end.'

Shrugging fatalistically, Cleone did as she was bidden. The portrait in its great gilded frame was heavy and she wondered if Saxon had carried it up these narrow, twisting stairs unaided.

'Where will you hang it?' she asked, as they stopped half way, to catch their breath and flex their cramped, clutching fingers.

'Facing my bed.' Ianthe had it all worked out. 'There's a blank wall. I'll be able to look at it there at night, and in the morning. It . . . it's sort of lonely not to have a mother, Cleo. All my friends have mothers.'

The unconscious pathos of the remark determined Cleone that this picture was going to hang in Ianthe's room come what may and they renewed their efforts, negotiating the rest of the attic stairs without mishap and arriving at Ianthe's bedroom breathless but triumphant.

'You stay here,' Ianthe commanded, 'while I go and get a picture hook and a hammer. I know where they're kept.'

Left alone, Cleone propped the painting against the wardrobe and in the better light regarded it searchingly. Ianthe should have added a duster to her list of necessary equipment, she thought. The work must have stood in that attic for a very long time. But the dust could not disguise the quality of the painting or the beauty of the subject.

She could see what had prompted Amyas's description of Tessa as a 'Helen of Troy'. Such beauty was the kind that men committed murder for. She shivered at the unbidden thought. Where was Tessa Turville? It was pretty obvious that Saxon and his wife were separated, but was she alive or dead and if dead, how had she died?

Could that grim man, Ianthe's father have been responsible for his wife's death? Cleone didn't like to think so.

So intent was she upon the portrait, so immersed in the thoughts it induced that she did not hear the long, swift strides along the carpeted corridor, knew nothing of Saxon's arrival, until a grip like steel encased her upper arm and she was shaken like a rag doll, while his voice cleaved her thoughtful silence—a cold axe of sound.

'What the hell are you doing with that and by what right? How dare you poke and pry ... how dare you bring to my daughter's attention something best forgotten?' His handsome features were no longer icily controlled but contorted with white hot fury.

Cleone was startled; and her worst fears had been realised. Ianthe had assumed wrongly that Saxon's permission implied carte blanche for any item above stairs. But shock and fear were overridden by indignation and the necessity to move further away from six foot two of angry, overpowering masculinity.

'Let go of me. You're hurting—and how can you say, or even believe, that it's best for a child to forget its mother's existence?'

'That depends on the mother,' he returned harshly. His grip slackened slightly, but he did not release her, 'and as the question does not concern you ...'

'But it seems it does ... inadvertently ... since I've helped Ianthe to bring down her mother's portrait and since ...' she looked defiantly up into the glacial grey eyes ... 'since I am going to help her hang it on that wall.'

'I forbid it!'

'I think you're very wrong,' Cleone interrupted earnestly, her golden brown eyes unconsciously pleading. It was a time for reason, not for anger. 'By your behaviour, you're giving far more importance to the matter, making it more of a desirable mystery in Ianthe's eyes than if you just quietly allowed her to have the picture. Do you realise just how deprived the child feels? that she hates being different in the eyes of her friends? They all have mothers and ...'

'So!' Anger seemed to increase his stature and he jerked her closer to him, so that she had to tilt her head backwards to look up at him. 'Not only have you encouraged my daughter to defy me . . . you've conspired to discuss private matters . . . to criticise me behind my back. . . .'

'I've done neither! Ianthe genuinely believed that you'd given her permission to bring down any item from the attic.'

'Not that attic.'

Cleone was thankful in a way that he had interrupted, for she could not, with truth, assert that Ianthe had never criticised her father; in fact it was worse than that; the child had stated her belief that her father had actually done away with Tessa. That was something he must never know, but Cleone wished that she at least might know the truth, so that she could put Ianthe's mind at rest, of course.

'Well, anyway, it was a misunderstanding and I don't think you should start shouting at Ianthe.'

'I do *not* shout. . . .'

'*You* might not think so, but I can assure you that the tone you've taken with me could be very alarming to a sensitive child. . . .'

'It doesn't seem to be very effective where you're concerned.' There was less anger now; replaced by exasperation.

'I'm neither a child, nor am I particularly sensitive and I won't stand for being bullied.' She succeeded in wrenching her arm from his slackened grip, moving away from him.

'By God, you're right! You're not sensitive,' he muttered, 'or you would realise just what you've done . . . trampling where angels fear to tread . . . bringing that portrait back into the light of day.'

Cleone felt a momentary pang of compunction at the look of very real pain which fleetingly contorted his rugged features . . . was he still so much in love with his estranged wife . . . would he be prepared to take her back? . . . Menelaus had taken back Helen of Troy. But sympathy waned at his next words.

'Very well ... Ianthe wants her mother's portrait ... she shall have it, but I do not want to hear it or her mentioned and while it hangs here I shall not cross the threshold of this room.'

Cleone bristled, her golden eyes snapping molten fire.

'*How childish!* No ... on second thoughts, it's not. Even a child wouldn't bear a grudge that long. After all these years, isn't it time you faced facts? OK. So you didn't hit it off with your wife ... can't you talk to your daughter about it, explain, sensibly? She's very mature for her years ... instead of leaving her to imagine all kinds of ...'

'Why, you little. . . .' He moved in on her again, then stepped back hastily, as they heard Ianthe returning.

The child burst breathlessly into the room.

'Sorry to be so long, Cleo ... I. . . .' Then, seeing her father, 'Daddy!' with incredulous joy, 'have you come to help me hang my picture? *Isn't* she lovely? At least now I'll be able to tell my friends what my mother looked like. None of their mothers are half so pretty.'

Cleone felt a sudden lump in her throat, a mistiness in her eyes and she looked at Saxon, willing him with her soul in her eyes not to destroy his daughter's innocent pleasure. After one hasty glance, he avoided her liquid, golden gaze and taking the hammer from the child enquired huskily:

'Where do you want it to hang?'

His capitulation was still the subject uppermost in Cleone's thoughts next morning, as she made her way uphill to the site of their projected excavation where she and Amyas were to meet up with Eric and the students.

Why had Saxon suddenly relented? Was it the sight of his daughter's touching enthusiasm, or had her own impassioned diatribe had its effect? Whatever it was, it was another proof that he was not as inflexible as she had supposed. He had given in over the archaeological investigation and now he had succumbed to his daughter's desire to possess her mother's banished likeness. Cleone sighed. It was too much to hope, she supposed, that these two incidents marked the beginning of a thaw in his nature. Then, not for the first time, she caught herself up sharply. Why should she be so preoccupied with Saxon Turville's lack of humanity or otherwise? Apart from the fact that she had developed a fondness for Ianthe, his character, his behaviour should be matters of supreme indifference to her. That was it, of course; it was on the child's behalf that she was concerned. This point satisfactorily settled in her mind, she was able to concentrate on the dig.

A week later, the site looked very different; gone the mossy greensward that had covered hillside and hollow. All had been carefully lifted away and layers of soil removed to show the Cotswold stone footings of an undoubtedly Roman building. Among the earlier layers had emerged scraps of dirty pottery and scattered tesserae. The area had now been divided into 'boxes', trenches having been dug, with narrow causeways left for access, causeways which would eventually be removed slowly. Layer by layer, century by century, the past was being laid bare.

The archaeological party, clad in a common uniform of dirty jeans and T-shirts, the men stripped to the waist by midday, worked first with spades, then with trowels and handbrushes, carefully revealing the solid walls beneath, cleaning out the hollows and channels of long-cold hypocausts that had once heated the many bathrooms the Romans had apparently found necessary. Broken tiles, fragments of glass, the occasional coin, their positions carefully noted, were dusted and taken to the site hut for examination and recording.

Ianthe was a persistent visitor to the site, begging to be allowed even the most menial of tasks, so that she might feel a part of the work going on and, to Cleone's surprise, Saxon did not fail to visit the excavation each day, remaining for some time and putting searching, even knowledgeable questions to the workers.

Eric, predictably, was resentful of what he termed 'officious supervision' on the part of the landowner and where once Cleone might have agreed with him, she found herself hotly defending Saxon's right to be on site and attributing more charitable motives to him.

'Have you established a date yet?' Saxon asked on one of these occasions, crouching on his powerful haunches to stare down at Cleone as she worked on her allotted section of the site.

She looked up at him, acutely aware that she was indescribably filthy, her hands and clothes permeated by the soil in which she delved. She brushed back her heavy braid of hair, unconsciously adding a smear of dirt to her cheek.

'We're not certain yet, except that it must belong to the second phase of Rominisation, somewhere between AD117 and 138. Villas weren't built until new towns or tribal centres had been established.' To her surprise she was conscious of a warm glow of gladness at his unexpected interest, glad for Ianthe's sake, she told herself, in an attempt at rationalisation.

Though mostly the weather was hot and sultry, it did not always treat the archaeologists so kindly and one morning Cleone arrived on site to find that an overnight rain had left it a morass of sticky mud, workable but decidedly unpleasant. She was alone, for Amyas had secured the services of one of his students to drive him back to Oxford, to collect Nerys, and he had given everyone else permission to do some necessary personal chores and shopping, for which there had not been time in those first days of frenzied activity.

In all that had happened, both on site and in her tension-filled encounters with Saxon, Cleone had almost forgotten that Nerys Kennedy was to join them. Amyas's fiancée had waited until advised that the excavation was viable, that it was well under way, before announcing her wish to join them; and quite frankly, Cleone was dreading her arrival. Nerys, she knew, would be bored and restless inside twenty-four hours, trying to distract Amyas from his work—not that she would succeed of course; but she would soon become sulky and create an atmosphere, of which everyone but Amyas himself would be made uncomfortably aware.

The Professor had suggested that his niece too should take a break, but she had elected to work. She had no particular desire to go shopping and the alternative, an unthinkable one, would mean being at a loose end at the manor; even Ianthe's company was denied her, for the child had gone out for the day with a friend.

'I could find you some occupation here?' Saxon had suggested, when plans were being mooted over breakfast. 'You won't achieve much up there on your own, especially after last night's rain.'

But Cleone refused emphatically, not wanting to be beholden to him in any way. Besides, knowing there would be very little activity up at the site, he was unlikely to come bothering her and she would be able to work uninterrupted. She quite enjoyed being alone, feeling that the enterprise was solely hers. It gave her a chance too to absorb the nature and atmosphere of her surroundings.

These foundations they had uncovered, the buildings they represented, who had once occupied them? ... a Roman of high rank or a Romanised Briton? Here people had lived, loved, laughed, wept and died. Today, without the distracting chatter of others, she really felt, as she had on other, similar occasions, that the past was actually a part of her, part of the present, the future too. She could imagine Roman life as it must have been in the Cotswolds, even though to some people, it must seem so remote as never to have happened.

As she worked, she was conscious all the time that, beyond the nearby belt of trees lay her first discovery, the ruined priory; and she could not help musing on its potential. Amyas, consenting to study the maps she had consulted, agreed that the area adjacent to that on which it stood was undoubtedly the Abbotsfield, or, formerly, the Grove of Libertina.

'If we have an opportunity, we'll open up a preliminary trench ... but you know, there won't be time for a full investigation. Perhaps next year,' he had muttered vaguely.

Next year! By then Amyas would be hot on the trail of some other site, probably in a totally different part of the British Isles. So Cleone was determined to keep him to his promise of at least testing out her theory, before they left Salpeth, and if she could not pin him down, then she would do the necessary work herself, she vowed.

She had asked permission to use the manor kitchen to make some sandwiches, so that she need not walk back to the village; and around midday, she rested from her labours, sitting on a tree stump to eat.

The only sounds and signs of movement now were those of the wildlife; blundering bees, flickering, insubstantial butterflies, and a rabbit. Emerging from the wood, it ceased its bobbing run to pose alertly upon a newly excavated piece of wall, an incongruous sight, and yet was it? she mused. Hadn't the rabbit as much right, if not more, to be here, since the Romans had been instrumental in introducing the species into England?

About two o'clock, a light rain began to fall, but Cleone worked on doggedly.

'You're asking for a chill!' an annoyingly familiar voice observed, making her swing round, so that she teetered precariously on the dampened soil of the trench.

Blow it! Why had he bothered to come up here today, his spaniels in attendance as usual? There was very little that was fresh for him to see.

'Why not call it a day?' he suggested. 'This is going to get worse. I've got the Land Rover just down the track. I'll run you back to the house.'

Stubbornly, she shook her head, even though the heavier rain he had predicted was already sweeping down through the trees. She had been determined to come up here today, to avoid him, she was not going to seek his company instead.

'No thank you. I'm not ready to pack up yet.'

'For heavens sake, girl! I believe you'd automatically refuse any suggestion I made.'

'Probably,' she muttered.

Why didn't he just go away? From her manner, it should be quite clear that she didn't want him hanging around. She couldn't concentrate with him standing over her like this, glowering no doubt, if she were to look up, only she wasn't going to give him the satisfaction.

Ostentatiously, she moved to another section of the site, less well drained, but further away from where he stood, his legs, she could see from the corner of her eye, arrogantly astride, his hands resting on tautly trousered thighs.

'You're wasting your time you know, trying to work in this.'

Drat the man! He'd followed her. She turned sharply, in order to tell him to get lost, to quit pestering her. In her annoyance, she forgot to be wary and after floundering helplessly in an effort to regain her balance, measured her length in the rain-filled trench. She was drenched from head to foot, jeans, T-shirt and even her heavy braid of hair coated with sticky grey mud.

Already seething, it did not improve her mood to hear him actually laugh—a full-throated, booming sound of pure amusement—at her expense. In her mortification, it did not at first occur to her that this was the first time she had ever heard him laugh; but as she looked up to spit her fury at him, the words died on her lips at the sight of his transformed features.

Laughter had been all that was needed to make Saxon Turville the most distractingly handsome man she had ever seen.

Genuine amusement had warmed the usually cold grey eyes and etched in tiny laughter lines at their outer corners. From being a hard, grim line, his mouth curved upwards, the relaxation revealing a sensuous fullness to his lips that had not before been apparent, lips that parted to show strong, white, even teeth. Cleone was frightened by the inexplicable wave of feeling that seemed to shake her to her innermost being.

'Damn you!' she managed to hiss, 'it's not funny.'

'Isn't it?' he queried. 'You should be where I'm standing.' He reached down a hand to her and with his words and the gesture, the idea was born, matured swiftly.

Without pausing to consider the consequences, she took the proffered hand and pulled, *hard*.

'And you should be where I am,' she cried, as she did so.

CHAPTER FIVE

SECONDS later she had the satisfaction of seeing him rise from the trench as muddy as she; and only now did she begin to realise that her rash act might have dire results; they were alone here, a long way from the village. If Saxon chose to exact retribution, to chastise her in some way for her prank, there would be no one to hear her cries for help; and right now he looked capable of murdering her.

He also looked very silly, like something out of a child's science fiction comic, 'the beast that rose from the primeval slime' she thought; and with the thought came a nervous giggle, which she seemed unable to control and then she realised that, astoundingly, he was laughing with her!

Incredulity stilled her own mirth, as he put his muddy hands about her slim waist and swung her shoulder high to place her on the edge of the trench, vaulting up himself to join her. For a few, tensely palpitating moments, he rested his hands on her shoulders, his face suddenly serious and she gazed up at him, aware of a sudden breathlessness. Then, abruptly, he took her elbow instead, propelling her away from the site and down the track towards the Land Rover.

'We must look a pretty pair,' he observed, as he handed her up into the vehicle, then swung himself in behind the wheel. 'What we both need right now is a bath.'

Relieved at the prosaic trend of his conversation, Cleone sighed, squinting down at her mud-plastered braid.

'And I shall have to wash my hair ... and it takes simply ages to dry.'

On learning that she had not brought a hair dryer in her luggage, since she had planned to visit a hairdresser when her long, thick tresses needed attention, he had a suggestion to make.

'I think I know where to lay my hands on an old dryer. It hasn't been used for ages, but it should still work.'

Cleone washed her hair under the shower, then luxuriated in a hot bath. As she soaped, she mused upon Saxon's totally unexpected reaction to her prank. She had expected him to be furious. She wouldn't have been at all surprised if he had exacted some kind of retribution, much as he might have treated Ianthe in a similar situation. But instead, he had been amazingly good-humoured, and there had been something else in his manner too, which had puzzled her, made her feel oddly tremulous. In fact, it was laughable of course, but she could almost have imagined that he was about to kiss her.

Wrapped in a large towel, she was attempting, with a second towel, to rub her hair dry, when, with a brief knock, Saxon, himself clad only in a brief robe, descended the two steps into her room. She tensed, clutching her towel about her, then relaxed. He was carrying the promised hair dryer, one his wife had left behind? she wondered.

'Thank you,' she said, and waited expectantly for him to go.

But instead, he bent to plug it in and before Cleone had realised his intention, he took up a handful of her red-gold hair and with calm matter of factness began to dry it for her.

Cleone was startled and extremely disturbed. It seemed such an intimate gesture, quite untypical of such a reserved man, and yet, beneath that reserve, hadn't she already sensed ...? What had she sensed? For the moment, in his presence, she dared not dwell upon it. But the whole atmosphere of her room was suddenly fraught with intimacy, the pair of them scarcely decent, together in a bedroom, the touch of his hand upon her hair. He was dealing very efficiently with his self-imposed task, and yet, somehow, his actions were not impersonal. She had the feeling that he was enjoying himself. Had he been accustomed to dry Tessa's hair like this? she wondered, remembering the long, sable cloak of it that the painting had depicted, his *wife's* hair. . . .

'Please . . .' she said breathlessly, 'you shouldn't . . . I mean ... you mustn't bother. I can manage quite well. ...' She tried to twist her head to look up at him, hoping to see agreement in his face, but he held her immobile by his grip on a handful of hair.

'Be still,' he growled huskily. 'It would take you ages alone. ...'

Recognising his tenacity of purpose, she had to accept the inevitable, despite the unease his attentions were causing her. She tried to pass off her embarrassment by remarking brightly:

'Long hair is a nuisance. Sometimes I think I should have it cut really short.'

The grip on her hair tightened in a sudden, painful jerk that made her wince.

'It would be criminal to cut off hair like this,' he asserted almost angrily. 'Some girls would give their eye teeth for it. "If a woman have long hair,"' he quoted, '"it is a glory to her."'

The words sounded Biblical, Cleone thought. She hadn't visualised Saxon as being a religious man, but then he was a total enigma to her anyway. This was just another facet to his complex nature.

It took twenty minutes by Cleone's bedside clock, before Saxon seemed satisfied that her hair was sufficiently dry, twenty minutes in which she sought desperately to unravel somewhat tangled emotions, caused by the pleasurable sensations his ministrations were causing her. Could this really be the same Saxon Turville, normally frigid and unapproachable? Here in her room, touching her hair lingeringly, as if he too were enjoying the experience.

Finally, he turned her around switching off the dryer and yet seemed reluctant to release her hair, running his fingers through the silky, glowing tresses, a wavy fire which almost consumed her slight, graceful body, as though to assure himself of the thoroughness of his work.

'Yes ... you have beautiful hair,' he said softly, his hands moving down to lightly encircle her slender neck, then lifting the auburn waves in two great swathes, letting it flow through his hands like molten liquid.

Yet he was not looking at her hair; he was looking

down at her visibly quivering mouth, into her bewildered golden eyes, bewildered for she just did not recognise or understand Saxon in this softened mood; and there was a strange expression on his rugged face too, which she found impossible to interpret. Nervously, she ran her tongue over lips suddenly parched and backed away from him, so that her hair escaped his caressing fingers.

'Th . . . thank you.' She almost whispered the words. 'That was very kind of you . . . especially after the dirty trick I played on you.'

He shrugged.

'I've been muddier . . . on a rugby field. Although, I did think,' he added, with a seriousness which had her deceived for a moment, 'of having you perform a suitable penance . . . such as scrubbing the mud off my back. . . .'

For a second, her eyes widened, as, irresistibly, she imagined the scene, then, realising he was joking, she smiled nervously. This new Saxon was definitely more alarming than the other; and she wasn't quite sure how to cope with her reactions to him.

'I . . . I ought to get dressed,' she said, hoping that he would take the hint and remove himself.

'Mmmm . . . me too.' But he made no move to leave and Cleone's unease grew, as did a shameful desire to have him touch her once more. 'Cleo,' he said thoughtfully. 'Ianthe calls you Cleo and so does Badger. Is it short for Cleopatra?'

Now she could smile naturally at such a thought, with the full effect of her lovely, generous mouth.

'Goodness no! Nothing so pretentious. It's "Cleone" actually.'

'Cleone! Cleone!' He experimented with it, the deep tones of his voice makes a subtle caress of the name. 'Yes . . . I believe it suits you. I couldn't really see you as a Cleopatra.'

No, she thought with sudden despondency, nor as a Helen of Troy. Both had been reputedly beautiful women. Strange that it should concern her so much that she was not. It had never troubled her unduly before. In fact, she had always thought that lovely women were not really to be trusted. They were too assured that anything would be forgiven them, because of their looks.

Saxon was looking consideringly at her hair again.

'A shame that it has to be dragged into that awful pigtail again. I suppose it is necessary?'

She resorted to flippancy to break the mesmeric effect his presence was having upon her.

'Heavens, yes! Can you imagine me delving in trenches with it like this? Totally impracticable.'

'Then why not unbind it, in the evenings, when work is over?' he suggested.

'Why on earth do you. . . .? I mean. . . .' She stumbled over the words, not wanting to ask him the question, what did it matter to him, how she treated her hair?

He shrugged.

'Shall we say . . . to satisfy a whim of mine? that I have a partiality for long hair . . . worn loose?'

He was thinking of his wife of course. But it was impossible to tell from his face, or his manner, whether he regretted Tessa's absence, or otherwise. But why should the way Cleone wore her hair concern him? Why should he think she should want to please him? Did she want to? Strangely enough, it seemed to her that she did, but she wasn't going to let him realise that, and yet, perhaps she might wear her hair loose, just now and again? so that it didn't make her seem too eager to comply?

'I really would like to get dressed now,' she said hopefully and this time he did turn towards the door.

But was it because of her request, or because he had heard the sound of a car drawing up? the chatter of children's voices, raised in farewell? Ianthe was home and the odds were that she would come directly to Cleone's room to retail the details of her day. Saxon would hardly wish to be found there. Ianthe was old enough to wonder why and perhaps to draw the wrong conclusions. But somehow Cleone felt that, if it had not been for this timely interruption, he would have delayed his departure still further, and the thought both frightened and excited her. What was happening to her? Why was it suddenly difficult to dislike Saxon Turville any more?

But Ianthe did not appear after all and Cleone was able to complete her dressing uninterrupted. This strange new obsession made her consider with care just what she should wear. She had an urge to appear as feminine as she knew she had looked with her glorious mane of hair flowing loosely about her. She knew it, because, willingly or not, Saxon's eyes had told her so; and any other man, she felt, would have voiced what his eyes revealed. But not Saxon. Despising women as he did, she felt he would not lightly bestow compliments, perhaps that was why she felt impelled to make the effort. A compliment from him would be worth more than that from a man to whom pretty speeches came easily.

The glazed cotton dress she finally chose echoed the tawny gold of her eyes, hugged her trim waist and flared softly over her flat hips, making them seem less boyish, more mature. But best of all, the pintucked bodice tightly caressed her small, tip-tilted breasts, revealing that she was very much a woman. After some hesitation over her hair, she divided it into two braids instead of the usual one and coiled it several times around her head, the fiery coronet giving her small, piquant face a look of regality.

Though a pulse beat agitatedly in her throat, she had a strange new confidence in herself, as she went downstairs in search of Ianthe—and Saxon.

She entered the sitting room, where Ianthe, more relaxed than usual in her father's presence, was gravely relating what seemed to be the entire plot of a children's matinee film she had attended, and, wonder of wonders, Saxon was showing an absorbed interest in his daughter's words. But he was not so absorbed, Cleone realised, that he was unaware of her entrance, or of her appearance and she knew a small glow of triumph, as the grey eyes made a comprehensive survey, ending with the new hairstyle; and she thought a tiny hint of a smile quirked his well-shaped mouth at this compromise between his request and her own determination. But he made no comment. Instead, he enquired of Ianthe if, after hours immured in a stuffy cinema, she did not feel in need of fresh air?

'You mean . . . we should go for a walk? You and I?' Ianthe's doubtful tone revealed all too clearly that this was not a common occurrence for father and child.

His swift glance at Cleone gave her the impression,

though afterwards she decided she must have been mistaken, that this was not what he had in mind, that he was anxious that Ianthe should leave the two adults alone. But another look at Ianthe's wide-eyed expression and he inclined his head.

'But ... but it's raining,' Cleone protested. She felt oddly deprived that, having comfortably settled herself, looking forward to a cosy, almost domestic situation with Saxon and his daughter, they should be about to leave her alone. She should be pleased for Ianthe's sake, of course, that he was suddenly showing an interest in his daughter's well-being but....

'It's stopped,' Saxon pointed out, 'a long time ago.'

And indeed, now that Cleone had eyes for anything but the two occupants of the sitting room, she could see that this was so. With late afternoon, an unpleasantly wet day had become one of golden light.

'Oh ... yes ... so it has.' She felt foolish, as though he could see through her objection; but her heart lifted at his next words.

'Would you care to take a walk with us, Miss Bancroft?'

Despite the little surge of pleasure, she looked at him doubtfully. Did he really want her company too, or was he just being polite? Had she shown her disappointment? She hoped not.

'Daddy!' Ianthe said earnestly. 'Why do you call Cleo "Miss Bancroft"? It makes her sound like a schoolteacher ... and she isn't a bit like a teacher.'

'No?' The old Saxon, the one Cleone knew best, was back in that sardonic lift of a brow. 'I think Miss Bancroft feels she has rather a lot to teach us.'

'Well, I call her Cleo, and I think you should too. It's ... it's friendlier,' she concluded firmly, but with a doubtful look at her father, as if a little scared by her own temerity in thus admonishing him.

'But you haven't asked Miss Bancroft's opinion,' he reminded her mildly. 'Nor do I have her permission ... as you presumably have?'

'I'm sure Cleo wouldn't mind ... would you, Cleo?'

Cleone didn't know where to look, for she had a

sudden illogical longing to hear him say her name, as he had done earlier, in that deep, rich voice of his. A little helplessly, she raised her delicately arched brows at him, at the same time giving an expressive lift of her shoulders, hands slightly spread.

'Would you mind?' he asked and although the words were simple, she had a feeling that not only Ianthe waited tensely for her answer; but why should such a little thing matter to him?

'N ... no....!' she murmured shyly. 'I ... I don't mind. I....'

'Then I shall call you "Cleone",' he said with decision. 'I feel that "Cleo" belongs to Ianthe, and to many others, and you must call me Saxon?'

She scarcely heard this last remark as she speculated on his decision. Was he trying to maintain a semblance of formality, in using her full name? or was he trying to imply that he wanted his own, special, personal name for her?

Rubbish! Sentimental self-delusion! Of course he didn't mean any such thing. Why should he? Why should he indeed, but she realised with a sick feeling of shock that she wanted him to think of her in some special intimate way that belonged to him alone. The little scene in her bedroom, when he had dried her hair had lent a new dimension to sensations of which she had been vaguely aware ever since they'd met. But even now, Cleone did not realise the full significance of what she felt towards Saxon Turville.

'And now, how about that walk?'

At the last moment, Ianthe declined to accompany them. The gardener's cat, she informed them, had littered that morning and she was anxious to see the new kittens. Cleone was dismayed. She had only agreed to accompany Saxon because she had been sure of Ianthe's presence. But it would look too pointed if she now refused to go, as if she was making unwarranted assumptions, that she felt she had something to fear from being alone with him; and she realised too that he now expected her to use his first name. It would not come naturally to her lips, she knew. Perhaps she could avoid calling him anything at all?

Up on to the smooth contours of the hillside overlooking the manor, a landscape of sweetly flowing lines, chequered by the long, low, wandering stone walls, velvety with moss.

'Once this was all open downs, grazing land.' Saxon swept his arm around in a comprehensive gesture, 'at the time of the great wool merchants. Now a great deal of land is enclosed, for crops. But some of it is still sheep country, especially on my estate.'

'I had heard that you were interested in sheep,' Cleone said cautiously.

'Not just sheep,' he emphasised, 'but a special kind of sheep. I'm keen to conserve the original Cotswold breed. They would interest you too, since they're supposed to be descended from stock imported by the Romans.'

She darted a suspicious glance at him, looking for mockery, but she could find none.

'They were noted for their large size, long necks and thick, white wool, their heavy fleece, which earned them the name of "Cotswold Lion".'

How appropriate, she thought with amusement. The name could apply not only to the breed but to their breeder. He had something of the fierce arrogance and disdain of a lion, an animal sure of its own power, its ability to fend for itself.

'You said you're "conserving" them?'

'Mmmm. The wool trade declined in the eighteenth century and the Lion was replaced by smaller, quicker-fattening sheep. There are very few of the original breed left today.'

This upper part of the valley in which Salpeth stood, was very different to the wooded and sheltered lower reaches. Cleone imagined that, in winter, it could be very bleak. Here, on the thin, clean turf of the wold pastures, grazed the sheep they had come to see, sturdy, square-built aristocrats, heavily fleeced, the thick wool curling down over their foreheads and down their legs. Roman noses flared below their shaggy forelocks.

'The Cotswold Lion was mostly replaced by merino for wool and smaller breeds for meat. But I believe, if farmers were to persevere, the Lion would regain its popularity, simply because of the demand nowadays, by supermarkets, for larger joints.'

As Saxon spoke with enthusiasm of his sheep and of agriculture in general, Cleone listened attentively, her eyes fixed upon his handsome face; she was fascinated to discover yet another new side to him, this man who farmed his land with authority and scope.

Before they retraced their steps, Saxon insisted that she must inspect the lambing pen, empty now, but ready for the next season. The pen was an enclosure of about thirty by twenty yards, which, in winter, would be weather-proofed by bales of straw. All round the outer wall ran a narrow passage, thatched over at about four feet in height, with hurdle partitions and openings to a central space. Cleone shuddered to think of the ewes giving birth up here on the bare wold, in the cold, early months of the year and she was relieved to see that the passage which Saxon described as the maternity ward, was dark, snug and safe from wind. In the middle were feeding places for other sheep, with lambs. Beside the pen stood a small caravan with a stove chimney.

'At lambing time, I move up here, until all the ewes are safely delivered.'

Cleone was surprised and said so.

'But surely that's the shepherd's job?'

'When it comes to the "Lions", I assure you, I am their shepherd. I let old Ben tend the main flock, but these I give my own attention.'

The interior of the caravan could be made snug enough, Cleone supposed, though once the door was shut it seemed to her that it was a little cramped. But perhaps this was because of Saxon's large stature, the discomfort she felt at being this closely confined, his muscular figure between her and the door. To distract her mind from this problem, she looked about her. There were all the needs that one man alone might have, but she still felt that it must take great dedication to spend much time there, particularly in winter.

'Aren't you afraid of getting cut off in bad weather?'

He smiled tolerantly at her doubtful expression and Cleone felt an uncontrollable need to swallow, a convulsive movement of her throat. She had seen him smile several times just recently, but always it struck her afresh how marvellously a smile complemented his striking features.

'It's happened to me more than once,' he admitted. 'The snow can be banked higher than a car roof in the lanes. So you can imagine what it's like up here.'

'But what do you do? The time must drag endlessly.'

'My time is full enough.' He sounded amused. 'I have to keep a continual check on the animals; then there's snow to be dug away round the van . . .'

'Aren't you ever lonely?'

His face was suddenly bleak, his voice harsh.

'There have been times when I've been lonelier down at the house.' Then, with a lightening of his tone: 'But no . . . I have Shep, my collie, for company . . . and my books.' He indicated a shelf full of the classics. 'I never feel I'm alone when I have a book. Would you agree?'

'Mmmm . . . up to a point. But I'd rather have people.'

'Yes.' He looked at her consideringly. 'I believe you would. Tell me . . . just how old are you, Cleone?'

Her golden eyes dancing, she teased him.

'Don't you know you should never ask a lady her age?'

'Oh, come off it!' His own tone was similarly light. 'If I didn't know you were just a child, I might agree. Since . . .'

'But I'm not a child.' Cleone felt aggrieved that he should still have that impression. 'I told you that once before, and if you must know, I'm twenty two.' She lifted her small, pointed chin proudly, squaring her shoulders, unknowingly bringing her firm breasts into prominence. 'I'm a woman!'

His eyes narrowed as he surveyed her and subtly she felt the atmosphere change.

'Yes, you're right . . . you are . . . and yet I would have guessed eighteen at the most. If I'd known . . . perhaps . . . perhaps. . . .'

His pause was charged with so much tension that Cleone, suddenly nervous, anxious to break the pulsating silence, blurted out:

'Perhaps what?'

'Perhaps I wouldn't have held back,' he said softly, 'waited so long . . . for this.'

A second later, incredibly, he had pulled her, with rough urgency, into his arms and was kissing her, with all the pent-up emotion of a man who had not held a woman for a very long time; and it was as though, the stony dam of control which had held him in restraint for so long once broken, he could not stem the floodtide of his feelings. His hold, his kisses were ruthless in their intensity and in her inexperience, Cleone had not realised how swiftly it was possible for a man to become so fully aroused . . . nor that it was possible for her own response to be equally swift. But this was all wrong. He shouldn't be doing this, and she shouldn't be allowing it.

'No . . . please. . . .' Her words were inaudible against his lips and she struggled frantically; unable, because of the tight proximity in which he held her, to beat against his broad chest. Instead, a nameless fear wrenching the pit of her stomach, her fists rained blows upon his back and sinewy shoulders, to no avail. It seemed he did not mean to give up his possession of her mouth until he had dredged all its sweetness, slaked his long-denied passions, reduced her to shattered compliance with his will.

Cleone had never been kissed like this and she was fighting for her very breath now, her breasts rising and falling in long, shuddering gasps, seeking the air her lungs were being denied. But he seemed to mistake their agitation for a response to his ardour and with a strong hand he felt for and captured one palpitating mound of softness, rousing unbearably urgent sensations, whose like Cleone had never before known.

Was this the man she had thought incapable of passion? She had always been aware, of course, of his physical attractions, but she had never dreamt that anything like this could ever happen between them. Underneath his icy exterior there lay an unsuspected, raging fire and gradually, insensibly, she was submitting to his onslaught, no longer wishing to resist. Her beating hands grew more feeble in their attempts to repel him, faltered, then, as though she had no control over their independent action, fluttered up over his shoulders and neck, seeking the thick, sun-bleached hair, where at last they came to rest, deeply plunged into the virile growth.

With her submission, the willing parting of her lips, her body curving against his without need of restraint, he became more gentle, freeing her mouth to explore with his lips the soft skin of her cheeks and neck. His hands fumbled impatiently with the pins that secured her hair, until it tumbled down around them both. He buried his face in its living flame, his fingers spreading the disorder they had begun, until the silky tresses seemed to engulf the two of them ... a state of affairs which seemed to increase the depth of his sensuality.

'I would like,' he said, his voice husky, slightly shaky, 'to see you naked, except for this hair of yours.'

The outrageous statement brought Cleone to her senses with a start. Until he spoke, she had scarcely realised what was happening to her. She had been overtaken, lifted and swept away by the tide of his passion, which had blotted out for her all other considerations. But what had begun as a kiss, ravishing her senses, fogging her intellect, was now threatening to develop into something quite different, something whose implications she could not accept.

Today, she had been glad that, gradually, Saxon was becoming friendlier, less unapproachable. But if she had suspected for one moment that his attitude towards her could undergo such a dramatic change, she would never have agreed to take this walk alone with him ... or at least she would never have entered the close confines of the shepherd's van.

Yet hadn't there been a hint of this change in him earlier, when he had insisted on drying her hair? Hadn't she known then, subconsciously maybe, that their relationship was no longer a hostile one, or even an impersonal one? Hadn't she known for quite a while now that Saxon Turville was not a man she could easily forget, physically or mentally? Hadn't this been the reason for the apparently senseless fear she had always felt, that she had told herself she did not want the impression he made upon her to go any deeper, for the sake of her peace of mind? She realised now that, right from the first instant of their acquaintance, she had been unwillingly responsive to his masculinity, even though she believed she did not like him. Recently, she had begun to discover new depths to his character, a side of him that perhaps he did not show to everyone, and now? Now she was aware of yet another fact, one which he had no right to demonstrate to her, his undoubtedly virile needs, all the more dangerous, she felt, by the fact that for so long they had been so tightly restrained.

A strong, warm hand had begun to slide down the zipper on the back of her dress and Cleone knew that, at this moment, he was driven by the desire he had expressed to see her clothed in nothing but her hair.

'No!' she told him sharply, as she fought against him. 'No ... stop it. Let me go at once. Have you taken complete leave of your senses?'

'Perhaps I've just realised that my senses still exist,' he said softly. 'Cleone ... has no one ever told you how very desirable you are?' His voice thickened, 'How lovely you could be in a man's eyes ... with just your hair to cover you?'

It was necessary to think quickly. To deny it would be to imply that she was free of any other involvements, that she was available to him, and she wasn't, she told herself vehemently, whatever her treacherous body might be telling her. All she had wanted had been a cessation of their hostilities, not this rapid swing to the opposite extreme. After all, she knew, for want of any concrete evidence to the contrary, that he was still married. Thus, she should not have any thoughts of him, thoughts of any involvement other than those occasioned by the needs of common courtesy.

'Has anyone ever told you?' he repeated, while, insidiously, his hands still sought to achieve what she denied.

'Of course I've been told that,' she said, successfully achieving calm matter of factness, belied by the inward pulsing of her blood.

'Oh!' He sounded disconcerted, annoyed. 'Who has told you that?' he demanded.

Who? That was a good question. Though Cleone had

been dated by several men of her own age, there had been nothing so intense in the relationships as to elicit such a remark ... except that....'

'Eric!' she improvised quickly.

It was partly true anyway. He had made the remark about lady Godiva.

'That long-haired....' Grim-mouthed, he bit off the epithet.

But her claim had achieved the desired effect, for he released her and moved as far away as the tiny dimensions of the van allowed. This was what she had wanted, Cleone assured herself. But why then did she feel so bereft, limp, as though a necessary support had been removed? She couldn't want something that wasn't right, or proper? could she? Her indecision showed in her eyes, limpid still with the reactions she could not hide to his recent lovemaking.

'Don't look at me like that!' He said savagely. 'Or I won't be answerable for the consequences. Come on, we'd better go, if Eric is to have you back undespoiled.'

Oh dear! In her desperation, had she created a situation for herself that would be awkward now to deny? Yet what did it matter? What need to deny it? Better that he should think her committed elsewhere, as indeed he himself was. Even if his marriage was a failure, Cleone still believed in the sanctity of the vows he had taken. He was not free to make love to other women.

The mood of their return to the house was very different from that in which they had left it. Then, their conversation had been easy, unstilted; now it was non-existent, yet the silence seemed to say more than the most heated of words. But it wasn't her fault, Cleone cried out inwardly. Much as she had welcomed the thaw in Saxon's manner of late, she could not be expected to permit such familiarities as he had seemed bent on inflicting. Indeed, on reflection, she could not think why he should act as he had. With the rest of the archaeological party, her presence here was resented by him, and she certainly hadn't encouraged that scene in the van.

Only once did he break the tangibly, uncomfortable silence, just as they reached the door of the manor house.

'And I could have sworn that you had revised your opinion of me, that you were even beginning to like me a little.'

Cleone stopped and looked up at him, her golden eyes unwittingly betraying to him the depths of her bewilderment, at his unprecedented behaviour, at her own shameful reactions.

'I had . . . I do . . . I did . . . I mean. . . .' she faltered.

'Yet you object to me kissing you? making love to you?'

'Of course I do!' she replied, indignation lending strength to her tremulous voice. 'It wouldn't be right. Even you must realise that. I mean . . . you're a married man . . . and. . . .'

'Cleone!' His hand came out in a swift movement towards her, a movement which she avoided. 'Is that why . . .? what you really believe . . .? because. . . .'

'We . . . ell. . . . Hello there!'

Absorbed in their exchange, neither of them had noticed the svelte figure approaching across the lawn. Nerys had arrived; and she couldn't have chosen a worse moment for her interruption. Or could she? What had Saxon been about to say? Cleone did not think she could have borne it if he had derided her cherished beliefs, had declared himself unheeding of moral and social tenets. She forced a smile to her lips.

'Hallo, Nerys. This is Mr Turville. He owns the land we're working on. S . . . Saxon. . . .' She must now, perforce, say his name, 'Miss Nerys Kennedy, my uncle's fiancée.'

'And Nerys to you, of course.'

It was apparent to Cleone that the older woman had registered all of Saxon's attractions; and Nerys herself was looking particularly glamorous, Cleone was reluctant to admit, her sleek, black hair swept up in a sophisticated chignon, her strange green eyes, an unusual combination with dark hair, deliberately widening as she held out a slender hand for Saxon's encompassment.

'And I shall call you Saxon!' It was an assured statement. Nobody ever refused Nerys Kennedy anything, when they looked into those avid, provocative eyes and Saxon, Cleone was disgusted to see, was no different to anyone else.

'How could I object?'

Cleone turned away and entered the house, aware of a very uncomfortable emotion boiling within her. It was incredible. She had no right even to feel this way. She was jealous! She was searingly jealous, because Saxon was so obviously appreciative of Nerys's sophisticated loveliness. She found herself thanking heaven that the other girl was engaged to Amyas. But it was small consolation after all. Would it make any difference to either Nerys or Saxon? Cleone had no illusions about the other woman and had always deplored her uncle's involvement with her. Now she was not so certain, as she had been on first acquaintance, that Saxon was totally impervious to women ... or if he had been up to now, the thaw was certainly setting in. Indignation swept her. For she felt that she had, in part at least, been responsible for humanising him, over these last few days. Was Nerys to come along now and reap the benefit?

Well you can't anyway, she reminded herself sternly, and neither can Nerys, though she doesn't know it yet. And when will you stop forgetting? *Saxon is married.*

They had followed her into the house and Cleone heard Saxon remark:

'I must say it's very pleasant to see a new face here in Salpeth. I fear we are a very small, isolated community.'

Oh, the hypocrite! One story for one person and a different version for another. He had told her that strangers were not welcome in Salpeth. He'd certainly changed his tune for Nerys. Why?

Then the other woman was exclaiming over the manor house. She and Amyas, it appeared, had arrived about an hour ago.

'And I've been just dying for you to come back and give me a guided tour of this too divine home of yours.'

Predictably, Saxon offered to show her round and Cleone went upstairs to her own room, still seething. Why had Nerys to come? She would spoil everything. She always did. She had always made Cleone feel very gauche and immature, but this time it would be worse. Now Cleone had another reason, besides that of her

uncle's wellbeing, for wishing Nerys at the other end of
the world. Nerys would ruin her newfound friendship
with Saxon. In her dread of this all too-certain
occurrence, it did not occur to Cleone that only moments
before, she had been denying herself any right to such a
friendship.

It was comforting to find that one other person saw
through Nerys Kennedy's sickly charm.

About half an hour later, Ianthe came in search of
Cleone, her little nose wrinkled with disgust.

'Cleo ... I admit you were right ... about me liking
your uncle. He's such a nice man. But however can he be
engaged to that awful woman? She ... she *gushed* at me.'
Ianthe's tone was so appalled that Cleone had to laugh,
despite her own gloom over Nerys's arrival. 'She said I
was a "sweetly pretty child" and what a charming idea to
have called me after Shelley's daughter, her favourite
poet, she said ... "so appropriate for the daughter of a
man with an M.A. in Literature." Oh, she's dreadful,
Cleo, and she's found out more about Daddy in ten
minutes than anyone else ever has, and he's answering all
her questions ... talking as if he likes her.'

Good, Cleone thought, with a sudden, savage,
revulsion of feeling. If that was the sort of woman Saxon
Turville admired, then good luck to him. Perhaps Nerys
would be so besotted, she'd give Amyas up for the
landowner, and they would just about deserve each other.
Resolutely, she told herself that she had succeeded in
quelling her earlier sensations of jealous outrage. Saxon
was not for her, but perhaps Nerys would not be as
scrupulous, and apparently he had no remaining feelings
of loyalty towards his wife, his estranged wife. Cleone did
not want to see her uncle hurt, of course; but she felt that,
in the long run, it would be for his greater good to have
Nerys weaned away from him, before their marriage
could actually take place.

Over dinner and throughout the evening, the
conversation was totally monopolised by Nerys, her
efforts, of course, directed at Saxon. As Ianthe, with her
childish perception, had pointed out the older woman

seemed bound and determined to wring from Saxon every possible personal detail, even if to do so she had to hear about the village, his farm, his special flock of sheep, things which Cleone knew could not possibly interest Nerys in a thousand years. No, it appeared that she had been bowled over by his looks, his home, his local status, and not least, his apparent affluence. Saxon would be a much more eligible catch for Nerys than a moderately comfortably-off Professor of Archaeology.

If Amyas noticed his fiancée's arch, flirtatious manner towards their host, he gave no sign of it. He was, he told Cleone, coming close to floor level up at the excavated villa and he had great hopes of what he might find in the way of mosaic paving.

'I suppose you are interested in archaeology too?' Cleone heard Saxon ask Nerys.

She was trying to attend to her uncle's conversation and yet straining her ears to hear what was going on between the other two.

Nerys laughed, a carefully cultivated light, rippling sound.

'Good Heavens no! Oh, I shall go up to the site no doubt, just once, to keep Amyas happy. But I intend to do as much sightseeing as I can while I'm in this part of the country.'

'That's what I tell Cleone she should be doing,' Saxon observed. 'There are other things in life besides ancient remains.'

Yes, Cleone thought scornfully, that's right, compare me unfavourably with the broad-minded Nerys. What you don't know is that Nerys's idea of sightseeing, means going round as many shops as she can find. She has absolutely no interest in culture as you and I see it.

'Well of course,' Nerys was saying in what were meant to be indulgent tones, 'Cleone is only a child as yet. She'll grow out of this obsession someday. But we mustn't hurry her.' She sighed. 'One grows old all too quickly, don't you think?'

Nerys was looking for a compliment, of course, and received it. But had Amyas's fiancée considered the construction that might be put upon her tactless words.

After all, Amyas, despite his fifty-two years, had never lost his interest in ancient history. It sounded as though Nerys was trying, subtly, to belittle him. If that were the case, nobody else seemed to have noticed, except, perhaps, Ianthe, who was looking first at Cleone and then at Amyas, a thoughtful expression on her elfin, yet worldly-wise little face.

'How long will you be able to stay in Salpeth?' Saxon enquired of Nerys.

She shrugged gracefully.

'I suppose that rather depends upon the duration of the dig.' She contrived to look prettily wistful. 'If this is the only way I am to see something of my fiancée during the Long Vac. . . .' She spread her hands expressively and Cleone thought sardonically that Nerys had never made any such effort in the past, so why now? 'But of course,' the other woman added with graceful deference, 'I am totally dependent also on the extent of your hospitality. Perhaps you'll tire of having me around?'

Oh, why had she never noticed before just how sickly and cloying Nerys Kennedy was? She was crawling and grovelling, metaphorically speaking, to Saxon in the most obnoxious way and he, poor fool, was apparently lapping it up.

'Perhaps you would care to begin your sightseeing tomorrow?' he suggested, 'since the length of your stay is uncertain?'

Probably only Cleone noticed the small frown that marred Nerys's brow. Evidently, this was not what the other girl had expected. No doubt she had wanted Saxon to declare that his house was hers for as long as she cared to stay. But even in his apparently besotted state, he was not that incautious.

'The problem is . . .' Nerys was saying, in tones that were meant to be sweetly troubled, but that Cleone knew were subtly insinuating, 'I don't drive myself. I'm totally dependent upon my fiancé for transport, and even then he gets Cleone to drive him everywhere.' She sighed heartrendingly, 'and I suppose they'll both be immersed in Roman remains all day, every day.'

Here it comes, Cleone thought, as Saxon drew breath.

This is what she was angling for, the cunning, conniving. . . .

'Then you must certainly allow me to offer my services. I believe I can be spared from the farm tomorrow at least.'

And if Nerys had her way, on other days as well, Cleone brooded.

On this note, the evening ended and as Cleone and Amyas bade Saxon goodnight, Cleone noted that Nerys contrived to linger, to be the last to leave the comfortable sitting room. She glanced swiftly at her uncle. Wouldn't he expect a few moments alone with his fiancée? But he seemed untroubled. Dear Amyas, Cleone thought affectionately, he was just too vague to notice deviousness or bad behaviour in those around him.

Cleone showered and sat before the dressing-table to brush out her hair, a task which she performed with religious thoroughness every night. Despite her full day, she did not feel really tired and she sat musing on the day's events; Saxon's surprising good humour, when she had hauled him down to join her impromptu mud bath; the way he had dried her hair afterwards; and, her cheeks warmed so that the colour was visible in her mirrored reflection, and the way he had kissed and caressed her that afternoon, in the confines of the shepherd's van. But she chivvied her brain past that seductive memory and moved on to the time of Nerys's unwelcome arrival and her subsequent blatant attempts to draw Saxon's interest. It seemed she had succeeded. Oh, well, Cleone thought, at least it would distract Saxon's attention from herself. He might find Nerys a more complacent proposition, if he was proposing to make up for his years of rigid self-control.

This led her on, by natural progression, to another thought. Had he lived a monk-like existence since his parting from his wife? Surely there had been women? discreet relationships, of course, since he would be jealous of his good name before his tenants and estate workers. Cleone wondered if there had ever been a divorce and if so why Saxon had not remarried. Judging by this afternoon's demonstration, he had a lusty, healthy, sexual appetite, and he certainly knew how to ravish a woman's senses. What would it be like? she wondered. Though she knew it to be totally wrong, foolish, she allowed her imagination a little licence, what would it be like to be possessed by him? Cleone had often wondered about marriage, the intimacies involved, things which were totally beyond her ken, or her powers of envisaging. What *was* it like, to be the recipient of a man's physical love? Would she ever know? She felt that perhaps she had come close to knowledge that afternoon, when needles of some sharp, ecstatic pain had assailed her, deep, deep down in hitherto ignored portions of her anatomy. Was that what it was like to desire a man?

She shifted restlessly, as the remembering induced a pale shadow of that unfamiliar sensation. Suddenly, she longed for experience, to know the full meaning of her body's urges. But, oh why had these dormant yearnings to be awakened by this man? Why couldn't her first kiss, her first inner stirrings, have been caused by someone she could like and respect, someone who was free to love and be loved?

She attacked her hair with new vigour, trying by self-inflicted pain to wipe out the sensuous memories that threatened to engulf her. She must not think these thoughts in connection with Saxon Turville. He was nothing to her, nor she to him, other than half an hour's dalliance and now he had Nerys eager and panting to bear him company.

The bedroom door opened and she half turned on her stool, expecting to see Ianthe. Sometimes the child, who was never sleepy at her allotted bedtime, would come to Cleone's room for a gossip. But Cleone's eyes widened with horror, her cheeks, still rosy with the warmth of reminiscence, flushed deeper yet at the sharp pang that ran through her at the sight of the man who stood in the doorway, closing the heavy wooden panel behind him.

It was an effort to force any sound from her strangled vocal chords.

'Wh . . . what are you doing here? What do you want?' Trying to sound indignant, she only succeeded in revealing the depth of her panic.

He did not answer, but came towards her, holding her immobile by the locking of his eyes with hers. He moved, she noticed with fascination, with all the nonchalant grace of a prowling lion, his thick, sun-bleached hair increasing his resemblance to the beast. Wordlessly, he removed the hairbrush from Cleone's now nerveless fingers and, still without speaking, began to draw it to and fro, separating her long tresses, stroking, smoothing, in a sensuous rhythm that held her mesmerised.

Through the mirror, covertly, she studied his absorbed face, sensing, as she had before, his enjoyment of his task. But then, after a few minutes, he set the brush down on the dressing-table and only his hands continued their insidious caress.

Cleone swallowed convulsively, as he lifted her hair to find her shoulders, their smooth skin visible through the transparency of her nightdress. His eyes met hers in the mirror now, watching her gravely, as he continued his exploration, down over her shoulders, finding the V of the nightdress, his hands slipping inside, seeking, finding, possessing, arousing.

With the sudden wave of feeling which washed through her, Cleone threw off the langorous stupour his touch had induced. Angrily, she dragged at his hand, inhibiting its audacious marauding.

'Don't do that . . . don't touch me. Get out! Oh . . . how *dare* you come in here and. . . .'

'I came here to conclude some unfinished business.'

Was he referring to his lack of success that afternoon in the caravan? Did he really suppose she would be more amenable, more vulnerable here, in a house full of people? Or did he think that the availability of her own bed would make the whole thing more acceptable, more respectable in her eyes?

'All that was finished this afternoon. I made it quite clear. . . .'

'You made it clear that you would have nothing to do with me, because you believed me to be married. I didn't get a chance to tell you that I'm not.'

A vast surge of . . . relief? excitement? . . . within her was sternly quelled.

'That still doesn't give you the right to come sneaking into my room. If you wanted to tell me that ... though why you should think I'd be interested ... you could have told me tomorrow ... downstairs.'

'Why you should be interested!' he repeated. 'Are you telling me you're not? That it doesn't make the slightest difference to you?'

'Why should it?' she asked with assumed indifference.

But she wasn't indifferent. She could admit, at least to herself, that she had wanted him to make love to her again, to continue the tuition of her senses that he had begun. That afternoon, she had refused both his advances and her admission of her own need because of her belief that he was not free.

Now, despite her attemps to submerge the rising turmoil within her, she knew that his intimation that he was not in fact married had released the floodgates of her emotions, setting free a tide of realisation of something which until now she had sternly refused to recognise. Despite his earlier coldness of manner her disapproval of the fashion in which he treated Ianthe, subconsciously she had always realised that there was a hidden warmth, that perhaps his nature was more the result of being sinned against, than having sinned. Now she knew with a mind-shattering certainty that, despite her inner battles, imperceptibly, but nonetheless true, she had been falling in love with Saxon, and now there was no need to hide the truth from herself, though it must be hidden from him a while longer.

Now she waited with bubbling anticipation for his declaration, his confession, that his heart, frozen by the experiences of an unhappy marriage, had responded to her, as it had done to no other woman in years, that, albeit against his will, he had fallen deeply in love with her, wanted to marry her.

It was in the tradition of all the best romances and now, surely, it was about to happen to her. Of course she would not admit anything, not just yet, but she would not keep him waiting too long for her answer.

She tilted her head to look up at him, conscious coquetry in the gesture, inviting him to speak.

Minutes later, she was spitting contempt at him, wishing she were strong enough, agile enough to evade his iron grip, so that she could rake her nails across his arrogant face.

No one, in all her life, had ever offered her so unwarranted, so gratuitous an insult.

CHAPTER SIX

MORE sinned against than sinning was he? That was a laugh! What a naïve, credulous little fool she'd been, and how mistaken in her interpretation of her feelings. Well, that was soon remedied. She'd show him she was not to be insulted in such a way.

At first, she'd thought she must have misunderstood. For the introduction to his suggestion had been innocent enough.

'Cleone . . . do you realise? you're the first person in a long time who has ever made me laugh. Today, I've felt more light-hearted than I have for ages.'

'I'm glad,' she told him simply.

Then his hand closed about the nape of her neck, stroking, caressing, inducing feelings of drowsy sensuousness, as he continued:

'Right from the first, I felt there was something about you that, against my will, I might add, drew me to you. And then I tried to disguise it. . . . I'd vowed never to get involved again. But you felt it too, I knew, by the way your body responded to me. You were very aware of my touch . . . my nearness . . . and then, this afternoon . . . when I did this . . . and this. . . .'

Cleone was unable to disguise her trembling as he bent over her, his lips following the molten trail his fingers were setting. She was, she felt, on the brink of emotional fulfilment. Could it really be her, ordinary Cleone Bancroft, capable of moving this incredibly attractive man to such heights of arousal . . .? And what was to follow? Breathlessly, she waited.

His voice throbbed strangely, as he continued.

'You must know that I want you, Cleone.'

The urgency in his voice, the sincerity, stirred her terribly, so that she wanted to turn to him and give him the promise that, surely, he was about to seek; but prudence restrained her, until he had spoken the actual words she waited to hear.

'I want to take you to bed, Cleone . . . now . . . to make love to you properly. I want you to know the ecstasy that my body can give you . . . that yours can give to me.'

She waited, expectantly. He wanted to do what he said, she understood that, it was only natural. But of course, he knew that it was impossible, until . . . and soon . . . soon he would ask her . . . to marry him.

But he seemed to have done with talking, as he lifted her from the stool, pulling her into his arms, his strong hands slowly, sensually exploring the warm, responsive curves of her body.

With thudding pulses, she allowed her own hands to slide up his back, pressing him closer to her, lifting her mouth, wanting him to possess it, wanting to experience more of those deeply disturbing kisses.

The compliant softness of her parted lips aroused him still further and he pulled her more tightly against him, and she allowed him to do what he would with her mouth, permited the intimate invasion of his tongue, as it searched, explored, tutored.

Daringly, she imitated, returned his kisses, savouring the taste of his mouth, as his breath mingled with hers.

But she stiffened, as his hands began to slide the flimsy nightdress from her shoulders.

'Don't resist me, Cleone,' he whispered, 'just let me undress you. I want to see you first . . . covered only by your hair . . . before . . .'

'No!'

Understanding dawned. He had meant what he said. With an outraged cry, she thrust him from her, the ecstasy her body had begun to feel drowned in a cold flood of reason.

'What are you thinking of? How dare you suggest . . .? You're not going to do anything of the sort . . . not now . . . not until we're . . .'

'Stop arguing . . . just kiss me.'

Savagely, he hauled her back against him, his thighs moulded against hers, leaving her in no doubt of his urgent need, a knowledge which caused a treacherous, responsive weakness in her. But her fighting blood was up. Twisting and turning, she avoided his mouth, so that she could speak the words of rejection.

'Get *out* of my room! Right now! What you're suggesting is . . .'

'Is what we both want . . . and you know it. Why this sudden prudery? You can't deny that you were enjoying . . .'

'Your kissing me . . . yes . . . but nothing more. I certainly won't let you . . .'

'What!' He stared down at her, cold disbelief in his grey eyes. 'You lead me on . . . return my kisses . . . tempt me with your body . . . and now this? Do you know how long it is since I've made love to a woman? How long it is since I've wanted to?'

She flinched at the bleak note in his voice. Was she being unfair? Part of her longed to comfort him, to assuage his deepest needs. But she couldn't, not . . . not before marriage. It was against everything she believed in.

'I . . . I'm sorry. . . .' she began, but it was a mistake, since Saxon took her apology as a sign of weakening on her part.

'Then you will?' he said confidently. 'Don't be afraid that I'll rush you. I won't take my own satisfaction until you are ready too. I . . .!'

'No!' she cried again, angry with herself for giving him the wrong impression, with him for misunderstanding. 'I didn't mean . . .'

'Cleone. . . .' His voice was husky, sultry with passion. 'I *know* you're not indifferent to me. You don't have to pretend, play hard to get. I won't think any the less of you for acquiescing readily. I . . .'

'So just what do you think of me?' she snapped. 'That I'm the kind of girl who climbs into bed with any man, just because he has a sudden, urgent need?'

He shook his head in bewilderment.

'No, of course not, not just any man. But I do believe

we could have a marvellous relationship, for as long as it suited us both. I wouldn't tie you down, just stay with me, let me make love to you, until . . .'

'You're . . . you're suggesting an . . . an affair!' she accused disbelievingly.

'Well, of course, if you reduce it to its basic. . . . What did you expect? You didn't think I . . .? Good Lord, Cleone, you didn't think I was about to go down on one knee and offer you hand and heart? It's not in me to do that . . . not any more. Once bitten, twice shy. Marriage isn't for me.'

Cleone felt bitterly insulted. Later, she knew, there would be other sensations, hurt, betrayal, but for the moment, anger reigned.

'And you really thought I was the sort of girl who would settle for something less, something casual, impermanent. . . .?'

'It certainly wouldn't be casual,' he said urgently, with a renewed attempt to hold her. 'I feel very far from casual at this moment, and it needn't be so impermanent. If we found that it worked, that we were happy together, it could go on for years, perhaps for ever.' He shrugged. 'Who knows? But I won't be tied down by a few lines on a piece of paper . . . not again.'

'Then, if all you want is a liaison,' she said bitterly, 'you've chosen the wrong girl. And I was beginning to think you weren't so bad after all. My God . . . just how wrong can one be! You're *despicable!*'

'Cleone!' he protested. 'Listen to me. I know I could teach you so much. You already want me and I could make you happy, much happier than you've ever been, or ever will be, with that long-haired layabout, Eric Morton.'

'W . . . with Eric . . . but I never. . . .'

'Oh, you didn't need to *tell* me about your relationship with him. If I didn't know about that I wouldn't have suggested. . . . But it was all too obvious.'

'Oh, was it?' Cleone said grimly.

'Yes. It's obvious you know how to respond to a man.'

It was only what he himself had just taught her, she thought drearily, but he'd never believe that.

'But admit it ... it was only an adolescent, teenage affair,' he continued.

'We're neither of us teenagers,' she snapped, without thinking what her denial might imply.

'All right! So it was a mature involvement. But I can offer you so much more, and I sensed your physical responsiveness to me, right from the start.'

Cleone cringed inwardly. Had it been that obvious? She had only just realised herself what her instinctive shrinking from contact with him had meant; but he, with his greater experience, had, apparently, known it all along. But it was necessary for her pride that she should deny it, or at least belittle the evidence in some way. She shrugged with an attempt at a coolness she was far from feeling.

'OK. I admit you have a certain ... charisma. But then, so have a lot of men and I don't leap into bed with every man whom I find sexually attractive.' No use telling him she'd never been to bed with any man. She could just imagine his expression of incredulity and there was no way she could prove it, except ... and that wasn't going to happen. 'I'm sorry, Saxon,' she said nevertheless, 'you've jumped to the wrong conclusion about me.'

'You're lying,' he said savagely, 'and I'll prove to you that I'm right ... that you need me, as much as I need you. ...'

Just what he would have done to vindicate his theory, Cleone never knew, for a knock at her door, followed by Ianthe's voice asking permission to come in, put a swift termination to their tense confrontation.

Swearing under his breath, Saxon moved away from Cleone, as she called out for his daughter to enter. The child looked faintly surprised at seeing her father there, but made no comment, merely waiting for him to depart, which he did with ill-concealed chagrin.

Pausing in the doorway, he fired his parting shot.

'This isn't over yet, as far as I'm concerned. I *know* I'm right.'

'What did Daddy mean?' Ianthe asked curiously, as the door shut behind him, with a control that, to Cleone, was more speaking than if he had slammed it.

'Oh,' Cleone improvised, though it was hard to concentrate upon answering the child, when all she wanted was to be alone to cry out her disillusionment and disappointment, 'we were discussing the "dig", nothing important. Now,' with a tremendous effort at self control, 'what's on *your* mind?'

Fortunately, Ianthe was readily diverted.

'Cleo ... I've been thinking. The villa site is really your Uncle's "dig", isn't it?'

Cleone nodded, wondering what the child was leading up to.

'Well ... don't you think it would be nice if *we* could have a "dig" of our very own?'

In spite of her misery, Cleone smiled. Did the child want her to go and dig up some corner of the garden, in the hope of making some small find that she could call her own? But she should have realised, she chided herself, that Ianthe had more maturity of mind than that.

'I was thinking,' Ianthe continued, 'that it would be wonderful, if we could have our own secret dig and surprise everyone. I know you'd like to in ... investigate the land around the old Priory. I've heard you say so. Why don't we see what we can find—just the two of us?'

It was true that Cleone had been greatly tempted to make a personal survey of what she thought as the Grove of Libertina, but could they make any useful progress on their own, a girl and a child? Looking at Ianthe's eager, but anxious face, she knew she couldn't discard the idea out of hand, little as she felt like concentrating on such a thing at this moment.

'I'll think about it,' she temporised.

Her reward was in Ianthe's glowing looks.

'I know that means "yes" really. Because once you've thought about it, you won't be able to resist the idea. Goodnight.'

Having, as she thought, gained her point, Ianthe slipped from the room, leaving Cleone, at last, to her thoughts. But if the child imagined these dwelt upon archaeology, she was very wrong.

Cleone sank down upon her bed, thankful to be alone to reflect upon the amazing scene that had occurred prior to the child's visit. Had Saxon *really* stood here ... doing those ... those intimate things to her? Had he really made that ... that unprincipled suggestion? She could scarcely credit it. Nor could she credit the depth of her resultant pain—the pain of disillusionment.

She had been ready to admit her love for him, to accept his proposal of marriage, and his totally unexpected proposition had shocked her to the core, had profaned all her dreamy illusions about men and romance. Weren't men romantic after all? Did they always relate 'love' with sex? seeing everything in terms of physical satisfaction? Had they no mental or spiritual needs? She felt as if someone had stamped upon and crushed a cherished, childish daydream—her long-awaited knight in shining armour had turned out to be sadly tarnished.

Despite her pain, the knowledge that it would take her a long time to forget her misplaced love for Saxon, now that she knew the kind of man he was, she would, she told herself, avoid him. She would totally immerse herself in the 'dig' and when Amyas did not need her on the site, she would adopt Ianthe's suggestion and conduct her own private investigations into the Grove of Libertina. Somehow, she would occupy every moment of every day; she would never allow herself to be alone with Saxon again. She wouldn't even resent it, she tried to convince herself, when Nerys tried to gain his attention; she was welcome to it, all of it. But in spite of this brave defiance, something lost, lonely and hurt wept within her ... and she knew why only too well.

Cleone decided to begin her campaign of avoidance by remaining in her room next morning, until she could be certain that Nerys and Saxon had set out on their 'sightseeing' expedition. She hoped, unlike most men, that he liked being dragged around shops. But she had reckoned without her host.

Ianthe arrived with a message that she, Cleone, was wanted in the office right away. It was useless, though she contemplated it at first, to refuse. Saxon would have absolutely no compunction about coming up here if she did not obey his summons; and that would bring about what she most wished to avoid, being alone with him. Still, she would keep the child with her, she determined, as they descended the stairs. He could not indulge in his reprehensible behaviour, enlarge upon his disgraceful ideas in front of his daughter. But oh, why hadn't she planned her campaign differently? Why hadn't she slipped away while they were all at breakfast and gone up to the site?

She did not require chaperonage after all. Both Amyas and Nerys were in the farm office and, amazingly, Nerys, who ought to have been happy at the prospect of her contrived outing with Saxon, did not look at all pleased.

'Ah, there you are, Cleone,' Saxon said pleasantly, as if, she thought, indignantly, his outrageous behaviour of last night had never taken place.

'What do you want?' she asked, her tone so hostile that it caused even Amyas's brows to arch enquiringly.

'Saxon has requested that you be released from the site for today,' her uncle explained. 'I told him that you have no regular duties, that it's all purely voluntary. But he was courteous enough to consult me anyway.'

Thus cleverly putting her in the wrong, Cleone thought savagely, if she refused his request, whatever it was. What could it be? she wondered with an access of nerves. At least he couldn't repeat his immoral suggestion in front of Amyas and if he thought she was going anywhere with him, unaccompanied. . . .

'I find myself in something of a predicament,' Saxon said smoothly. 'I had quite forgotten that my car is booked in today for a thorough servicing. But as I'm anxious not to disappoint Nerys. . . .'

'It doesn't matter,' Nerys muttered.

Cleone looked at her sharply. Why the sudden change of heart?

'Oh, but it does,' Saxon contradicted. 'I wouldn't dream of letting you down, when you're so set on sightseeing.' He turned to Cleone. 'What I proposed, and your uncle has kindly agreed, is that you and Ianthe should come on this expedition. Allow me about an hour to take my car in to Cirencester, then you can bring Nerys and Ianthe in the Humber and pick me up.'

No wonder Nerys looked aggrieved and was indifferent as to whether the outing proceeded or not. She wouldn't have anticipated the inclusion of Cleone and Ianthe in her day out with Saxon. Cleone would have experienced unholy glee at the other woman's crestfallen expression, if she hadn't been so disillusioned with him herself. What would Nerys make of his proposition to her, if she knew about it?

As Saxon had foreseen and anticipated by his public request, Cleone could not refuse to do as he asked, without seeming unreasonable and churlish, and besides, Ianthe's eyes were aglow at the prospect of an outing with her father.

But why on earth did he want the two of them along? She would have expected him to jump at the prospect of a day in the all-too-eager Nerys's company. It couldn't be due to any principles on his part that he did not want to be alone with the other woman, she thought scornfully, because Nerys was another man's fiancée. He hadn't any principles.

An hour later she was steering the old Humber along the now familiar narrow lanes, to the accompaniment of Nerys's grumbling.

'I don't see why I couldn't have gone with Saxon in the Mercedes, instead of travelling with you in this old rattletrap. You could just as easily have picked the two of us up.'

'My Daddy never takes ladies out on their own,' Ianthe's voice piped up from the rear seat. 'He says it gives them "ideas".'

Hastily, Cleone smothered a chuckle. But he'd not made any objection to being alone with her, she mused. But then he had been the one with the 'ideas'.

'Precocious brat!' Nerys muttered.

She was all sweetness to Ianthe in Saxon's presence, but Cleone knew that, in reality, the other woman had no time for children. She had always declared that this would be one of the advantages of marrying an older man, since he was unlikely to be interested in starting a family. Besides, Cleone thought with a rueful grin, in Amyas's case, the poor darling would probably forget that his offspring existed.

Was Nerys changing her mind? Was she after Saxon and prepared to endure the thought of taking on Ianthe too? But of course, the child's worst fears would be realised in that case. Nerys would undoubtedly see to it that Ianthe was sent to boarding school.

A wave of indignation swept Cleone. Why should Nerys Kennedy just swan down to Salpeth, annex Saxon and summarily dispose of his delightful little daughter? It was almost enough, she thought, to make her accede to his suggestion, just to put Nerys's nose out of joint of course, and to safeguard Ianthe's future.... Almost enough, but not quite. She wondered if Nerys would agree to an affair, given the chance; and suspected that Nerys too would hold out for marriage, though for different reasons, in her case, security, not necessarily moral scruples.

Saxon was waiting at the appointed rendezvous and, to Cleone's disgust, he indicated that she should move into the back with Ianthe, while he drove the Humber. He might as well have borrowed the car in the first place and had the garage pick up the Mercedes. Then he need not have included her in his plans; but had he deliberately done so? Was he hoping that further exposure to his company, to the charm he could undoubtedly turn on when he liked, would bring her round to his way of thinking?

Cleone sighed. In one way she was glad to be here. Despite her resolution to avoid him, she knew it would have been torture, thinking all day of Nerys enjoying his sole attention.

And Nerys, her good humour now restored in Saxon's presence, chose to be provocative. She smiled up at him coyly.

'Really, this is just like a family outing. Husband and wife in front and the children in the back.'

Cleone felt a distinct urge to smack Nerys's face. Was the older woman really seeing herself in the role she described? Children in the back indeed! No way was she, Cleone, young enough to be Saxon's daughter, she didn't feel like his daughter; and he didn't think so either.

Immersed in these thoughts, she had not really noticed

which direction they were taking, until Ianthe's incredulous cry of delight broke across her reflections.

'Oh! Daddy! I didn't know you were going to bring us here! How super!'

Cleone could see nothing to excite such rapture. They were driving through one of the many attractive villages which she had now come to associate with the Cotswolds. Church and manor house; barns with buttresses and gothic windows, a little terrace of cottages and an inn, a stream running along the lower village street, where there was also a chapel, post office, general store and a school.

'Where are we?' she asked.

'Didn't you see the sign?' Ianthe marvelled, before her father could answer. 'This is Chedworth. We are going to the villa, aren't we, Daddy?'

Saxon inclined his blond head, while Cleone stared incredulously at the back of his neck . . . her fingers could still recall its muscular strength. What was his motive in bringing them here? Of course she had expressed a desire to see the villa; but surely he wasn't doing this for her sake—especially after her rejection of him? and he needn't think she'd change her mind either, if this was part of his tactics.

'Villa?' Nerys was asking with dawning suspicion in her lovely, now discontented face.

'Mmmm!' Ianthe bounced up and down, receiving as a result a quelling glare from Nerys. 'It's one of the most famous excavated Roman sites in the whole of the British Isles.'

Cleone saw and could not help rejoicing over Nerys's brief expression of fury, before the other woman said with false sweetness:

'You didn't tell me your little girl was obsessed with the archaeology bug too. Takes after dear Tessa, does she?'

Cleone glanced sharply at her. What did Nerys know about Tessa Turville? The way she spoke, it sounded as though they were even acquainted. But of course, she thought. If Tessa and Saxon had been up at Oxford together, they might well both have been contemporaries of Nerys. But then why hadn't the older woman mentioned the fact? She had said nothing when Cleone introduced her to Saxon. Nerys had taken an MA in literature and so had Saxon. Was that why Nerys had been so keen to accompany this expedition? Cleone pondered ... because she had known on whose land it was to be? Had she wanted to meet Saxon again, known that the Turvilles were no longer married, seen this as some kind of opportunity? These and other unanswerable questions whirled chaotically around Cleone's brain, as Saxon drove uphill, out of Chedworth village, over the wold and through Withington Woods, five miles of light-filtering beeches and oak trees, then up the narrow approach road, thronged with traffic.

The National Trust owned property was a delightful place to visit, aside from its historical interest, standing on a slope, almost entirely surrounded by magnificent woods, the ground plan of the villa laid out and easy to grasp. It was simple, for instance, to see that once its buildings had fitted snugly into the side of the coombe. As a site, it had none of the melancholy and desolation of a ruin, such as that which permeated the old priory at Salpeth.

As Saxon checked the security of the Humber's doors and boot, Ianthe took the opportunity to whisper to Cleone:

'I don't think this is what Nerys meant by "sight-seeing".'

'I'm sure it wasn't,' Cleone replied with a conspiratorial giggle.

'Why do you think Daddy brought us here?'

Cleone was burning to know that too.

'Why don't you ask him?' she prompted.

Saxon overheard this last remark.

'Ask me what, poppet?' It was the first time Cleone had heard him address an endearment to the child.

'Why you brought us here?' Ianthe repeated dutifully, 'I didn't think you liked Roman remains?'

He answered her gravely, courteously, as he would an adult and suddenly, Cleone had an insight into his treatment of Ianthe. Perhaps it was not a lack of affection for the child, which made him seem so stiff with her.

Perhaps it was merely that, unlike some adults, he did not talk down to her.

'I thought,' he said, 'as it seems we are likely to be the possessors of a comparable site, that we should take a look, get some idea of what to expect. Also . . .'

'You mean, we'll get visitors . . . and have a proper little museum and sell postcards and . . .'

'Steady on! Steady on! Maybe. We'll have to wait and see. Anyway, you didn't let me finish. I also thought this would be a very good place to begin Nerys's sightseeing. After all, as the wife-to-be of an eminent archaeologist, she ought at least to have seen one of the most important Roman sites.'

So it was for Nerys's sake they had come here. But didn't Saxon realise . . .? But then he had the temerity to send Cleone a telling wink, which informed her very clearly that it was not for Nerys's benefit; he knew this was not what Nerys had had in mind.

Cleone refused to acknowledge his signal. She held no brief for Nerys, but she would not be drawn into any conspiracy of humour with him. It was despicable of him to flirt with the other woman and then mock her behind her back. She pretended she had noticed nothing.

'Perhaps, as the only expert present, Cleone should tell us about Chedworth,' he went on to suggest.

'Oh really, Saxon,' Nerys drawled, 'you mustn't give the girl an exalted idea of her own importance.'

'You might get a shock, Cleone thought, if you knew just how important he seemed to find me last night. But she turned her attention to Ianthe, ignoring her two uncomfortable companions.

'The villa dates back to between AD 100–150. If you look, you can see it's a series of buildings on three sides of a sloping valley. It's one of about twenty-two sites in this area. Salpeth, we hope, will make it twenty-three. A villa like this wasn't just a house. It was a centre for self-supporting, agricultural life, and it incorporated all that was best in Roman culture, their civilisation, peace, order, the arts. This room here, number thirty-two on your plan, is the point where discovery of the whole site began, in eighteen sixty four, when a gamekeeper was digging for a lost ferret.'

'Why did the Romans ever go away and leave their lovely houses?' Ianthe wondered.

'The legions were withdrawn in the fifth century to defend Rome,' Saxon interjected swiftly. 'Cleone's not the only one around here who knows her history.'

Cleone had often wondered how the local inhabitants, protected by the might of Rome, had felt about their withdrawal. It must have seemed to them, originally, that their way of life would go on forever, an idyllic existence, pleasant setting, country sports, fresh, home-grown food, served by two Roman roads; the Fosse, some four miles to the east and the White Way across the uplands to the amenities of nearby Cirencester. And yet they had been abandoned, except for the defence provided by a Roman-trained warrior, better known nowadays as King Arthur of Camelot.

And how had the Romans felt about leaving all that they had built up for themselves? She had only been here a short while and yet, already, she felt it would be a wrench to leave. But would that be solely on account of the beauty of her surroundings? She was honest enough to admit to herself, that this was not her only motive.

'I suppose there isn't anywhere here where one can get a decent cup of tea?' Nerys's fretful enquiry broke in upon her reflections. 'My feet are killing me.'

No wonder, Cleone thought, looking at the impossibly high-heeled, strappy sandals. Fine for a leisurely browse around smart shops, but scarcely the thing for an archaeological site.

'Oh, do we have to bother with tea yet, Daddy?' Ianthe objected. 'We've scarcely arrived and there's so much to see.'

He smiled indulgently. The rarity of a smile on Saxon's face still did strange things to Cleone, even though, she told herself, she utterly despised him after last night. Hastily, she averted her eyes from the disturbing sight.

'Suppose you and Cleone look round, while I take Nerys to find her cup of tea?'

Did he really prefer to keep Nerys company? Cleone wondered disconsolately, as their party split up, the other woman visibly purring. Why, she wondered, when he had so entirely alienated her by his behaviour, did she still feel this twisting knife of jealousy, that he should prefer to go off with Nerys? It was totally illogical and the sooner she snapped out of this mood of introspection the better. She forced herself to concentrate on explaining the layout before them to Ianthe.

The site and the villa faced east, but the bite of the wind would have been tempered by woods and undulating slopes and the villa would have received the full power of the morning sun. A spring had provided a plentiful, pure water supply; and behind the site rose steep hills, while before it lay the narrow valley of the Coln with its flat bottom.

'Our villa may well be like this,' Cleone told Ianthe. 'It was probably built around the same time, when a certain style of building would have been popular. This is a courtyard type, three sides of a square, surrounded by buildings. There were bathrooms in the north wing and more here, in the west wing.'

'They must have bathed a lot,' Ianthe observed.

'Perhaps they kept falling into muddy trenches!'

A start of surprise, and reluctantly, she admitted it, pleasure, brought colour to Cleone's cheeks. Saxon had come to join them after all.

'It's a common hazard on Roman sites, isn't it, Cleone?' he said, with a quizzical lift of his eyebrows and Cleone was glad that only the child was there, to witness this hint at the shared intimacy of a joke.

Ianthe was looking puzzled.

'Your Daddy's just funning, darling,' Cleone told her. 'Yes, they did bathe a lot.'

'Why can't you call me "darling" with such fervour,' he murmured, annoyingly, insidiously at her ear.

'Because,' she hissed, 'you don't deserve, or require, such endearments from me. You're only interested in one thing. Words . . . emotions . . . mean nothing to you.'

'But you'd like to bestow them, is that it? the words . . . the emotions?'

'Yes,' she riposted, 'but not on you, on someone who'd appreciate them.'

'Such as the long-haired Eric?' he sneered.

'That's my business ... and Eric's,' she told him demurely, and was rewarded with a look of fury. Could he be jealous? she wondered, with a spurt of elation that was inconsistent with her firm self-assurance that he meant nothing to her any more.

'I thought you were going to have a cup of tea with Nerys,' Ianthe suddenly interposed.

'So did Nerys,' he remarked, 'but it wasn't really "my cup of tea".'

'Daddy!' Ianthe said incredulously. 'You made a joke!'

'I believe I did. What do you think of that, Cleone?'

'That it was high time you did discover a sense of humour,' she replied tartly, 'for Ianthe's sake, if for no other reason.'

'And what about you? Do you like a man to have a sense of humour?'

'Among other things ... yes. ...'

'You must tell me sometime what attributes you consider the perfect man should have.' His grey eyes were roaming insolently over her slim form, as though to indicate clearly what attributes appealed to him.

'What's the point?' she retorted smartly, 'since you don't have them.'

And that was a lie, she reflected soberly. Because, apart from his avowed distaste for marriage, he had everything. Looks, sexual charisma and now, she was beginning to discover, other qualities of the mind which appealed to her. Taken altogether, it was a formidable combination of charm. But he need not think that he would charm her into forsaking her principles.

'Daddy? Cleo?' Ianthe asked with interest. 'Are you arguing or flirting?'

Cleone was stunned into embarrassment. Sometimes, this child was disconcertingly perceptive. Saxon, however, was unperturbed.

'Both,' he said calmly. 'I'm flirting and Cleone's arguing.'

'Does that mean you like her, but she doesn't like you?'

'Something like that,' he agreed.

'Oh, Cleone,' Ianthe said with uncomfortable directness, 'I do think that's a pity. Because if you liked Daddy,

as much as he likes you, you could get married and stay
here for ever and ever.'

'And you'd like that, would you?' Saxon enquired
gravely, while Cleone fought to prevent the hot tide of
warmth that threatened her.

'Oh yes!' Ianthe declared. 'If I can't have my real
mother, then I'd just as soon have Cleone. Of course, I
wouldn't want anyone like that awful Nerys. You don't
like her, do you, Daddy? Will you marry Cleone, Daddy?
Do you think I could be a bridesmaid? I've never been a
bridesmaid.'

Goodness, how the child did rattle on. A decidedly
pink Cleone was almost glad to see Nerys trailing towards
her, her face petulant.

'What an age you've been. If I'd realised you were
going to abandon me completely, in that dreary
tearoom. . . .'

'Nonsense,' Saxon said briskly. 'As if I should be
cavalier enough to abandon anyone so lovely. I was
merely unavoidably detained.' He gestured towards his
daughter and Cleone.

The hypocrite, Cleone seethed, trying to lay the blame
on them. He thought he could treat women any way he
pleased and then charm himself out of trouble, as witness
Nerys's restored good humour, as Saxon slipped a
supportive hand under her elbow and steered her in the
direction of the car.

'Time to move on. I think we've all had enough of
Roman remains.'

'*I* certainly have,' Nerys said with feeling.

About a mile down the road, Ianthe, who had been
unusually silent, dropped another bombshell.

'I suppose,' she said sadly, 'that Eric is your boyfriend,
Cleo? Do you prefer Eric to Daddy?'

Cleone was aware of Saxon's swift, considering glance
at her through his driving mirror, of Nerys's even more
speculative look over her shoulder; and indeed, it was
Nerys, always swift to take advantage of a situation, who
took it upon herself to answer the child's question.

'You mustn't forget, Ianthe dear, that Cleone has
known Eric for a long time. He is nearer to her age too,

shares her interests. Your Daddy . . .' with a coy glance at Saxon 'nice though he is, must seem very old to Cleone.'

'I don't see why he should,' Ianthe objected imperturbably. 'Daddy doesn't seem very old to me. And after all,' she added, with the quaint elderly wisdom which still surprised Cleone, 'a lot of ladies like older men. You should know that. Your fiancée . . . Professor Pringle . . . is much older than you.'

And that's put you in your place, Cleone thought gleefully, as Nerys's expression hardened. The older woman would not like being defeated in argument by a child. Cleone prayed that Nerys would never be in a position to quell Ianthe's bright spirit, and again she wondered, would Nerys be more willing to settle for the kind of illicit relationship which Cleone had rejected? Would she get the chance? would any woman do now that Saxon seemed to be coming out of his long hibernation?

The nearer they drew to Salpeth, the greater the improvement in Nerys's mood, as, subtly, she worked towards the gratification of her tastes on the following day.

'And I do think a little shopping trip would benefit Ianthe,' she pointed out, with a critically appraising look at the child's skimpy dress. 'Haven't you noticed, Saxon darling, her skirts are positively indecent? Suppose we were to take her into town and buy her a few things? Really, the poor little mite looks like an orphan.'

However much the same thought might have crossed Cleone's mind, she would have hesitated to express the notion and from the tightening of Saxon's strong jaw, she was glad she had not been responsible for its utterance. She was sure that Nerys intended to exclude her, Cleone, from the projected shopping expedition; the older woman was certainly making an all out play for Saxon. How could she when she was already engaged to another man? But Cleone felt hopeful that Nerys's tactics were entirely wrong.

These hopes, however, were shattered, when Saxon turned towards Nerys, a smile on his arresting face, so that Cleone felt she must have mistaken his earlier fleeting expression of anger.

'A splendid idea, Nerys. I must thank you for drawing my attention to my daughter's pitiful condition.'

Nerys's consequent smile of self-satisfaction was almost more than Cleone could endure. She looked askance at Ianthe, to see the child's reaction. The expression on the little face was one of wrinkled disgust. She leant against Cleone's shoulder and whispered:

'I can just imagine what sort of clothes she'll choose. Why can't you take me?'

Cleone wished she could, but she hadn't been invited to do so.

'Tomorrow then?' Nerys was continuing complacently, 'and now, Saxon darling, a little more horsepower if you please. I think I could fancy a nice hot soak in a scented bath, followed by a little drink before dinner.'

But Nerys's sybaritic pleasures were to be deferred a little longer.

'In view of your generosity, forfeiting your own pleasure on my daughter's behalf, we must make sure that none of today is wasted,' Saxon insisted. 'You took such an interest in my family history, that I'm sure you'd enjoy a conducted tour of the church they endowed, and where their memorials are displayed.'

As he spoke, he braked to a halt outside the church that, for centuries, had served the manor house, and courteously he assisted Nerys to alight.

Cleone could just imagine Nerys's feelings, but the other woman would not wish to show herself up by protesting her indifference to the church and its contents.

'Ianthe, of course, is familiar with the building and Cleone prefers Roman remains. So perhaps the two of you would rather run along? Then you won't be bored if Nerys and I take our time over the church?'

Nerys's look of profound annoyance had gradually given way to a smug smirk, as it seemed Saxon was trying to engineer a tête-à-tête with her; and certainly that was how it struck Cleone too, so much so that a demon of jealousy prompted her to thwart the attempt.

'Oh, but I'd like to see the church too, really I would, while I have the chance.'

'And I'd like to help show it to Cleo, Daddy,' Ianthe

announced; and Cleone had the distinct feeling that the child's motives were identical to her own, to prevent any deeper intimacy developing between Saxon and Nerys.

If looks could have annihilated, Cleone and Ianthe would have vanished from the face of the earth, under Nerys's darkling gaze, but Saxon merely seemed amused, an amusement which he succeeded in concealing from Nerys, but not from Cleone, who had come to recognise the slightest nuance of his expressions, so rarely did humour exist there. Just what was he up to? Could he possibly like Nerys and still laugh at her behind her back? It seemed unlikely and yet Saxon Turville was a very unpredictable man. Normal tenets of behaviour did not seem to apply to him.

'It's fifteenth century, built by Cotswold craftsmen and, over the years embellished by their successor,' Saxon explained, as they walked through the churchyard, Nerys clinging to his arm, her excuse the slightly uneven paving. 'Not one of the really great wool churches, but well enough. My ancestors could afford to pay for the best masons, sculptors and glaziers.'

The door was of English oak, with iron studs, latch and bolt and in the porch, a carved sheep's head looked down upon them, a symbol of the good sheep country that once had surrounded the village.

This was not the last of the building's extraordinary features. At every corner, it seemed, little grimacing gargoyles, representations of peasants and dragons, looked down. The afternoon sun shining through Biblical scenes made a blazing scarlet and gold of the interior, while the other furnishings, such as brasses and carved pews, were just as rich. Great roof beams were supported by angels, flying out above the upturned faces of the sightseers. In the aisles were the wool tombs, the merchant Turvilles, hands folded, sightless eyes gazing piously upward, their feet resting on the sheep and woolsacks which gave them their wealth. Memorial brasses bore the merchants' marks, which once were stamped upon their wool bales.

Nerys, after a pretence of absorbed interest, was flagging noticeably, but Saxon appeared oblivious to her growing discomfort and boredom; and, as she sank fretfully into a pew, massaging her aching ankles, he merely bade Ianthe keep her company, then continued to stroll around the building, extolling its virtues for Cleone's benefit.

'Now this is a history to be proud of,' he claimed. 'This is my kind of history, where I can see permanent, lasting proof of existence, a past linked to today.'

'So is Roman history linked with the present,' Cleone replied. She sought for a convincing argument, then said, triumphantly, 'What about your famous sheep, for instance? You said the Romans introduced them. But for that you might not have been breeding them now.'

Smilingly, he shrugged his acknowledgment of her point.

The church was obviously well used and well cared for, Cleone noted, as unobtrusively, Saxon steered her further and further away from the others. The woodwork was lovingly polished, as were the many brasses; and numerous vases of flowers lit up the interior of the church and of a side chapel which comprised the family pew of the Turvilles.

Here, out of sight of Nerys and Ianthe, Saxon turned upon Cleone, dropping all pretence of describing her surroundings, as he demanded to know whether she had thought any more about his proposition.

'It's obvious to me that Ianthe would be happy to have you remain here. The child has grown very fond of you in these past few days.'

But Saxon himself had not, Cleone thought. It was not gratification of heart and mind that he sought, but satisfaction of quite another kind.

'And do you really think Ianthe would be satisfied with the sort of arrangement you had in mind? What sort of example would that be to set your daughter? No, what you ask is quite impossible. It . . . it's totally opposed to everything I believe in and it's not as if . . . as if . . . I even liked you . . .' she faltered over the lie.

His eyes gleamed a warmer shade of silver grey, reflecting the pleasant tones of the Cotswold stone around them.

'Is that so?' he murmured, a hand coming out to trap her pointed chin, elevated at him in defiance. 'And is it so hard, Cleone . . . to like me?'

It wasn't. She knew it wasn't. It was very easy indeed and if only she did not have these reservations about his motives. . . .

'It certainly wouldn't be hard to make you want me,' he murmured suggestively.

That was very true. She had already received adequate proof of his effect upon her senses and she didn't require a further demonstration, which was what he seemed to have in mind. . . .

'No . . . no . . . I . . . you. . . .'

She was hopelessly trapped in a dark corner of the pew, her chin still in his iron grip, her body restrained from all movement by the heavy pressure of his own; and his expression was signalling his intention of kissing her, perhaps even attempting further liberties, right here and now. Suppose someone came . . . Nerys . . . Ianthe . . . even the Vicar?

'No, Saxon . . . please. Someone might see. It . . . it's not right . . . to . . . to behave like this . . . tàlk like this . . . in . . . in a church.'

Slowly, reluctantly, he releasd her, but he did not move away and his eyes still held hers mesmerised, so that she was afraid she might fall against him, so tremulous were her knees.

'Perhaps you're right,' he said thoughtfully. 'This isn't the time, or the place. We can do without any interruptions. But we are going to resume this discussion . . . later . . . and next time, I won't take no for an answer.'

'If your question is the same as last time, then my answer will be the same,' she told him stubbornly. 'I will not have an . . . an affair with you.'

'Not with me?'

'Not with anyone!' Cleone emphasised, her golden eyes steady.

Saxon looked sceptical.

'Do you honestly expect me to believe that? after what you have inferred about Eric Morton . . . inferences, incidentally, which Nerys has confirmed?'

Oh she had, had she? Thank you very much, Nerys,
Cleone thought—but how could she refute Nerys's words,
when they had only echoed her own panic stricken
improvisations?

'No one as prudish as you claim to be, would have
reacted as you do, every time I come near you,' Saxon
stated. 'You must have learnt that sense of awareness
from someone.'

'No . . . I . . . .'

'Remember, I've been up at Oxford myself. I know
how students behave. Don't tell me the male students of
today are any less red-blooded than they were fifteen
years ago.'

'I wouldn't know,' Cleone snapped, 'and as to the
promiscuity of fifteen years ago, I'll have to take your
word for it. Though if you're anything to go by, I'm
inclined to believe you.'

'I didn't say I was promiscuous,' Saxon pointed out.
'In those days, there was only one woman for me . . .
Tessa. I wish. . . .' He broke off.

What had he been going to say. A searing pain smote
Cleone's heart. That he wished Tessa were still here now?
But she steadied herself.

'In those days,' she repeated, 'and what about now?
Couldn't you make it up with her . . . for Ianthe's sake?'

Cleone was aware that her heart was pounding
uncomfortably. Did she want to hear him say he still loved
Tessa, that he wanted her back? She knew she didn't.

Saxon was looking at her . . . strangely, she thought.

'You're not that naïve. So you must be an
accomplished actress. Don't try to pretend to me. . . .'

'Pretend what?' Cleone was totally bewildered. Of
what was he accusing her now?

'That you know nothing about Tessa . . . what
happened . . . that you haven't been listening to village
gossip. . . .'

'What chance have I had . . .?' she began.

'Oh, not you, maybe, but your Eric has been staying at
the Inn and . . .'

'Eric's told me nothing. Besides, what makes you think
the villagers gossip about you? I thought you were such a

close knit little community—one for all and all for one?'

'In the main, yes, my tenants are loyal to me, and similarly my estate workers. But there are a few people still resident in the village ... not true Cotsallers, who ...'

'Well, whatever enemies you may have, I haven't met them ... listened to any talk about you ... or. ...'

Except from Ianthe. The thought flashed across her mind and she faltered to a halt.

'You mean nobody has told you ... about Tessa's death?'

So Tessa *was* dead. Ianthe had been right. Did that also mean ...? All her old fears returned.

'I ... I ...'

Oh, if only she could just tell this one lie convincingly. But she had never been able to do so. Deceit was anathema to her.

'As I thought!' He pounced upon her hesitancy. 'You did know.'

'I ... I didn't know for certain.' Rashly, she plunged on. 'I heard a rumour that ... that Tessa *was* d ... dead. But the story I heard was so far-fetched, so ... so totally impossible that I. ...'

'Far-fetched! Impossible!' His eyes narrowed. 'Perhaps you'd better tell me just what you have heard ... and from whom ... since you say you haven't been listening to village gossip.'

Cleone felt the panic growing within her. Suppose ... suppose the dreadful story Ianthe had related were true ... and Saxon discovered that she, Cleone, knew? If it had been a closely guarded secret, known only to his loyal tenants, mightn't he try to do away with an outsider, whom he thought was in the know? He probably wouldn't have much compunction where she was concerned. It wasn't as if he were in love with her, it was only desire that he had expressed, and his personal safety would surely be a more important consideration. As to who had told her ... he must never know that it was his own daughter. Cleone set her lips and shook her head, trying to disguise the fear she felt by a show of stubborn bravado. Casually, she tried to edge past him.

'I ... I forget ... and Nerys and Ianthe will be wondering what's keeping us,' she murmured.

Iron-hard fingers pinioned her upper arms.

'The truth, Cleone! Now!'

CHAPTER SEVEN

WITH a little gasp of relief, Cleone realised that they were no longer alone. Tentatively, Ianthe had entered the side chapel and was regarding them doubtfully, her eyes going from Cleone's flushed, fearful face to her father's imprisoning hands.

'Daddy?'

At the sound of the child's high voice, Saxon swung round, muffling an oath, releasing Cleone as he did so.

'Daddy, Nerys was bored. She's gone back to the house. But I said I'd wait for you and Cleone. I ... I hope you don't mind?'

Cleone certainly didn't and it was impossible for Saxon to continue his inquisition with Ianthe walking between them, but, from the meaning glances he darted at her above the child's head, Cleone knew her reprieve was only a temporary one. She controlled a shudder. Somehow, between now and their next encounter, she had to make up a credible story, which would fit all the facts, convince Saxon that she knew next to nothing of his private affairs, and all without revealing Ianthe's involvement.

Cleone slipped surreptitiously out of a rear exit to the manor house and seeking concealment from every tree and shrub, made her way by devious routes to the site of the 'dig'. The morning held the promise of a glorious day to come and she spared a sympathetic thought for Ianthe, forced to trail round the shops in Nerys's wake. How would Saxon enjoy the experience? Vindictively, she hoped he would find it extremely tedious—and it would serve him right.

She was fairly certain that Nerys had gained her point:

that the three of them would be going into town, but
Cleone was taking no chances this time. Saxon should
have no opportunity to wangle her inclusion in his party.
So she had set her alarm clock for six-thirty, before the
rest of the household was stirring, donned her working
gear and set out. She would occupy herself up at the site
and if she fancied she heard any sounds of pursuit, would
conceal herself in the woods. Her uncle would not find it
strange to discover her already at work and, in fact, she
would be glad when he and the rest of the party joined
her. If necessary, she determined, she was going to seek
his protection from Saxon's importunities, even ask if she
might go back to Oxford for the remainder of the Long
Vac.

It would be a wrench to leave Salpeth, but it would be
better than this continual repression of her inclinations,
fighting Saxon's insidious attraction for her. She would
not weaken . . . would *not* become his mistress.

It was seven-fifteen when she reached the site, light
enough to see how things were progressing there. The
exposure of the mosaic floor was well advanced and
Cleone spent several minutes studying the work which
had been done yesterday in her absence. The exposed
tesserae were in very good condition, their colour
successfully retained over many centuries. They would,
she knew from past experience, have been embedded
in cement of fine quality, the high polish achieved by
using a piece of fine tile, to give a smooth, shiny
surface, bringing out the natural colour of the stones
used.

Amyas had stated his belief that the area so far
uncovered had formed part of a private chapel and
Cleone could see his reason for thinking so. The area
uncovered was on a lower level than the rest of the villa
and might well have been a 'cult' room, sited in a
basement below the ground floor. The design, similar to
others Cleone had seen, was composed of female figures
or naiads, a mixture of geometrical patterns, mythological
figures and natural objects. But there was also a central,
elaborate head, whose identity Cleone recognised
instantly as that of Minerva, the soldiers' god.

Amyas had reminded her of the smaller inscriptions on the older of Saxon's maps; 'Fortuna' and 'Minerva'. His theory was that the owner of this villa had been a high-ranking Roman officer, who had dedicated his private place of worship to the soldiers' god.

Cleone debated with herself whether or not she should begin work, before Amyas and the rest of the party arrived. With such an important find, however, her uncle might well prefer to oversee every part of the uncovering and recording for himself. It would be wiser, she decided finally, to await instructions. In the meantime, wasn't this a good opportunity to look at the priory site, whose unexplored existence still nagged at her?

Amyas was not as concerned with that area of investigation, so he would scarely make any objection, if she, tentatively of course, opened up a small area for study.

Her decission made, she fetched the necessary tools from the site hut, to which she had her own key and, her excitement mounting, made her way through the trees that divided the two sites.

She chose a promisingly uneven piece of ground a few yards away from the crumbling stones of the old chapel, expecting that the raised areas would yield up the outlines of more walls. She had removed a long strip of turf and was about to probe the soil beneath, when she heard the sound of voices, over at the villa site. She looked at her wristwatch—only eight-thirty! Amyas had routed out his students very early. That was if it *was* Amyas. Suppose, suppose it were Saxon, come in search of her? But in that case, to whom would he be talking?

Cautiously, she moved through the screening trees, until she could see without being seen. There were three men moving about the site and they were all complete strangers to Cleone. Without considering that she might have more to fear from these unknown men than from Saxon himself, she stepped out into the clearing, challenging their right to be there.

'Hey! Who are you? and what are you doing here?'

They turned and Cleone saw that two of them carried cameras, whose style immediately proclaimed them as press photographers. How had they learnt of this discovery? Following Saxon's strict injunctions, the archaeological party had been careful to keep their operations secret.

'You're trespassing,' Cleone informed them as she moved closer. 'This is private property.'

'Are you the owner, Miss?' one of the men enquired, his manner conciliatory.

'No,' she admitted. 'But I . . . I'm a friend of his and I know he'd be . . .'

'A friend?' another man enquired, as he whipped out a shorthand notebook. 'Perhaps I could have your name?'

'Certainly not! We don't want any publicity.'

'Oh, why's that then, Miss?'

'Because the landowner doesn't want hordes of people traipsing about all over his land. Hey . . . what are you writing in that book?' she asked suspiciously.

'Just noting down the owners objections to trespass, Miss,' the man said smoothly. 'We wouldn't want to annoy him, would we?'

'Oh . . . well . . . that's all right then. So would you please leave now! What . . . what's he doing?' she pointed to one of the photographers, who had taken the opportunity of her involvement with his colleague, to take a few shots and had now turned his camera on her.

'A few pictures, just for future reference,' she was assured, 'when we get permission to print, of course . . . to save us coming back again.'

The men seemed quite content now to leave the area of the 'dig', but Cleone decided to see them off Saxon's land and make sure they did not turn back.

'You're not from these parts are you, Miss?' the man with the notebook said pleasantly, as they walked.

'No . . . I come from Oxford actually. I'm just staying at the manor.'

'Oh?' Quickly, the intentness in his eye was veiled. 'Undergraduate are you?' His tone was casual, disinterested.

'Heavens no!' Cleone laughed, lightheaded with her relief at having steered these men away from the forbidden area. 'I'm not that brainy. I help my uncle with his work, drive him about, keep his notes and so on.'

'Oh? Writer is he?'

'No, he's a Professor of. . . .' She stopped suddenly, folding her lips. This man was asking too many questions for her liking. He couldn't possibly be interested in her anyway.

By now they had reached a small saloon car, parked in an unobtrusive spot, not far from the Inn, and the three men got it. The man who had asked all the questions ran down the driver's window and gave her a courteous salute.

'Well, thank you for all your help and advice, Miss Pringle. . . .'

'Bancroft,' she corrected automatically. 'My uncle's name is. . . .' She stopped once more, as a look of satisfaction crossed the other's face, then he slipped the car into gear and drove away.

For a while, Cleone stood, looking after the car. She felt disturbed. Saxon had said 'no news media' and now the Press had ferreted out the existence of the Salpeth site . . . how? She was not naïve enough to suppose that this was the end of it. They would be back and others in their wake. But at least they hadn't got much out of her and she had got rid of them fairly effectively.

Should she tell Saxon about the reporters? she wondered, as she retraced her steps to the site. Somehow, she didn't fancy the prospect. He was bound to be annoyed and his annoyance always seemed to rebound on her. No, she would tell Amyas and leave it to his discretion as to whether Saxon should be informed.

She heard the roar of an engine coming up behind her. Surely those men weren't coming back? Indignantly, she swung round, ready to give them a piece of her mind. Then, her jaw dropped, her heart plummeting similarly, as she recognised the Land Rover. Oh, let it be one of the estate workers driving, she implored the fates. But even before she glimpsed the thick thatch of sun-bleached hair, she knew her prayer had gone unanswered.

She began to run, knowing it was futile; but if only she could reach the trees before the vehicle overtook her, perhaps she could evade him. The Land Rover could not pass between the stout grey boles of the ancient beeches.

But Saxon could. Even as she felt the sheltering trees enclose her, she heard the squeal of brakes and pounding footsteps coming relentlessly closer.

Excited dread stabbed through her, as she tried to increase her pace. Cleone might be slight of build, but she was fleet of foot and some years younger than the man who pursued her, though he was by no means unfit. In fact, she doubted if he had a spare ounce of flesh on his broad, muscular body. He was all bone and sinew, but she would give him a run for his money, even though she knew, with a queer, uncertain feeling that was half-terror, half-excitement, that capture was inevitable.

She had sought protection amongst the lofty beeches, but it was a tree that turned traitor, causing her downfall, its roots bring her to her knees, just as Saxon essayed a flying tackle on his own account. With his arms wrapped around her waist, instead of her knees as he had planned, they rolled together, over and over, down a grassy slope, ending up, limbs inextricably tangled. Cleone was breathless and indignant, Saxon breathing similarly fast, but triumphant in his possession of the upper hand, or rather, the upper position, for Cleone was well and truly trapped beneath the weight of his athletic body, his strong, muscular legs entwined with hers.

For a moment there was silence, broken only by woodland sounds, but a silence that was somehow turbulent with emotion. Oppressed, yet, at the same time, powerfully stimulated by the pressure of his large frame upon her soft body, Cleone fought to suppress the very improper longings sweeping over her, the tremors of pure sexual excitement, caused by the thought of what he might do to her, now that he had made her captive.

She feared to meet his gaze, yet, irresistibly, her eyes were drawn to his, to find, as she had feared, a glint in those grey orbs, which increased her discomposure. She shifted her glance, only to find herself studying the tanned attraction of his features, the sensual mobility of a mouth far too close to hers.

She was trembling, not just with reaction to the chase, the shock of falling, but with the knowledge of her own raw vulnerability to him. Not only was he in a position of ascendancy over her, but she doubted whether her own resolution was equal to fighting him off, should he attempt to make love to her.

He took her mesmerised paralysis for passivity and fastened his lips hungrily upon hers, as though he would deprive her of the little breath she had left. It was a hard mouth, possessive, punishing, bruising her lips apart, until she had no choice but to open to him; and yet, gradually, it was becoming a not unwelcome invasion. Against her will, she was beginning to respond, not only with her lips, but with the whole of her body, which seemed to know instinctively to arch against him, aware of his throbbing desire as he sought to purge his frustrations.

Now, his hands joined in the war of attrition against her remaining resistance, his strong fingers slowly, sensually exploring her body. Piercing sensations began to well within her, speeding up the surge of her blood, as she knew the anticipation of an ecstasy which, once realised, would make her his for ever. Her heart pounded erratically, and a moan of mingled desire and pain escaped her as, for the first time, she realised the power of the body's demands over the brain's reason. His thighs were growing heavier as his urgency grew, his broad chest crushing her small breasts.

'Cleone, I need you,' he mouthed huskily against her lips.

Desperately, she fought for sanity. She must pull herself together, before it was too late. But he was arousing such wanton urges within her that she was fighting, not only him, but herself. She had no doubt that he was an expert lover, nor that he intended to possess her here and now, to achieve by the seductive force of his body what words had failed to gain for him. Then, he would taunt her with having no reason to refuse his proposition, since he had already made her his.

Even whilst she gathered her strength to resist, subtly, his kiss had altered, savagery becoming a seeking, sensual potency, increasing her tremulous weakness.

'Cleone!' Once more her name was a groan on his lips. 'Do you know what you do to me? Let me love you . . . now!'

His movements against her were expertly seductive, the heat of him vibrant, so that her own flesh ignited at his touch. She knew he must be aware that her own needs were rising, for the movements of his hands were becoming rougher, speaking of a control almost snapped and as she felt him seek the zip of her jeans, sanity prevailed and with what remained of her strength, she fought him, pushing away the hands that sought too great a privilege, kicking with her sandalled feet against the legs that weighed her to the ground. Now that she had begun to fight, anger seethed within her, reaching almost insane proportions, so that, despite her puny efforts, she managed to thrust him from her, rolling from beneath him and on to her feet in one swift movement, trembling hands going to her clothing to assure herself of its security.

Fury now white hot, she glared down at his still recumbent form.

'You ... you ought to be locked up,' she declared, her voice savage, half-strangled in her throat. 'You're nothing but a ... a common rapist.'

He rose to his feet, the look in his eyes one of muted violence, the twist of his well-shaped mouth cynical.

'You always draw back at the last moment, don't you Cleone?'

'There was no question of "drawing back",' she told him furiously, 'I never wanted you to touch me in the first place ... you forced yourself upon me ... your company ... and then ... this, this ... I ....'

He ignored her accusation.

'Why did you go out so early this morning?'

Anger made her reckless.

'To avoid you, of course ... why else? I'm ... I'm sick of you ... of ... of your lewd suggestions ... the way you look at me ... touch me. You revolt me.'

'You have a very strange way of showing your revulsion,' he murmured, his voice soft but deadly.

'I hate you,' she reiterated, 'despise you ... I do ... I do ... and if you don't leave me alone, I shall ... shall tell my uncle.'

'Run with tales to Uncle Badger?' he scoffed. 'I don't

think you'll do that, Cleone. It wouldn't be wise.' He paused, then added with great significance, 'I think Badger would like to finish his work here. He wouldn't be very pleased, if I were to withdraw my permission.'

'Do you mean ... you'd ...? Oh, that's ... that's filthy. It's blackmail. But it won't work. Do you seriously think my uncle would put his work before ... before my welfare?'

'No,' he agreed, 'but I think *you* might. Be sensible, Cleone. This find could make your uncle a very famous man. Many papers, many learned books will be written about Salpeth. Would you really deny him the chance of going down in history as the man who discovered the second most important villa in England?'

She stared at him. She had no doubt that he meant what he said.

'My God!' she said softly, 'you must be hard up for ... for satisfaction ... if you have to stoop so low to get what you want.'

'There are plenty of places where I could take my "satisfaction", if that were all I wanted,' he told her. 'It's *you* that I want, and I should have taken you whilst I had the chance, before you decided to play hard to get. Because there was a moment, when you didn't want to stop me ... when you were as inflamed as I was.'

She opened her mouth to deny his accusation, but she couldn't. He was right and it hurt dreadfully to know that he could read her so easily, that her weakness had been laid bare to him. It was humiliating that her body should betray what her words denied. But at least he thought it was only a physical reaction. He could not know how hopelessly she was in love with him, so that she was almost tempted to accept what he had to offer, rather than lose him totally.

'Why are you so determined to reject me?' he asked abruptly. 'Is it Eric ... tell me about him ... do you respond to him like that?'

How he did harp on that subject. She supposed it must be jealousy, of a kind, and she wanted to tell him that she did not respond to Eric in any way, but that would imply too much.

'My feelings are none of your business,' she said shortly.

'Are you in love with him?' he insisted.

'Love?' she repeated the word sarcastically. 'What would you know about love? You're only interested in "relationships" . . . sexual gratification. You're not even capable of fatherly love . . . towards Ianthe . . . you. . . .'

'So that's what you think! Why, you. . . .' She heard his teeth snap together. 'I'd like to. . . .'

'You're altogether too full of what you'd like,' she swept on, heedless of his anger. 'Now I'll tell you what I'd like. I'd like to be allowed to get on with my work here, without being harassed by you. You shouldn't even be here this morning. You're supposed to be shopping, with Nerys and Ianthe. That poor child. . . .'

'I got someone else to drive them into town,' he said shortly. 'I wanted to talk to you, not to waste my time trailing around shops.'

'Well, you're wasting your time here too,' she snapped. 'And how could you do that to Ianthe? She'll hate Nerys's choice of clothes. I know she will.'

'You accuse me of indifference towards Ianthe's feelings,' he said heatedly, 'which, incidentally, is not true. But what about your indifference to her fate? She'll hate it even more if Nerys stays here with me . . . instead of you.'

Cleone stared at him, aghast. Did he really mean it? Would he offer Nerys what she had refused . . . could he really even think of weaning away another man's fiancée? Had he no consideration for Amyas's feelings?

For once, Cleone refrained from rushing into impulsive speech. Instead, she considered the implications of what Saxon had just said. What would be the outcome of such an action on his part? How would it affect those involved? True, she would be glad to see Nerys out of Amyas's life and though her uncle might be hurt at first, Cleone knew him well enough to suspect that it would only be a temporary condition, soon submerged in the fascination of his profession; Amyas was not really a marrying man. Saxon and Nerys, each in their own way, would probably achieve some sort of satisfaction. The only people, she thought drearily, to be really wounded, would be herself and Ianthe.

But much as she had come to love the child, even for her, Cleone could not set aside her scruples. Ianthe was young. She had her whole life before her; and she would not always live in her father's house. As for herself, unconsciously, she tilted her chin and squared her slender shoulders, accepting the burden, she would manage. She would never forget Saxon, but she would not let the fact ruin the rest of her life. She might never marry now, she did not feel that she could ever look at another man without comparing him unfavourably to Saxon, but she could become a career woman, follow her uncle's example.

'Well?' Saxon said impatiently. 'Is it to be Nerys, or you?'

How dared he present her with such an ultimatum.

'Go to hell!' she said clearly and distinctly, then, turning, she marched away, hoping that the trembling of her legs was not visible, quite expecting that she would be overtaken and hauled back.

But after a while, she realised that he was not following her and once she was certain she was out of his sight, she began to run, anxious to reach the refuge of her bedroom, a locked door between her and Saxon, behind which she could give vent to the tears of misery which welled up behind her eyelids, causing her to stumble, half-blinded, as she ran.

Saxon had not attempted to follow her, nor did he attempt to pester her during the two days that followed. In fact, Cleone was unhappily certain that he intended to carry out his threat, for his attentions to Nerys became assiduous and ostentatious and Cleone was forced to witness them, so that she was hard put to it to hide her pain. Somehow, she succeeded, though unhappiness affected her appetite and painted deep violet shadows beneath her golden eyes, darkened to brown with her misery.

But, as she had resolved, she tried to drown her emotions with hard work and with Amyas's permission toiled away at the priory site, Ianthe an eager and willing assistant.

To Cleone, Ianthe spoke of fears, which, Cleone realised, meant that the child too had witnessed and interpreted Saxon's conspicuous actions.

'I thought my Daddy was beginning to like you, Cleone, but since Nerys came, he seems to have changed his mind. He couldn't marry her, could he, not when she's engaged to your uncle?'

'Engagements can be broken,' Cleone pointed out gently. 'Would you mind very much, if your Daddy . . .?' She hesitated to suggest to a child that her father might not be interested in marriage, but in a far less permanent relationship. 'If your Daddy did have a . . . a new wife?'

'I shouldn't mind, if she was you,' Ianthe said frankly. 'But if it was Nerys, I should mind . . . I should run away. She doesn't like me . . . and she'd make Daddy send me away anyway. Cleo. . . .' She looked up at the older girl appealingly. 'Daddy hasn't been half so strict with me, since you've been here. I . . . I was beginning to think he didn't mind having me around after all. But if Nerys. . . .'

'Ianthe, love. . . .' Cleone strove to be fair, for the child's sake, even though her own indignation with Saxon knew no bounds. 'I've watched your father and you together and I know he is fond of you, even though he doesn't always show it, even though he seems strict. I . . . I think he must have some reason for being particularly stern, something to do with your mother, though I don't know what. I . . .' she nearly choked on the thought. 'I don't think your Daddy has always been a very h . . . happy man. But whoever he's friendly with shouldn't make any difference to his feelings for you.'

'Something to do with my mother,' Ianthe said thoughtfully. 'Cleo, is she . . . has my father ever said . . . is she. . . .?'

'Dead?' Cleone said softly. 'Yes, Ianthe, I'm afraid so. He . . .'

'And . . . and do you think Mrs Griggs was right . . . that . . . that he . . . k . . . killed her?' Ianthe's eyes were large and fearful.

Cleone sat down on a tree stump and drew the child

on to her knee. She knew Ianthe well enough now to
know that this indication of affection would not be
rejected.

'I think you'd better tell me exactly what you heard,'
she suggested.

This was not indulging in malicious gossip, Cleone
assured herself, nor was it to satisfy her own personal
curiosity. Ianthe needed help and, hopefully, reassurance.

Ianthe wrinkled her brow with concentration, as she
sought to recall the exact sequence of events.

'It was at the beginning of summer. I was sitting up in
the apple tree, reading. I wasn't supposed to be there,
because the gardener said I'd damage the buds, spoil the
crop of fruit for this year. So I kept very quiet, when I
heard him coming. Mrs Griggs was with him, she wanted
some vegetables for the table. He . . . he was asking her
about my mother . . . he's new here, you see . . . and he
said "isn't there a Mrs T?"'

'I'm surprised that your housekeeper should gossip
with a new employee,' Cleone commented. 'I thought all
your father's workers were very loyal to him.'

'They are usually. But Mrs Griggs isn't a true
Cotsaller,' Ianthe said, with all her father's scorn. 'She
used to be married to one of Daddy's estate workers,
she's a widow now, and the gardener is her brother.
He couldn't get a job anywhere else, so he came
here and Mrs Griggs persuaded my father to take him
on.'

Was this what Saxon had been referring to, when he
had spoken of malicious gossip by outsiders? Of trouble
caused by people new to Salpeth?

'Mrs Griggs said that my mother was long gone, and
the gardener said "do you mean she upped and left him
or snuffed it" . . . isn't that a horrid word? . . . and Mrs
Griggs got all confidential, I could only just hear. "It's
my belief it was his blame, heard him several times I did,
saying as how he'd wring her neck some day . . .".'

'And is that it?' Cleone felt a wave of relief wash over
her, as the child nodded. 'Ianthe, dear, I don't think you
should take too much notice of that. It's quite a common
expression, when you're exasperated with someone, to say

you feel like wringing their neck. It's not meant to be taken literally.'

Ianthe regarded her steadily, hopefully.

'Are you sure, Cleo? I wouldn't want my Daddy to go to prison ... or. ...'

'No question of it,' Cleone said firmly. 'Just forget that you ever heard two silly people, who had no business to be gossiping, building up a mystery out of a few angry words.'

There had been no indication that Saxon meant to carry out his other threat, to evict the archaeologists, but the relative calm of those two days should have warned Cleone of the storm to follow.

On the morning that it broke around her head, she was working on what she now thought of as her own site, alone this time, for Ianthe, reluctantly it was true, had been persuaded that she was neglecting her friends of her own age and had consented to an outing to the seaside.

Much as she enjoyed the child's company, Cleone was not sorry to have a day to herself, to record and clean the sparse findings from the priory site. Her first attempts at investigation had not yielded much and she planned to move a few yards further and open up a new patch of earth.

It was almost lunch time. She had just rolled back an area of turf and was debating whether to take a break now, or to work on a little longer, to see if this plot would prove more successful, when she heard the familiar note of the Land Rover ascending the nearby track. She was not seriously alarmed, since her uncle too was still hard at work and since Saxon had not been near her for two days, it was more likely that he had come to view progress at the villa site.

Shortly afterwards, she could hear his voice, raised as if in anger, and the more muted rumble of her uncle's tones. But then there was such a babble of excited, indignant voices, that, against her will, she walked across to the adjacent site to investigate the cause of the uproar.

Saxon was the centre of the group of archaeologists, most of whom were craning their neck over something he held; and she had not been mistaken at the note in his voice. He was angry all right and then his glance fell upon her, as she approached and somehow she knew, with an agonised pounding of her heart, that his fury had been increased by the sight of her, that somehow she was the cause of it.

'So there you are! I wonder you're not afraid to face me. You deceitful, devious little bitch! What did you expect to gain by it? Did you think, by getting these lies published, that you could force my hand? Well, it won't work.'

Dazed she stared at him and then at the newspaper, which he thrust into her hands. It was some moments before she could still the trembling of her fingers sufficiently to hold it steady, or focus her eyes upon the newsprint. Then, as she began to read, she gasped, with annoyance at first, then with mounting fury and finally knew a sinking dread, as she realised the cause of Saxon's ire.

The article, which had been given a full page spread, was entitled 'Romance among the Ruins?' and beneath it was an excellent photograph of Cleone. This was bad enough, but the content of the rest of the page horrified her.

'*Is it Romans or Romance which has brought the lovely Miss Bancroft to a remote village in the Cotswolds? Miss Bancroft, who acts as assistant to her uncle, Professor Amyas Pringle, the eminent archaeologist and Oxford Don, was a little evasive on the subject, when interviewed recently by our reporter. Pictured here, on the site of what promises to be one of the most important finds of the century, she admitted, however, to be a very good friend of the landowner, Mr Saxon Turville, at whose house she is currently staying. It is significant that Miss Bancroft seemed to know a lot about that gentleman's likes and dislikes, together with his distaste for publicity and his attempts to keep this important archaeological find from the British public, whose right it is to know of its historical heritage. When will the facts about the Salpeth Villa be revealed and will another interesting announcement be made at the same time? Perhaps the undoubted charms of Miss Bancroft will soften Mr Turville's implacable refusal to allow access to the site.'*

There was more, about Saxon's first marriage, about his local standing, but Cleone had read enough. She glanced up, first into Saxon's cold grey eyes, then into those of her uncle who looked troubled, but who, unlike Saxon, was waiting to hear her explanation before making accusations.

'Th . . . this isn't *my* doing,' she whispered, knowing as she did so that her feeble effort carried no conviction.

'That *is* your likeness?' Saxon interposed harshly, before Amyas could speak. 'You're not going to tell me that you have, miraculously, a double?'

'No . . . but . . .'

'You did speak to these men?'

'Yes. I . . .'

'Then how can you say this is not *your* doing? How much are they paying you for this interview . . . for giving them an exclusive story?'

'Nothing . . . they're not paying me . . . they . . .'

'How very short-sighted of you,' he said sarcastically. 'How very unbusinesslike of you, since money was *all* you were likely to get out of it.'

'Wh . . . what do you mean?'

A swift wrench of his hand pulled her away from the listening group of students and his tone was low, venomous, for her ears only.

'Did you think by implying that your marriage to me was imminent that you . . .?'

'I did *not* imply any such thing!' Cleone's voice was stronger now, projected by her sense of outrage. 'Nor was I responsible for those men coming here. They . . . they just turned up.'

'You're not even a very good liar.' he said contemptuously. 'How else could they have known about Salpeth? We've been very careful to keep it quiet.'

'I'm not the only person who could have let it out,' she retorted.

'Then whom would *you* accuse? Your uncle; one of his students, your precious Eric, me?'

Cleone shook her head despairingly. No, she could not honestly believe that any one of them would have acted in such a way. Only Eric had ever protested over the secrecy, but he would consider himself bound by her uncle's promise of discretion.

'But it wasn't *me*,' she reiterated.

His only reaction was a look of disbelief.

'As I say, I can fathom your motives, but you've done them a disservice, not the reverse.'

Cleone stamped her foot.

'Will you get it into the . . . the empty space between your ears that I didn't do it . . . I haven't any motives. I wasn't after money, or publicity, and I most certainly wouldn't have implied that I was going to marry *you*. What would be the point of telling such an outright lie?'

'As I said . . . to force my hand. I know you wouldn't be adverse to being bedded by me, Cleone. But with you "wedded" comes first, doesn't it?'

'Yes . . . it does . . . and what's wrong with that? Just because I refuse to . . .'

'I'll tell you what's wrong with it. You chose the wrong man to try your tactics on. I've had one experience of marriage, and I swore no other woman would ever have a chance to do to me what Tessa did. . . .'

'Not all women are the same!' she cried. 'You can't go through life punishing every woman you meet for what your wife did. Why punish me?'

'So!' He gripped her arm fiercely, 'you admit it is a punishment to you? You do want to marry me?'

'No . . . no, no, *no!* I'll never marry anyone without love.'

Cleone became aware that the rest of the archaeologists were watching them curiously. Though their conversation could not be heard, their angry gestures and expressions were all too visible and Amyas was becoming restless. Before long, he would feel impelled to come to Cleone's rescue and she didn't want him to hear Saxon's wild accusations.

'For heavens sake,' she said urgently, 'everyone is watching us.'

He released her, but she knew it was only a temporary

reprieve. At the first opportunity that presented itself, he would return to the attack.

Somehow, no one had the heart to go on working that day. Silently, the archaeolgists packed up their tools and in ones and twos they drifted away in Saxon's wake. Their glances at Cleone were not exactly accusing, but they were decidedly speculative and she wondered just what they made of the situation.

Amyas was more direct.

'*Did* you notify the press about our findings?' he asked, as, together, they walked back to the manor house. 'Wait!' he held up one hand, as she parted her lips indignantly, 'Remember, if you say you did not, I shall believe you. I'm not accusing you in any way.'

She slipped an arm through his and hugged it.

'Bless you! No, I was telling the truth. I didn't get in touch with the news media in any shape or form. I was surprised to see them that morning. I meant to tell you about them, but somehow it slipped my mind. I got them off the site as quickly as I could. I thought they hadn't got anything out of me, but I suppose I must have let something slip.'

'They're very astute, these fellows,' Amyas said comfortingly. 'They can make a story out of very little. But they must have had an informant in the first place. I don't suppose we'll ever know who it was.'

In that supposition, Amyas was wrong. They found out very swiftly and unexpectedly. In fact, they had barely crossed the threshold before Cleone knew that her name was, to her unutterable relief, completely cleared.

As they entered the large, square hall, they encountered Nerys, descending the staircase, suitcases in hand, her progress watched by an all too obviously simmering Saxon. To the astonishment of both uncle and niece, they were accorded a venomous look from Nerys's green eyes, as she stalked towards them.

To Amyas, her only words were:

'Well, our engagement's over. You'll find the ring on my dressing-table. I'm off, and I hope I never see you or your abominable niece again.'

To Cleone, her remark was more obscure, but nonetheless unmistakeably underlined with malice.

'Cunning little bitch ... thought you'd steel my limelight did you? Well, now that you've got what you were angling for ... be careful you don't end up like Tessa.'

Amyas turned as if he would follow his fiancée and Cleone took his arm, but it was Saxon who deterred him.

'Let her go, Badger. She's not worthy of you. You've no idea of the machinations she's been up to, behind your back.'

Amyas might not have been aware of Nerys's underhand behaviour, Cleone thought, but she had, and Saxon's part in it had been just as ignominious. How hypocritical of him to denigrate the other woman, when he had encouraged her, flirted with her. . . .

'Cleone,' Saxon's voice cut across her thoughts. 'I should like to speak to you. Come into the library.'

Cleone shook her head, clinging more tightly to Amyas's arm. Not another confrontation. She couldn't bear it.

For once, Amyas's perceptions were not clouded by other considerations, as he looked down at her understandingly.

'I think I had better be present too,' he said firmly.

Saxon shrugged.

'As you wish.' But Cleone knew he was not pleased.

In the library, he seemed to find it difficult to begin. Then, with a palpable effort, he confronted Cleone.

'I owe you an apology,' he said stiffly, 'about that report.'

She nodded her acknowledgement that this was so. But she said nothing. She did not feel inclined to make this any easier for him.

'Nerys received a letter by the second post. She opened it in front of me and a piece of paper fluttered out of the envelope. I picked it up and as I was handing it to her, I couldn't help noticing that it was a cheque, for a very substantial amount, and the name of the account against which it was drawn.' He mentioned the name of the newspaper which had printed the offensive account. '

taxed her with having been responsible for the leak of information. . . .'

'And she admitted it?' Amyas enquired with a frown.

'Not at first, no,' Saxon admitted, then, grimly, 'but I got it out of her in the end.'

Cleone could imagine that he had. If one had a guilty secret, Saxon in a fury would be more than capable of extracting that secret. She shivered. She had to get away from here, before he elicited her own. But, meantime, she was concerned about her uncle. Just how badly had he taken Nerys's defection?

'Uncle Amyas . . .' she began, but Saxon cut in.

'Don't waste any time regretting Nerys's departure, Badger,' he said bluntly. 'She'd have made you an abominable wife. You need someone prepared to immerse themselves in your concerns, someone who's there when you want them. A conflict of interests is hell. I speak from experience,' he added bitterly. 'A wife should be totally loyal. Nerys's intention—she lost her temper and told me so—was that the reporters should contact her, interview *her*, it was Nerys's picture that should have appeared in that paper.'

Amyas was nodding his head ruefully.

'I suspect you are right, I'm not entirely blind, though I may seem so at times; and in one way I believe only my pride is wounded. I was already beginning to think that I had acted over hastily, getting engaged at my time of life. But I would have gone through with it, if Nerys had not. . . .'

'Then thank goodness she showed up in her true colours before it was too late,' Cleone said impulsively. 'Better no wife at all, than a bad one.'

'Exactly my feelings,' Saxon interposed smoothly. 'Which reminds me, now that you know your niece is completely exonerated from all blame, where the press report is concerned, now that you know I am not about to castigate her, perhaps you would allow me to speak to her alone?'

Cleone began to protest, Saxon could do worse things to her than allot blame, but Amyas forestalled her, by indicating his consent and by leaving the room. Appalled, she tried to follow him, but Saxon's next words arrested her attempt at flight.

'At least do me the courtesy of hearing what I have to say. I won't *force* you to remain, but. . . .'

'Well, that will make a change,' she could not resist remarking. Many of his words were etched upon her brain by virtue of the painful grip that had often accompanied them.

With a forebearance unusual in him, he did not challenge her retort.

'I want one last chance to make you see my point of view,' he said, and despite his promised restraint it was obvious to Cleone that he was labouring under strongly repressed emotions. He seemed unable to remain in one place, but roamed backwards and forwards across the library, like a caged lion, as he spoke. 'My marriage was not a happy one, at least, not after the first few months. I'm not claiming that it was all Tessa's fault. I daresay I was not an easy man to live with, and I made certain demands upon her, which she was not prepared to concede.'

Cleone's brain raced over the possibilities. Had Tessa been frigid? No, or Ianthe would never have been born. Had she, perhaps, refused to bear any more children after the first? And had Saxon demanded that she continue childbearing, until a son was born to inherit his estates?

'Tessa came from a poor background, it was a struggle for her to stay at university. I think she saw marriage with me as a twofold advantage. Perhaps she was in love with me at first, a little, but I think she saw my money as a means to pursue her profession. She was obsessed with archaeology. She had no intention of settling down to ordinary domesticity; and when Ianthe was born, she took no interest in the child; she couldn't wait to get back to her current project. I told her, over and over again, that the present was more worthwhile than the past, that living people should be of more concern to her than the long dead. We had some bitter quarrels.'

Overheard by Mrs Griggs, Cleone thought.

'I suppose that's why you dislike archaeology so much,' she ventured.

His lips tightened.

'One of my reasons . . . yes.'

Cleone remembered something that had puzzled her for some time, until other matters had superseded.

'You asked me once, why I liked archaeology . . . do you remember?' and as he nodded 'I said it was the fascination of trying to prove a theory, the excitement of discovering something wonderful.' She looked at him and finding his eyes intent upon her earnest little face flushed a little. 'You said my answer was also the answer to the question I'd asked you . . . why you had changed your mind . . . about letting us stay.' Again he nodded. 'I wish you'd explain,' Cleone pleaded, 'I've puzzled about it off and on ever since. What did you mean?'

'I meant,' he said slowly, his eyes still devouring her, feature by feature, 'that I had formulated a theory, a theory about you, that I was allowing you to remain, because I wished to test that theory. I thought perhaps,' his voice was soft, husky, 'that I might discover . . . something wonderful.'

She was speechless, and it seemed that the lack of power to move accompanied her inability to speak.

'I had never,' he continued, 'wanted any more strangers at Salpeth, not since a . . . a certain visitor completely disrupted my life, but I wanted you to stay, I still want you to stay. I know there are a lot of things about me that you disapprove of, you think I'm harsh with Ianthe. But don't you see, Cleone? I have to be firm with her . . . she's Tessa's daughter . . . I don't want her to fail at human relationships . . . that's why I dread her becoming obsessed with the past. . . .'

Cleone sighed. He was not cruel, only misguided in the way in which he had tried to protect Ianthe. He himself had almost been responsible for his daughter's failure to relate to anyone, to himself in particular. But perhaps it was not too late for that mistake to be corrected.

He had kept his promise not to touch her; he had not even moved as much as half a step towards her and yet Cleone knew that the brink between immobility and movement was a fragile one, that, at one word or sign from her, the gap between them would be closed. But she could not say what he wanted to hear, she could not compromise with her beliefs.

'*Will* you stay, Cleone?'

Slowly, she shook her head.

'Not on your terms . . . no.'

'You still want . . . marriage?'

No, she didn't, not just as a means of keeping her here, with no feeling or desire for such permanence on his part. So again, she shook her head.

His hands, which had lifted slightly towards her, as though he were about to capitulate, fell to his side.

'So . . .' he muttered, 'you *don't* l . . . and I could have sworn. . . . Very well. I won't persist. For the remainder of your stay here, I . . .'

'That won't be very long,' she assured him. 'There's just one small, personal project I have to complete, then. . . .'

'How long?' The harshness in his tone, following its former weary resignation, startled her.

'A couple of days,' she told him quietly.

'I see!' He swung away and continued his pacing and Cleone watched him helplessly.

Why couldn't things have worked out differently? If only his need of her had been a conventional one, one that she could accept. How could she bear to go away, thinking of him here alone, wondering if anyone else would ever fill the place that could have been hers? At least she did not have the fear that it would be Nerys; but that was small consolation for her sense of deprivation.

'Perhaps you'll meet someone else.' Something dragged the words from her, perhaps a desire to hear him deny it.

His reply was all that she could have hoped, yet the viciousness in his tone startled her.

'I'll make bloody sure I *don't*. Women are hell. I swore I'd never put myself at one's mercy again. I'm not husband material, Cleone. I expect, need, too much of a woman. Perhaps I should have lived a few centuries ago . . . but the modern woman has ideas, needs of her own, which she isn't prepared to subjugate. Maybe I was too intolerant, maybe I treated Tessa badly because of it, but she wouldn't meet me on *any* point . . . and then. . . . Well, I can't take the risk of another disaster.'

He took another turn about the room, whilst she longed, but did not dare to ask the question that burnt on her lips: What had happened to Tessa?

She was about to leave, when he made a request, the words coming almost humbly, if that were possible from such a man.

'Before you go . . . leave Salpeth I mean . . . would you help me . . . to know my daughter better . . . how to get close to her?'

How could she refuse, even though the exercise would mean a deepening of her own acquaintance with Saxon, a dangerous strengthening of her feelings towards him?

Inevitably, her agreement led to an extension of her time limit beyond the two days she had intended to remain. In the mornings, she insisted on working, but in the afternoons she accompanied Saxon and Ianthe on expeditions into the surrounding countryside, watching the understanding between father and daughter grow and, for her own part, becoming more attached to Saxon, to Ianthe and to the beautiful Cotswold countryside.

The minor roads they travelled led to many a charming secluded village and unspoilt stretches of landscape. These quiet lanes always held some little surprise, a rare, unexpected sight of some shy wildlife; sometimes a half hidden stile would tempt them from the car, to walk footpaths across fields, paths which suddenly emerged into villages by narrow back alleys.

And during these outings, quietly, almost unobtrusively, Saxon was gaining Ianthe's confidence. Little by little some of the unhappy story of his marriage was revealed; tactfully he made his daughter understand why he did not want her to become obsessed with her mother's interests. And Cleone too began to understand much about Saxon Turville. She could sympathise when he waxed indignant as he described one of Tessa's acts of defiance, shearing off her lovely hair, because it hampered her at her work. But never once did he mention his wife's death, or the manner of it.

Finally, Cleone taxed him with this omission. The time had come, she felt, to renew her resolution to leave Salpeth. Her work up at the second site had not fulfilled its promise. Discouraged by this and her unhappiness increasing with each day, in proportion to her longing for Saxon's love, she felt that she must make the break, procrastination was only prolonging her agony. She made her announcement just as she was about to retire for the night, cowardice having made her delay the intelligence until the very last moment.

Amyas had fallen into the habit of leaving them alone together, last thing at night. Perhaps, Cleone thought sadly, he hoped for a happy outcome to their apparent friendship. She had never told him the true facts of their relationship.

'I'm finishing up, at the site tomorrow,' she said, hovering in the doorway of the sitting room.

'Oh?' He regarded her warily. 'Then what?'

'Then I'm going home to Oxford, to get the house opened up and ready for when my uncle comes back.'

'I see. . . .' His expression was taut. 'So none of this has made any difference to you. . . .'

'Did you really think it would?' she asked sadly. 'I only stayed on for Ianthe's sake . . . you knew that.'

'Yes . . . I suppose I was a fool to think. . . . I had hoped it might be for *my* sake too.'

His movement across the room was so swift that she had not time for flight.

'Cleone!' His strong arms encompassed her and for the first time for days she felt the warmth flowing from him, insidiously ensnaring her in a mesh of desire. 'Do you still not understand—can't you accept me as I am? Stay here with me. . . . Surely I've proved to you that we could be happy, the three of us, I've tried not to interfere with your interest in archaeology . . . not to bind you. . . .'

The fool, Cleone thought. If only he knew how she wanted to be bound. She was no Tessa. How gladly she would abandon the dry dust of ancient bones for the warmth of living reality.

'Is there something still troubling you?' he asked, his tone tinged with desperation as he sought to beat down her resistance, pulling her closer to him, one hand seemingly irresistibly drawn to her hair. In another moment or two he would have succeeded in freeing it from its binding and from past experience she knew what effect its flowing luxuriance could have upon him.

She could not tell him what really concerned her, that she was ready and willing to give herself to him, but only for life, in the bonds of matrimony. She must distract him.

'You ... you still haven't been entirely frank with Ianthe,' she said. 'She ... she's always asking me *how* her mother died. It ... it seems to worry her ... she. ...'

His hands were stilled as she had hoped. Eyes narrowed, lips tightly drawn, he stared down at her.

'How can I speak of that to the child ... without telling her that I ... that I was responsible for ...'

'For Tessa's death?' Cleone gasped in dismay, 'then you *were* ...?'

'And you claimed not to listen to gossip!' he said bitterly. 'Yes ... so now you know. I *was* responsible for my wife's death ... and since I've confirmed your idle speculations, what do you intend to do about it?'

CHAPTER EIGHT

WHAT had he expected her to do? Cleone wondered later, as she lay in frozen misery on her bed. Had he expected that she would take some dramatic action, such as telephoning the police, blurting out her knowledge to them? However great her shock, her horror at his confirmation of rumour, she knew she could never do that.

If Saxon had killed his wife, it had been a crime of passion. Of that, Cleone was convinced. He was hot-blooded, quick-tempered and heaven knew Tessa had given him provocation enough ... for Saxon had gone on to tell her that he had discovered Tessa was having an affair.

'With a fellow archaeologist, needless to say, a man she'd known up at Oxford, a chap, who, in those days, was as poverty stricken as she was. But he'd come into money, and a title, through the unexpected death of a cousin. He shared Tessa's obsession and he had more than enough money to gratify their joint interest. She told me that they were planning to go to Egypt.'

Cleone hadn't waited to hear any more. She couldn't have endured it, to stand there and listen to Saxon's description of what had followed. But she assumed he must have struck his wife. Typically, his anger would have been immediate, it wasn't in him, she was sure, to cold-bloodedly plan a death. But how, she wondered, had he disposed of Tessa's body? She shivered. With such vast acreages at his disposal, it could be anywhere.

On reaching her room, Cleone had locked and bolted the door. Now she lay, still fully dressed, the bedside light still on as though to disperse terrifying shadows, staring up at the ceiling. She could not even cry to relieve her anguish. Her shock and horror went too deep for tears. Despite the frisson of fear that had gone through her, when Ianthe had first told of the housekeeper's idle words, Cleone had never seriously expected to hear them confirmed, and having heard a full account of the relevant conversation, she had genuinely believed what she had told Ianthe—that it was a misinterpretation of hasty words, spoken in anger.

As she lay there, with no expectation of being able to sleep, she made her plans, coldly, clinically. She would waste no more time tomorrow. She had no heart even to tidy up at the priory site. She realised now how little archaeology meant to her, in the light of living human relationships.

First thing in the morning, she would slip along to her uncle's room, give him some explanation, she hadn't quite decided what, for her desire to leave Salpeth. Then, she would drive down to the Inn, get one of the students to take her to the nearest railway station and bring the Humber back.

She rose from the bed and began to pack; nothing should delay the earliest departure possible.

This done, and it was not an onerous task for she always travelled light, Cleone knew she must get some sleep or go mad. The thoughts that teemed within her brain were too intolerable to dwell upon. Headache tablets were all she possessed, something she barely had occasion to use, but which formed part of a basic first-aid kit. A larger dose than normal might do the trick.

She awoke to full, brilliant daylight, shining through her uncurtained window. Her head felt thick and heavy with the unaccustomed drugged sleep. Still in a daze, she rolled over to consult her bedside clock. Disbelievingly she stared at the accusing hands. It was almost ten o'clock!

With a groan of despair, she fell back upon her pillows. So much for her overnight scheming. Everyone in the house, including Saxon, would be up and about. In fact, by now, her uncle and the students would be at the villa site. It would be necessary to toil all the way there, before her plans could be put into effect, with the consequent danger of encountering the man she most wished to avoid.

She had hoped too, cruel as it seemed, to leave without having to say goodbye to Ianthe.

Well, her plans might have been delayed, but they were still viable. Resolutely, she got up, stripped off the clothes she had slept in, washed and redressed in fresh things. She was ready to leave her room when she heard an excited babble of sound beneath her window and shortly afterwards her uncle's voice enquiring for her.

Seconds later, he was hammering at her door.

'Cleone? You awake yet? Come on, lazybones! Just wait till you hear what's been going on, whilst you've been sleeping your life away!'

She opened the door, only to see Amyas disappearing once more in the direction of the stairs.

'Wait!' she cried. 'I want to . . .'

But he merely gestured impatiently, indicating that she should follow him.

Cleone ran. She was determined to make her uncle listen to her, to enlist his help in getting away from here, now. But as she caught up with him, he was about to enter the library, followed by, of all people, Eric Morton. She had never thought to see him cross Saxon's threshold, either voluntarily or by invitation.

Irresolutely, she hovered on the threshold of the room. Saxon was there too and Ianthe and whatever it was that her uncle had to impart, it was obvious that he had awaited Cleone's arrival, for father and daughter looked utterly mystified.

'Fancy lying in, today of all days,' Eric commented, as Cleone obeyed her uncle's injunction to be seated.

'What's special about today?' she asked disinterestedly, except that it's the last day in my life that I shall see Saxon, she thought.

'It wasn't special until half an hour ago,' Amyas said. 'Cleo, I got curious about that site of yours, up at the old Priory. You weren't getting anywhere and yet I felt that you were right in your throries. So I decided to take a look for myself, with Eric's help. We left the students cataloguing the artefacts from the villa and went over there.'

'And?' Despite her all-enveloping gloom, Cleone could not help a tiny spark of interest lighting her eyes and she sat up a little straighter. After all, this was the kind of thing with which she must fill her empty life from now on.

'A couple of feet further over, and a little deeper, that's all it needed,' Amyas explained. 'It didn't take long with two of us digging.' He leant forward eagerly. 'We found——' he paused impressively, 'a skeleton.'

'Then I *was* right,' Cleone breathed. Her site *had* been a burial ground. She did not notice the small stir of consternation from the point where Saxon and his daughter stood listening.

Amyas nodded.

'It was in a very good state too, might almost have been a recent death, it was so well preserved. It's the skeleton of a young woman. She'd been brutally assaulted, beaten down with clubbing blows to the head and then, judging by the angle of the vertebrae, of the skull, she'd been strangled.'

With a piercing shriek, Ianthe flung herself across the room, her small hands beating against Cleone's breasts.

'You lied ... you lied ... you *lied* to me! She *was* strangled ... she *was!*'

Then, before Cleone could catch hold of the small body, the child was gone, running wildly, the sound of her hysterical sobs seeming to hang upon the air.

'What the hell was *that* all about?' Eric enquired.

White-faced, Cleone stared at her uncle.

'Was that the only body?' she enquired tensely.

Though as mystified as his assistant, he answered her promptly.

'In that grave, yes, but a few yards away there were several others. They'd all been treated in the same way ... a mass murder of some kind I should think....'

'And the age....'?

'Well, I haven't done any tests....'

'Just a rough idea,' Cleone insisted.

'Yes ... I can give you an educated guess ... at least two thousand years old.'

With a little shuddering sob, Cleone sank back against the chair, covering her face with her hands. For a moment, she, like Ianthe, had thought.... She started up. She must go after the little girl. But where would a frightened child run to?

'We *must* find Ianthe,' she said, her voice anguished. 'She thinks ... thinks....!'

'Thinks *what*, for God's sake?' For the first time, Saxon spoke, standing over Cleone, making one of the concerned trio of puzzled men.

'She thinks Uncle Amyas has found Tessa's body,' Cleone said flatly.

'What!' The exclamation was Saxon's; the other two men just looked blank. Of course, they didn't know, couldn't know.

But Saxon was quick on the uptake. Cleone recognised the precise instant when realisation struck him.

'Badger!' he said abruptly, 'will you and your assistant try to find my daughter? Bring her back here....'

'No!' Cleone cried. 'Let *me* go and look for her ... she....'

'*You* will stay here,' Saxon informed her, 'until I get to the bottom of this ... this outrageous....' Descriptive words failed him, but his grasp of Cleone's wrists effectively restrained her from following the two men as, still puzzled, they moved, nevertheless, to obey his request. 'And if I find that you're responsible ... that you've put these ideas. ...'

'Don't ... don't leave me here ... alone. ...' Cleone cried after her uncle. Just because the skeletons they had unearthed hadn't been Tessa's it didn't mean—and Saxon looked positively murderous.

All further thought processes were rendered impossible, as he shook her, until her teeth rattled and her head wobbled helplessly on her neck.

'Now,' he said grimly, forcing her down on to the settee and seating himself beside her, 'cut out the hysterics. *You* are going to explain this whole thing ... starting at the very beginning.'

Ten minutes later, it was he who sat, silent and incredulous—but not for long.

'You really mean to tell me that both you and Ianthe thought I had *murdered* Tessa? Such naïvety on the part of a child, I could perhaps credit ... but *you*!'

'It's your own fault,' Cleone cried desperately. 'You made me think. ... You told me so yourself ... you *said* you were responsible. ...'

'Dear God!' He brushed a hand over his face, his shoulders slumping in sudden weariness. 'But I didn't mean. ...' He straightened and turned upon her, taking her by the shoulders, gently this time, forcing her to look at him. 'Listen to me, and this time listen carefully, right to the end, with no interruptions, so that you won't go drawing your own misguided conclusions. You don't have to rely on my words, you can check every fact for yourself, but Tessa *left* me. She went off with her lover, he'd been working in these parts and they'd been meeting secretly. About a month later, she wrote to me, asking me for a divorce. I refused. I happen to believe in the marriage vows.'

'You said she was dead,' Cleone began accusingly.

'I told you not to interrupt. She *is* dead. A year after she left me, she came home, to ask me to take her back. Her lover had thrown her over, for some rich Egyptian woman. Tessa was destitute.'

'She asked you take her back ...?'

'Yes, but I refused. She'd destroyed every iota of love I had ever felt for her, by her treatment of me, of Ianthe, oh, in many ways. I offered to help her though, to make her an allowance, to tide her over until she met someone else. She would have done, you know. Tessa was never short of admirers.'

Amyas had said the same thing, Cleone remembered, that Tessa had been the toast of Oxford—Helen of Troy.

'She left here in a towering rage . . . after I'd told her a few home truths . . . refused to let her see Ianthe. At the inquest,' he said bleakly, 'they said she was driving like a madwoman . . . that the tractor driver wasn't to blame. She hit him broadside . . . she was killed instantaneously.'

'But you said it was *your* fault . . . why?'

'I've always felt that it was,' he said simply. 'I've always thought that perhaps I acted the hypocrite. I was the one who believed that marriage was for ever. If I'd been more forgiving, less harsh. . . . Perhaps I *should* have given her another chance . . .!'

'No!' Cleone cried emphatically. She couldn't help herself. 'She didn't *deserve* it . . . she didn't deserve *you*.'

A strange spasm contorted his features.

'Cleone?' he began, but she jumped up.

'I simply must find Ianthe . . . tell her. . . .'

'But you don't know where to look. Wait . . . I'll get the dogs . . .!'

Cleone shook her head.

'I must go alone. Don't you see . . . if she thinks you . . . well, she'll probably hide. I have to get her to listen to me . . . to explain. . . .'

As she spoke, she was already hurrying towards the door. It had suddenly come to her, an instinctive knowledge of where she would find the child.

Cleone ran through the woods, stumbling over the projecting roots of trees, but somehow always retaining her balance. She was hot and breathless, but she refused to slacken her pace. She *must* reach Ianthe before anyone else did, even before Amyas and Eric, for *she* was the only one apart from Saxon who knew the truth. She only prayed that she could make Ianthe listen to her. The child believed that she had lied to her once, would she be prepared to credit Cleone's explanation this time?

Cleone was sure, somehow, that Ianthe would have made for the priory site. To some it might seem a ghoulish conclusion, but, believing that her mother's grave, however unhallowed, had been found, she felt that Ianthe would go there. Had the child ever seen a skeleton? she wondered and what effect, believing it to be Tessa's, would it have upon the impressionable little girl?

There was no one to be seen in the hollow, but an inspection of the earth around the excavation convinced Cleone that her guess was correct. Ianthe *had* been here, but how long ago? and where was she now? She could not have reached the site too long before Cleone herself. Despite the delay for explanations, Cleone felt that her speed and stamina were greater than that of a child.

Where would she be likely to hide, if she had heard Cleone's approach? Instinctively, her eyes turned towards the ruined Priory. Apart from the trees, it was the nearest and best place of concealment. It was worth investigating.

Cleone picked her way over the crumbling stones that lay around the base of the building, mindful of her recent accident here. Only the smell of decay, of rotting vegetation was here, the faint rustlings of small disturbed animals and birds. But what about the so-far uninvestigated crypt? It was off limits to Ianthe, but would a child dare to go down there? A desperate child might. Resolutely putting all thoughts of bats out of her mind, Cleone began to descend the worn and slippery steps.

'Ianthe?'

Silence . . . and yet she felt it was not the silence of emptiness, but the stubborn silence of rejection. She tried again.

'Ianthe? Are you there?'

'Go away! I hate you! You're as bad as *he* is.'

The small, tremulous voice came from the furthest corner, dark and almost inaccessible.

'Ianthe,' Cleone said urgently, 'please . . . I have to talk to you. It's not what you think, truly. . . .'

'You said you were telling the truth before, and you

weren't. So why should I . . .? Oh, Cleo! Look out . . . *look
out!*' The child's scream of terror reverberated around the
enclosed space.

Too late, Cleone looked up. It would have been too
late in any case, in spite of Ianthe's warning. The first
piece of falling masonry caught her a glancing blow on
the temple; and she was not conscious long enough to see
the rest of the deluge of stones, which blocked
the entrance, trapping them both in an underground
tomb.

'Cleo . . . oh, Cleo . . . please . . . please don't be dead.
I'm sorry I called you a liar. It wasn't your fault if *he* lied
to you. I can't bear it if you're dead too.'

The sound of Ianthe's distraught words roused Cleone
from her half-dazed state and she tried to sit up, but
something was pinning her down, by one arm and one
leg. Mercifully, her body had not been crushed, she
thought, or she might not have lived to regain
consciousness.

'Ianthe . . . Ianthe, dear . . . it's all right. I'm *not* dead,
don't cry. How . . . how long have I been unconscious?'

'I . . . I don't know . . . but it seemed like ages. Oh,
Cleo, what are we going to do? We can't get out, I know
. . . because I've tried. I thought if I could get help. . . .'

'Then we'll just have to wait until someone finds us,'
Cleone said, trying to sound more cheerful than she felt.
Her head was throbbing and she felt a dreadful certainty
that the trapped arm and leg must be broken. Moreover,
would anyone ever find them? Would anyone think to look
here? Wouldn't it be the last place they would expect to
find either herself or the child?

Ianthe echoed her fear.

'No one ever comes here, except you and me.' Her
mind reverted to the reason for her own presence. 'Oh,
Cleo . . . did you . . . did you see . . . the . . . the
grave?' A series of little staccato sobs escaped her.

'Yes, I did.' Cleone was glad of something to take her
mind off their present plight, 'and that's what I wanted
to talk to you about. Ianthe, that . . . that skeleton isn't
your mother's . . . honestly. Those bones . . . my uncle

said so ... and you *know* he's an expert ... those bones are at least *two thousand years old*. They're what I was looking for ... the Romans' graveyard ... or perhaps that of the monks who lived here later.'

'He said it was a woman,' Ianthe objected. 'Women weren't monks.'

'Then she was a servant ... or a local woman,' Cleone said patiently, 'but she wasn't your mother. Your mother was killed in a car crash, miles away from here.'

There was a silence, then:

'And my father didn't ... didn't. ...'

'No, Ianthe, darling ... he didn't kill her. I told you that was all rubbish, didn't I? He does blame himself, because he made her angry, so that she drove carelessly ... but it *wasn't his fault!*'

In the darkness there was a great sigh of relief.

'Oh, I'm so glad ... but ...' and the voice faltered again, 'suppose I never get out of here ... so I can tell him so?'

'We *are* going to get out,' Cleone reiterated, 'either by our own efforts or because someone will rescue us. Now ... let's see if together we can move these stones that are holding me down.'

Between them, they made a valiant effort, but it was not enough and the pain it caused was so intense that Cleone fainted again, though briefly this time.

She came round to find Ianthe huddled against her.

'Don't try again, Cleo, please. I don't want you to hurt yourself. We ...' her voice trembled, as now she attempted to reassure, 'we'll do as you suggested ... we'll wait till somebody comes. I'm not frightened any more ... not really ... so long as you promise not to faint again.'

Cleone was doubtful of her own ability to keep such a promise, but she did not tell the child so.

Though outside, above them, burnt a sultry summer's day, in the dark underground crypt, it was damp and chilly and there was always the fear of more falling masonry. At first, Cleone wished she could see her watch, then was glad that she could not, since time seemed to be endless enough without watching it pass. Were they doing the right thing? she wondered, in remaining immobile, relying on others for their deliverance. Yet what else was there to do?

She thought for a moment that she was imagining the scurrying, snuffling noises, somewhere over her head; then her active imagination pictured the rats that might inhabit this crumbling ruin. But a short, shrill bark, followed by another, alerted Ianthe.

'That's Gwynne and Castlemaine,' she said positively, 'and if the dogs are up there, Daddy's there too.' Joyfully, urgently, she began to call out and with an incredulous leap of her heart, Cleone heard Saxon's deep answering tones telling them that they were indeed discovered.

But, necessarily, more time elapsed before he could bring a party of estate workers to their rescue; for one man alone could not remove the fall of heavy masonry that held them prisoner; though she learnt afterwards that Saxon had worked as hard and harder than any of his men, with an almost manic determination to reach her side.

They remained still, listening to the sounds of activity above them, then, as soon as a large enough gap appeared, Cleone insisted that Ianthe scramble through to safety and she could hear the child warning the rescuers of Cleone's plight, heard Saxon swear expressively.

Alone now, without the need for remaining calm, to reassure the child, Cleone felt reaction setting in. A great deal more work would have to be done before sufficient space had been cleared to enable the men to remove the blocks of stone that held her down; and from snatches of overheard conversation, she knew that there was a danger that more might fall.

The sound of Saxon's voice, husky, concerned, speaking to her from the far side of the obstruction, was the final blow to her self-control. Viciously, she bit at her lip, in an attempt to still its quivering, but she could not restrain the tears that poured down her cold cheeks, nor the little sob that accompanied them as she tried to assure him that she was quite all right.

She heard him curse savagely; and then his head and

shoulders appeared as he wriggled his way cautiously into her prison. Then he was beside her, cradling her head and shoulders, murmuring words of comfort and promise.

'Relax, darling ... I'm here and we'll have you out soon.'

But she was afraid for him too.

'You shouldn't be down here,' she told him between sobs. 'There may be another fall, I heard you say so, then you'd be trapped as well. You should be out there ... with Ianthe. Suppose ... suppose something happened to *you* ... she'd be all alone in the world.'

'And suppose, whilst I was out there, guarding my own skin, something should happen to you?'

'That's different,' she insisted. 'I don't have anyone depending upon my existence ...'

'Don't you?' he began. 'I think you're mistaken. ...'

But then the first of the men reached them and conversation was abandoned in the delicate task of freeing Cleone's limbs from beneath the weight of the ancient stones. Despite their care, pain was inevitable, increased as the blood was able to flow once more in compressed veins and arteries and with a little cry, Cleone fainted away for the third time that day.

She woke to more pain, but it was bearable now, because she was no longer claustrophobically immured below ground, because she lay in a comfortable bed, her injuries tended and not least, because Saxon sat on the edge of that bed, her hand held firmly in his.

'Nothing broken,' he assured her, as she murmured his name, 'just very bad bruises.'

'Ianthe?' she began.

'Quite safe and, thanks to you, quite happy. I can't thank you enough,' he said gravely, 'for making her understand that I. ...'

'Saxon,' she interrupted him, 'I'm sorry that I was ever silly enough to believe that you could ... could. ...'

His hand tightened on hers and he lifted her fingers to his lips.

'I know ... I know,' he said softly. 'But I can't blame

you for thinking as you did. You've had no reason to think of me as anything but a bad-tempered brute.'

She closed her eyes suddenly, so that he should not perceive just what she *did* think of him.

'Pain?' he enquired with swift concern.

'I . . . just a little . . . not too bad.'

Self-control asserted once more, she was able to look at him, only to find him curiously intent upon the shape and structure of the hand he held, as though *he* were unable to meet *her* gaze.

'Cleone . . . I . . . I had a lot of time to think . . . from the moment I discovered you were trapped down there . . . until I found you were not as badly injured as I'd feared . . . and I began to realise quite a few things about myself . . . things I didn't like. I don't know how to put this . . . perhaps an analogy would help? I gather you and Badger are keen rugby fans?'

Cleone could not help raising her eyebrows a little at the turn the conversation had taken, but she nodded.

'Yes . . . we watch the Tigers every Saturday afternoon.'

'It's a game, isn't it, about which the players have to be completely whole-hearted? They have to put all of themselves into it . . . body . . .' he paused, 'and heart and soul?'

Again she nodded.

'I used to play rugby. I was never afraid in those days to give it everything I'd got . . . I wasn't afraid of being hurt. . . .'

He was silent again and his grip upon her fingers was becoming extremely painful, as though he had forgotten that he held them, and yet she would not have had him release her.

He began again abruptly.

'The same goes for life, these last few years, and particularly just recently, I've been a coward.'

She stirred restlessly.

'Oh, yes I have, not physically perhaps, but mentally, spiritually. From the first moment I set eyes on you, I knew you were trouble. I was afraid that I might have to learn to live again. I was, literally, *afraid*. And I thought, if I could possess you, just for a while, I might get you out of my system, without committing myself irrevocably. . . .'

'Saxon, if you're leading up to. . . .'

'No, Cleone . . . I'm not. I'm not asking you to stay here, to be my mistress. . . .'

'You're not?' To her dismay, she felt the ready tears begin to fill her eyes, so that once more she must close them hastily. He was going to tell her that he had recovered from his obsession with her . . . that. . . .'

'No,' he said gravely and the steely strength of his fingers almost made her cry out. 'I'm asking you to . . . to marry me. . . .'

It had taken Saxon some time to convince her that he meant what he said, Cleone thought, looking back upon that eventful day, some three weeks later, three weeks in which painful bruises had had time to heal, three weeks of blissful tingling anticipation.

'Are you sure?' she'd asked him, 'you seemed quite ready to put Nerys. . . .'

'In *your* place?' He laughed huskily. 'Never . . . that was just a little ploy, to make you jealous. But you were a tougher nut than I thought.'

'But you'd known her before and. . . .'

'So she told me.' He shrugged. 'She apparently remembered me, but I couldn't recall. . . . Let's face it . . . it was a long time ago and in those days I only had eyes for one woman.'

There had been times when Cleone had thought the three weeks would never pass, that some time before then she must wake from a delightful dream to stark reality. But dream or not, she was still living in it—and today had been her wedding day.

Today, she had walked down the aisle of Salpeth church, as many other Turville brides must have done before her, in a full-length dress of ivory silk, the bodice a mass of dainty tucks beneath a lace, V-shaped yoke with its chiffon frill and high lace neck, her arms covered by sheer lace sleeves. Saxon had insisted that she wear her hair loose, beneath the cream, antique lace veil with its silver and wax orange-blossom headdress and the fierce warmth in his eyes had told her how lovely she looked, as she advanced towards him on Amyas's arm.

Ianthe had achieved her ambition to be bridesmaid, in a similarly high-necked Edwardian dress, with puffed sleeves, wide skirts and coloured sash.

But now all the pomp and ceremony, the fairytale details of the day were over, and Cleone was face to face with reality.

In Saxon's brown and cream bedroom, a room she had never entered before, she waited for him to join her; and there was still so much of which she was unsure.

He had never actually said that he loved her, that was the first thing. When she'd accepted his proposal, it hadn't seemed to matter so much, perhaps she'd assumed that love was implicit in his offer. But as the days, the weeks had passed, the word had still never been mentioned.

Did it matter so much? He wanted her, badly enough to risk marriage a second time around; and *she* loved *him*. Wouldn't her love be enough? She didn't know and yet, of one thing she *was* certain; whether her love be returned or not, she would rather be married to Saxon than spend the rest of her life without him.

She had elected not to have a honeymoon. She had wanted to spend her first days as Saxon's wife here, where she had first fallen in love with him; and they would be completely alone. The gossiping Mrs Griggs and her inquisitive brother had been sent packing, and Ianthe, with a tact beyond her years, had volunteered to spend the next two weeks at the home of a friend. The archaeological party had come to the end of their Long Vacation and had returned to Oxford, with Saxon's promise that they might return next year to continue uncovering the villa in the woods.

It had been early evening, when the last of the wedding guests departed and later they had dined alone. There had been little conversation, adding to Cleone's uncertainty, as she wondered whether her new husband was already regretting his capitulation.

He had made a strange request, as he suggested tha
she might like to go up first, in order to prepare for bed.

'Plait your hair and wind it around your head.'

Cleone had stared at him. It was the last thing she
would have expected him to ask. But she was too nervous
to query his command and now she stared at her
reflection in the long mirror of Saxon's wardrobe. The
realisation of the transparency of the sheer fall of silk
which was all she wore was sufficient to bring a flush to
her cheeks; and she could not but be aware that she
looked very lovely and very regal, her slender form
topped by the elegant, sophisticated hairstyle.

The creaking timbers of the old house betrayed his
approach. Cleone began to shiver with an ague that was
not due to cold; for summer still warmed the sheltered
little Cotswold village.

Unable to move, she stood, watching him enter, close
the door behind him. She had expected that he would
come straight towards her, to take her in his arms, that he
would immediately assert his long-awaited possession of
her. But after one long, simmering look that was of itself
as intimate as the caresses she had anticipated, he moved
into the adjoining bathroom.

Her legs suddenly tremulous, she sat down on the edge
of the bed. Somehow she could not bring herself to get
into it. It seemed too . . . too. . . . When he emerged she
was still sitting there, her gaze fixed mesmerically upon
the bathroom door. He had showered and now he wore
only the briefest of bathrobes, which left very little to her
fevered imagination.

She had seen men wearing less, bathing trunks for
example, but this was different . . . disturbing . . . the
sight of his strong muscular thighs below the hem of the
robe which was open above the waist to disclose to her
fascinated gaze the expanse of his broad chest, with its
soft, strong down of blond hairs.

He stood over her, looking down into her bemused,
golden eyes, then, with the greatest gentleness he had
ever shown towards her, he reached out and pulled her to
her feet, his eyes still holding hers in thrall, his hands
moving slowly to the simple ties that secured her gown;

and she heard the faintest whisper of silk, as it fell in a graceful pool around her slender ankles.

She trembled, turned her flushed face aside, as his eyes made a voyage of comprehension, as though he memorised every inch of her, ending with the molten, copper crown of her hair.

'Did you wonder?' he asked softly, 'why I asked you to bind your hair again?'

Wordlessly, she nodded.

'Because,' he murmured, 'I wanted to do this. . . .'

Then his hands were undoing all her work, loosening the red-gold, heavy waves, until they tumbled about her, their deep colour emphasising the marble whiteness of her body.

'It occurs to me,' he said a little later, as he lifted her in his arms, carrying her towards the bed, 'that I have never heard you express any feelings for me.'

'I could say the same,' she retorted, 'except that I know you don't . . . that you . . . you haven't any. . . .'

'I haven't?' He set her down and stretched himself out beside her, the hard muscularity of his body excitingly, tantalisingly close. 'Then why do you think I married you?'

'Because,' she said, with devastating frankness, 'it was the only way you could get what you wanted.'

He raised himself on one elbow, studying her with a puzzled frown.

'And you didn't mind that?'

She couldn't answer him. She had discovered that she did mind—terribly. But of what use was that? She had made her decision . . . taken what she could have of him and. . . .

'I've wondered why you agreed to marry me,' he said musingly. 'You've told me often enough that you don't even *like* me.'

'I . . . I didn't say that, not exactly,' she denied. It was difficult to speak, his closeness seemed to be having a very strange effect upon her vocal chords.

'And we never *did* establish just what your feelings were . . . for young Morton,' he continued, his manner would-be-casual, while one exploratory hand strayed over her neck and shoulders, wandered lower still, in caressive appreciation of the curves it found.

'I never had any feelings for Eric ... except friendship,' she managed to say. A strange languor was overtaking her and it was an effort now to even think clearly, for her mind seemed at one with his hand, concentrating with feverish intensity upon its insidious wanderings.

'That day ... at the caravan ... up by the lambing pen ... when I told you how you would look ... how I wanted to see you ... like this. ...' His voice was husky, staccato, his grey eyes silvered with passion as they slid over exposed flesh, adorned only by her flowing tresses, which offset, rather than concealed. 'You implied that Morton had ... had. ...' His voice became harsh and his hand closed over the breast it now held with sudden painful intensity.

Startled out of the sweet lethargy his caresses had been inducing, Cleone sat up and confronted him.

'Eric has *never* seen me like this,' she said firmly. 'He once made a joke ... about how, with all my hair, I could go to a fancy dress party as Lady Godiva, but that's all it was ... a joke. ...'

'Then why, for God's sake?' he demanded almost savagely, 'did you let me go on thinking ...?'

'Because ... when I ... when you ... because I thought then that you were married. I had to think of some way to ... and Eric's was the first name I thought of. I. ...'

'But when I told you I *wasn't* married ...?' he objected.

'Yes ... you told me,' she retorted, 'and in the same breath you told me you never intended to get married again ... that all you wanted was an affair. ...'

'You wouldn't enter into that kind of relationship with me ... yet you let me think you'd had an affair with Morton,' he persisted.

'Only because I ... I didn't want you to think ... to know. ...' She could not go on, his eyes were boring into her very soul and she felt as tongue-tied and embarrassed as if they had just met.

'Ianthe asked you if Eric were your boyfriend,' he reminded her, 'and you didn't deny it to her either.'

'Well *you* were listening,' she defended, 'and then Nerys had to shove her oar in and you seemed to believe her ... and by then I thought you and Nerys ... I did tell you ... later on ... that I wasn't involved with Eric in any way, but you refused to believe me.'

'What was it, Cleone, that you didn't want me to know?' His voice was casual, but his hands were insidiously coaxing.

'You ... you seemed so sure that I ... that I ... wanted you,' she whispered the final words, unable to look at him. 'And it seemed ... I felt....'

'And didn't you?' His hands were continuing their disruptive downward path and Cleone fought to conceal the trembling that threatened to overwhelm her.

'I ... I....' she mouthed soundlessly.

'Even when I *offered* marriage, you refused ... so that I began to think you meant what you said ... that you disliked me ... that I had been mistaken about your response to me.'

'I thought,' she forced the words from between quivering, hungry lips ... oh, if only he would put an end to this inquisition ... kiss her.... Her mouth, her body could tell him so much more easily, that which she found difficult to speak. 'I thought you had been driven to proposing ... because it was the only way you could ... could....'

'Have my wicked way with you?' he said teasingly and his hand made a sudden, unexpected move, which set her gasping ... not at his audacity ... she wanted him to touch her so, to go on doing it until.... No, the gasp was at the shattering effect of that touch upon her already palpitating senses.

'I wish I'd met you first, instead of Tessa,' he mused now, as he bent his fair head, his lips intent upon following the trail his hands had blazed, his arms a sudden prison, his body a barricade.

A gurgle of nervous laugher, almost resembling a sob, escaped her.

'You'd have been arrested for cradle snatching.'

'Does that bother you?' His eyes were intent, 'the difference in our ages?'

'No ... of course not ...' she began indignantly, unwarily, 'when you're in love, age *shouldn't* make any ...' She stopped, realising what she had nearly revealed.

'But then *you* don't love *me*?' It was said tenderly, earnestly; and somehow, under the twin caresses of eyes and hands, at the feel of hard muscles that tensed and strained against her, it was not so difficult after all to compromise with foolish pride, to admit something which, she was beginning to realise with joyful incredulity, was what he wanted to hear, because ... because. . . .

'I *do* love you,' she whispered, adding shyly as the violence of his reaction shuddered through him, 'so very, very much ... that I. . . .' She could not go on, but instead allowed her body to yearn against his in tremulous surrender ... in supplication. . . .

Now she had betrayed her carefully guarded secret; and yet it did not matter, for she witnessed the dawning of a great joy in his face, felt his body's answer to hers.

'And *I* love *you*,' he muttered, his lips close to hers, 'only I didn't realise it, or didn't want to admit it, until I thought I might lose you.' He shuddered, and remembered fear seemed to increase his potent urgency, 'if those stones had fallen differently. . . .'

Then she knew, from the quivering pressure of him, by the touch of his lips on hers, that no more words need be spoken, before, with his body held fast to hers by the gentle bondage of her tumbled hair, he proceeded to show her the exact depths of his love, his own fulfilment expressed in a rising growl of ecstasy—the Cotswold lion tamed at last.

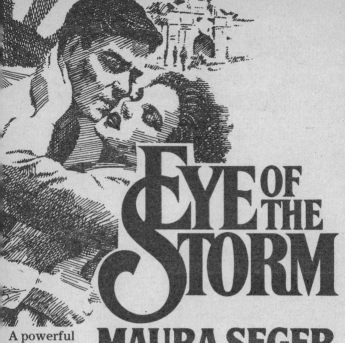

EYE OF THE STORM

MAURA SEGER

A powerful
portrayal of
the events of
World War II in the
Pacific, *Eye of the Storm* is a riveting story of how love
triumphs over hatred. In this, the first of a three-book
chronicle, Army nurse Maggie Lawrence meets Marine
Sgt. Anthony Gargano. Despite military regulations
against fraternization, they resolve to face together
whatever lies ahead.... Author Maura Seger, also known
to her fans as Laurel Winslow, Sara Jennings, Anne
MacNeil and Jenny Bates, was named 1984's
Most Versatile Romance Author by *The Romantic Times.*

You're invited to accept 4 books and a surprise gift Free!

Acceptance Card

Mail to: **Harlequin Reader Service®**

In the U.S.
2504 West Southern Ave.
Tempe, AZ 85282

In Canada
P.O. Box 2800, Postal Station A
5170 Yonge Street
Willowdale, Ontario M2N 6J3

YES! Please send me 4 free Harlequin Romance® novels and my free surprise gift. Then send me 6 brand new novels every month as they come off the presses. Bill me at the low price of $1.65 each ($1.75 in Canada)—an 11% saving off the retail price. There are no shipping, handling or other hidden costs. There is no minimum number of books I must purchase. I can always return a shipment and cancel at any time. Even if I never buy another book from Harlequin, the 4 free novels and the surprise gift are mine to keep forever.

116 BPR-BPGE

Name _____ (PLEASE PRINT)

Address _____ Apt. No. _____

City _____ State/Prov. _____ Zip/Postal Code _____

This offer is limited to one order per household and not valid to present subscribers. Price is subject to change.

ACR-SUB-1

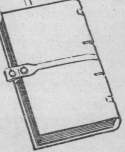